The Frontier Garrison

P. HOWARD
(Jenő Rejtő)

Translated from the original Hungarian text
by Balint Kacsoh

ETALON PRESS
the archetypal yardstick

TRANSLATOR'S DEDICATION

To my children.

CONTENTS

I am grateful to Dr. Jon Martin for his help and never ending patience and encouragement. Thanks are also due to Jenny and Nash Mayfield and my daughter Dori Kacsoh for their valuable help in polishing the translation.

PREFACE

In 1969, when I was not quite ten years old, my brother – fifteen years my senior – gave me a book for my name day.[1] Among all my name day and birthday presents, unexpectedly, this little book had one of the biggest impacts on my life. Decades later, I translated it into English – and this is the book you are about to begin reading: *The Frontier Garrison* [*Az Előretolt Helyőrség*].

You might wonder: why would a medical school professor translate a novel? The reasons are many. I have lived over half of my life in the USA. My children speak Hungarian, but they would struggle reading Hungarian novels in the original language. One of my motives was to make this book accessible to my children and the children of many other Hungarian expatriates who want to become more familiar with their cultural heritage. Of course, I secretly hope that English-speaking fans of fiction, regardless of their ethnic background, will read it too and develop an appreciation for the author, Jenő Rejtő.

Who was Jenő Rejtő? When I read this book as a ten-year-old boy, I had no idea. At the time, he was not listed in the Encyclopedia among the prominent Hungarian literary authors. In fact, most critics dismissed Rejtő as a pulp writer, and he was not taken seriously. However, Rejtő's books have defied the critics and have maintained unwavering popularity since their original publications in the 1930's.

Rejtő was an enigmatic figure in Hungarian literature. He was born to a Jewish Hungarian family as Jenő Reich in Budapest on

March 29, 1905.[2] He later changed his name to Rejtő, which means "hider" (to hide = *rejt*). He indeed tried to hide his identity under several layers of cover. He used several pen names to publish his books. Most of them, particularly the ones set in the French Foreign Legion, were published under the name of P. Howard. To use an English name was his publisher's idea (Dávid Müller, the owner/editor-in-chief of *Nova*) as a marketing ploy – British bestsellers were the fad of the day in Hungary – but Rejtő came up with the name P. Howard on the spot in Müller's office. The year was 1936.

Rejtő could not escape the tragic realities of the times. To understand the era and its impact on Rejtő's life, a brief digression is unavoidable. WWI and its immediate aftermath devastated Hungary.[3] At the end of the Great War, President Mihály Károlyi and Minister of Defense Béla Linder left the country without proper military defense before the completion of peace negotiations, which contributed to Hungary's territorial losses. After the Romanian army, in violation of the cease-fire agreement, advanced to the River Tisza, the Vix Note (named after a French Lieutenant Colonel who represented the Entente Powers) was handed to the Hungarian government. It essentially mandated that Hungary recognize the Romanian territorial gain with the Tisza being the provisional border. Since the citizenry affected by the advancement of the Romanian army was nearly 100% ethnic Hungarian, the government did not want to oblige, nor did it have the power to resist. In this situation, the inept Károlyi practically handed the rule over to Béla Kun's communist government in March of 1919.

The Hungarian Council (*i.e.*, Soviet) Republic was viewed at the Versailles Peace Conference as a threat to capitalism, and the communist leaders were deemed unsuitable as partners in diplomacy. Thus, Hungary was not invited to the Peace Conference until after the collapse of the Council Republic, by which time all meaningful decisions had been made. In Hungary, the Red Terror of the Council Republic provoked a backlash: increased antisemitism, a transient period of White Terror, and strong, lasting anticommunist sentiment.

The last accord of the Versailles peace negotiations, known as the Treaty of Trianon, was signed on June 4, 1920. By then, Hungary was reestablished as a kingdom (headed by Admiral Horthy whom the Parliament elected as Regent). The Treaty (in reality, a dictate), in the name of ethnic self-determination, broke up the territorial integrity of the multiethnic Hungarian Kingdom (where Hungarians were in majority) disregarding the distribution of ethnicities, and generated several small multiethnic Successor States, where Hungarians were a large minority. Hungary lost two thirds of her territory, and one third of her ethnic Hungarian population; *i.e.*, every third Hungarian was condemned to a minority status – without self-determination – in hostile countries, which surrounded Hungary. These countries formed the Little Entente. In "maimed Hungary" (the leftover core) – by far became the least multiethnic Successor State – Jews comprised the largest ethnic and/or religious minority (~5 to 6%).

Hungary tried to regain at least those territories where ethnic Hungarians were in majority. This diplomacy led to Italian and German alliance and to the First (November 2, 1938) and Second (August 30, 1940) Vienna Awards, which returned the southern part of Slovakia and Northern Transylvania, respectively, to Hungary by diplomatic means.

Hitler played Hungary and the Successor States against each other, enticing the Successor States (and threatening Hungary) with annulment of the Vienna Awards. The machinations led to Hungary formally joining the Axis Powers – Germany, Italy, and Japan – of the Tripartite Pact on November 20, 1940. Romania and Slovakia joined the Pact on November 23 and 24, respectively.

Under pressure from Hitler's Germany, in 1938, 1939, and 1941, the Hungarian Parliament passed three increasingly harsh Jewish Laws and, upon the bombardment of the city of *Kassa* allegedly by the Soviet air force (which was either a Nazi false flag operation or an error of the Soviet pilots), Hungary entered WWII against the Soviet Union. Although the Arrow Cross Party (a Hungarian Nazi party) became a governing force only in October of 1944 (in a coup d'état with help from occupying German forces that removed the mostly lame-duck, albeit reemerging Regent), they had been a significant and vocal political minority since 1939. Under Regent Horthy (an ardent opponent of both the Arrow Cross Party and the communists), the Hungarian government refused deporting the Jewish population to Auschwitz. This and Horthy's bailout attempts (secret armistice negotiations with the British in Turkey) that Nazi intelligence had discovered prompted the German military occupation of Hungary on March 19, 1944, and led to the Holocaust in Hungary. Horthy was formally left in charge, but the real power rested with Veesenmayer, Hitler's plenipotentiary to Hungary. Prime Minister Miklós Kállay had to find refuge from the Gestapo at the Turkish Embassy, former PM István Bethlen went into hiding from the Germans, and Regent Horthy was forced to appoint a new Prime Minister (Sztójay) and cabinet (in essence, a Quisling government), almost exclusively as dictated by Veesenmayer, down to the level of undersecretaries. To this date, it is fiercely debated whether Horthy should have resigned and to what extent he was culpable for the Holocaust.

Jenő Rejtő became a victim of these events, although he died before the German occupation. When Hungary entered WWII as an ally of Germany, the ill-equipped 2nd Hungarian Army was sent to the Eastern Front. An estimated 45 to 50 thousand of the approximately 243,000 men perished in the operation, most of them at the battle of Voronezh in January of 1943, or died due to the harsh conditions (cold, lack of nutrition, diseases). The Hungarian Army consisted of an armed force and a labor service; both were mostly draftees. Jews were drafted to the labor service. Of the original 207 thousand men of the 2nd Hungarian Army sent to the Eastern Front in the summer of 1942, approximately 17 thousand were in the labor service.

Jenő Rejtő was in poor health, when a newspaper of the Arrow Cross Party (*Egyedül Vagyunk* [*We Are Alone*]) published an article about him on October 9, 1942, in which they raised objections to Rejtő not having been drafted and having been able to continue writing his novels at his usual table in a Budapest café in spite of being a Jew. Sympathizers (and members) of the Arrow Cross Party were present in several institutions. The newspaper article achieved its intended effect, and Rejtő was soon drafted to labor service with instructions to report to the railway station in *Nagykáta*, an agricultural town about 40 miles southeast of Budapest. On November 27, his squadron was dispatched to Soviet territory, where he soon died of typhus (a disease spread by lice – an infestation that reached epidemic proportions during the war) on January 1, 1943.

There is no doubt that Rejtő was singled out by the Arrow Cross Party's newspaper because of antisemitic hatred. Rejtő's success as an author made him visible in spite of his "layers of identity cover." This hatred cut short the life of a talented, prolific author. He was 37 years old when he died.

Of course, when I read *The Frontier Garrison* (still my favorite book by him, along with *The Three Musketeers in Africa*) at the age of ten, I was completely oblivious to Rejtő's biography. However, growing up in Hungary, particularly in the 1960's (merely twenty years after the end of WWII) made it impossible to remain unaware of the war and the Holocaust even at such a young age. Every family was affected by tragedy, and every family had vivid memories.

I knew that my paternal uncle was a career officer of the Hungarian Army who died at "the Bend of the River Don," *i.e.*, the battle of Voronezh. He was no Nazi. Like our family in general, he despised the Nazis and communists alike, and was against attacking the Soviet Union. Alas, no one asked his opinion. He wanted to attend War School (to become a General Staff officer), but his application was turned down. According to family stories, it was because the Army had also turned down his marriage application somewhat earlier. In the end, he married his wife in a fairly secretive fashion at a very private ceremony. To this date, I am not sure what the Army found objectionable about her, but I suspect that she might have had some Jewish ancestry. Marriage between a Jew (as defined by ancestry) and a non-Jew was banned by the Third Jewish Law. Thus, instead of War School, my uncle was dispatched with the fighting forces to the Eastern Front. His body was never recovered. He is probably resting in a mass grave near *Ostrogozhsk*, Russia.

Nearly 28,000 of the fallen soldiers of the 2nd Hungarian Army are listed in a thick volume: János Bús, Péter Szabó: *May They Rest in Peace*.[4] My father (who was never able to come to grips with the loss of his brother) gave this book to me. My uncle is listed among the fallen on page 511: Captain *Endre Kacsó*: January 19, 1943, *Ostrogozhsk*.

And there is another entry on page 658: *Jenő Reich*: January 1, 1943, *Evdakovo*.

My uncle, a Captain of the Hungarian Army, and Jenő Rejtő, draftee to the labor service, died far away from Hungary, yet within 15 miles of one another and 18 days apart. They were both victims of Nazism.

As an added strange coincidence, my mother's family was from *Nagykáta* – the town where Jenő Rejtő boarded the train as a draftee of the labor service.

Against this backdrop, I believe it is understandable that I feel a special connection to Jenő Rejtő.

Jenő Rejtő
(1905-1943)

After WWII, during the hard line communist era, Jenő Rejtő's books were not published. They were not on the banned list, and used copies exchanged hands for exorbitant prices. The communist regime, however, deemed his books "pulp" not worthy for printing. But times changed, and so did perception and cultural policy. When a bestseller remains popular for well over seventy years, it becomes a classic. The author who wrote several such classics cannot be dismissed as a "pulp writer." Rejtő earned his place in the pantheon of Hungarian literature.

Rejtő's books are among the most popular and widely read in Hungary. From preteens to retirees in their 90's, from those with minimal education to those with the most advanced degrees, people enjoy his writing. A friend of my parents, the late András Komán, was a medical doctor who specialized in laboratory medicine. I still remember his enthusiasm when quoting passages from Rejtő's books by heart. He told me that the students attending medical school immediately after WWII, when exhausted from studying their textbooks, had turned to reading "P. Howard" as a relief.

To have such a broad cross-cultural appeal, no book can be very sophisticated in a Shakespearian sense. But what holds the interest of the intellectuals? I seriously doubt that it is the story line or the stylish use of the language.

One of my professors in medical school (the late Tamás Ács – a deeply humanistic geneticist) once suggested that I should read books by Dostoyevsky and Rejtő. He went on to say that Rejtő had a gift of creating memorable characters in a few sentences. He was right. In addition to his offbeat humor, this is exactly the secret to Rejtő's broad appeal and staying power. *The Frontier Garrison* is an excellent example of Rejtő's character-creating talent – not just the main characters, but also those in supporting roles, like one of my favorite P. Howard characters, Hümér Troppauer, the legionnaire poet.

There are a couple of well-known movies that have a sense of humor that is reminiscent of P. Howard's. One of them is *The Mummy* (Universal Pictures, 1999), which was categorized as "period, horror, action/adventure, and romance." Incidentally, an early scene of *The Mummy* includes a fight between the French Foreign Legion and Bedouin tribesmen. If *The Frontier Garrison* were a movie, it would be categorized similarly: "period, espionage, action/adventure, ghost story, and romance." In addition, both movies would be (or should be) categorized as comedy. In a scene of *The Mummy*, Evelyn (Rachel Weisz) wants to make sure that Rick (Brendan Fraser) is telling the truth. She asks Rick: "Do you swear?" Rick replies: "Every damn day!" This exchange could have leapt from a page of a P. Howard book. Another movie that has P. Howard-like offbeat sense of humor is *Shrek*. Lord Farquaad (voiced by John Lithgow) proclaims in a scene when he is sending off champions to rescue Princess Fiona from the dragon to become his bride: "Some of you may die, but that's a sacrifice I am willing to make."

Rejtő's books present certain challenges to the translator. Today, Rejtő has a cult-like following in Hungary, and the Hungarian readers are very familiar with Rejtő's style of humor. It is almost in the air. However, when English speakers read the translation, the humor might fall between the cracks, particularly if the reader has a critical mindset and attributes odd phrases, paradoxical statements, semi-obvious platitudes, and the like to poor translation.

Regardless of the quality of translation, the uninitiated reader might even find Rejtő's repetitious usage of attributive adjectives as parts of noun phrases objectionable, such as *"the fat Yvette (who had a perfect baby face)"* or *"the chunky poet with a gorilla jaw."* However, Rejtő was certainly not the first one to use satirical juxtaposition of Homeric style *epitheton ornans* and mundane characters. Another example of such parody in Hungarian literature is *The Hammer of the Village* [*A helység kalapácsa*] by the 19th century poet Sándor Petőfi.

There are other recurring elements, phrases in every Rejtő book, characteristic of his style. The recurring elements are used in several ways, but they are primarily used for generating a pattern, a certain rhythm for the prose, thereby conveying a poetic undercurrent. But it would not be Rejtő if it were done without an eye on humor. This style of humor is called offbeat for a reason:

one is lulled into a rhythm, which is then unexpectedly broken, or the recurring phrase is placed in a surprising context.

Rejtő was very fond of using onomatopoeic words, some of which are difficult to properly translate to retain the meaning and comparable onomatopoeia. A similar challenge was to convey the emotional state of the characters by using various words describing body posture or gait. Hungarian is particularly rich and nuanced in such expressions, and Rejtő used them very effectively. Finding the perfect match in English puts the translator to the test. In addition, of course, some of the humor stems from playing on words or expressions, which might not be amenable to comparably humorous translation. On occasion, to retain the humor, the original text was translated with some poetic license.

Rejtő sprinkled his books set in the French Foreign Legion with French military jargon, such as addressing the sergeant as *Oui mon chef!* (Yes, Sir!), or an officer giving a command as *Rompez!* (one of Rejtő's favorite French words in his Foreign Legion books, meaning *Dismissed! Break up! Fall out!* [to leave one's place in the ranks]). Rejtő intended to create an atmosphere by inserting French words; therefore, these were left unchanged in the English translation (*i.e.,* only the Hungarian text was translated). To aid the reader, the English translation of the French expressions were included in the End Notes in the order of first occurrence and alphabetized in the Glossary. Rejtő, who was proficient in German, made occasional errors in his French texts; *e.g.,* the lyrics to the march of the Legion were quoted incorrectly, and some French words were misspelled. These were corrected. I am grateful for her help to my daughter, Dori – an astute student of the French language – who was instrumental in presenting the French expressions correctly.

The spelling of some of the names in the story was changed. These names were spelled with Hungarian phonetics in the original, even though they were not Hungarian names. An example is the Czech name *Hlaváč* transliterated into English as *Hlavách*. If you look up the flower *scabiosa* (the meaning of *Hlavách*) in Wikipedia, and then chose Czech as the language, you will see the proper spelling. *Hlavách* was spelled as *Hlavács* in the Hungarian original text of the novel. Some names were translated into English, such as *Elek Rongy* as *Alec Rags*. This example is a literal translation of the meaning of *Rongy*. The character was not Hungarian, indicating the Hungarian word used as his name was an epithet. *Alec* was chosen as the cognate English name of the original *Elek*.

Temperature, weight, volume, length, and distance were given in the novel in metric units. In most cases, these were converted into the traditional units used in the United States (*e.g.*, °F in lieu of °C, inch for centimeter, pound for kilogram, *etc.*).

I am the first to admit that the best way to translate is to translate a foreign language text into one's mother tongue. Thus, I would have been better equipped to translate an English book into Hungarian rather than the other way around. To make sure that the text reads well in English, I recruited some of my friends who are native speakers of American English. I am particularly grateful to Dr. Jon Martin for his help and never ending patience and encouragement. Jenny and Nash Mayfield (who are professional high school English teachers) and my daughter Dori Kacsoh also provided valuable help in polishing the manuscript.

In Hungary, Jenő Rejtő is often remembered as the *Immortal Legionnaire* because many of his books are set in the French Foreign Legion, including *The Frontier Garrison*. I hope you will enjoy this true classic "P. Howard" novel.

Balint Kacsoh
Macon, Georgia, USA
January, 2014

CHAPTER ONE

1

Pigeon sailed through the air and slammed against the wall. The next moment he punched the boatswain in the mouth with such force that, in his surprise, the boatswain swallowed the quarter-pound wad of tobacco he had been chewing, and he then had the hiccups for minutes.

This was the moment the helmsman was waiting for. He grabbed Pigeon with his huge arms to play his usual trick, which was to twirl his opponent with a twist and fling him to the farthest corner of the pub. The helmsman was well known for this stunt in most major ports around the world.

His gigantic arm was already lifting his opponent when, somewhere from the direction of the man it grabbed, a steel-like object fell on the helmsman's face, knocking him out for a moment. Later, his friends would swear under oath that the heavy object was Pigeon's fist.

A couple of seconds later, the helmsman got up from the floor, still dizzy, and opened his eyes.

He immediately got slapped, and the blow knocked him back to the floor. When he made another attempt to get up, Pigeon delivered a barrage of blows, making him fall down again.

Now he remained seated and meekly said:

"I am Alec Rags. If I might ask you, could we please suspend this for a while?"

"Certainly. My name is Jules Manfred Harrincourt.⁵"

Rags got up.

"Listen here, Jules Manfred Harrincourt. You can be proud of yourself. For your information, I have never been beaten before. This is the very first time."

"All beginnings are hard. From now on it will come to you easier. But tell me, sir, why did you gentlemen want to kill me?"

"Have a seat at my table, and I'll tell you."

The preceding close encounter and the subsequent cordial conversation took place at a popular entertainment locale in the Port of Marseille that was known to the gentlemen of the underworld as the *Rabid Dog Café & Restaurant*.

Rags, the helmsman of the schooner *Brigitta*, and Paul, its boatswain, had been at sea in the Pacific for two years. Naturally, they were unaware that, in their absence, certain things in Marseille had changed.

Thus, presumably, they did not know about Pigeon. Pigeon had arrived from Paris about a year ago at a time the *Brigitta* was sailing somewhere around the West Indies.

Pigeon was tall, perhaps a bit lanky and relatively wide-mouthed, but overall, a rather handsome young man. He was perpetually smiling, and his large blue eyes looked at everyone with unlimited trust.

Where he came from, what he did before, nobody asked. Here, in the neighborhood of the Port, it was utterly impolite to inquire about the past of one's acquaintances. Everybody comes from wherever he pleases – or from wherever he is being released.

Pigeon arrived with a straw hat on his head. His striped, rather shaggy jacket was thrown on his forearm; he was smoking and kept a bamboo walking stick spinning between his fingers, whistling a quiet tune. His classy, sophisticated appearance immediately stood out among the Port's simple folk, who consisted of porters and robbers. They most admired his beautiful shoes. One of them was especially elegant, a buttoned lacquer shoe with a white insole.

Putting much care into one's appearance will draw attention. The proof of this was the small crowd, which patiently followed the distinguished stranger for many blocks.

Music could be heard from the *Tiger* restaurant, and the stranger entered.

Later, after the riot police and the emergency crew had restored order and collected the injured, the desperate restaurateur could only say this to the captain of the police:

"A lunatic with a walking stick came in, said he wanted to play the harmonica, and then destroyed the room."

The innkeeper did not lie. Harrincourt had indeed stepped to the middle of the pub, and with the widest and most polite grin said:

"Ladies and gentlemen! Please allow me to borrow the harmonica from the conductor of the orchestra and play a few pastoral dreams for you. Afterwards, if I might beg for your financial support for a poor but talented musician."

The restaurateur politely asked him to go to hell. A porter, who was a generous soul, was of the opinion that the lunatic should be allowed to play the harmonica.

Pot, the 250-pound gangster, who had broken up with his lover earlier that day and because of that was in a foul mood in the first place, shouted at Pigeon:

"Leave at once! You idiot!"

Harrincourt jokingly threatened him by waving a finger:

"Now, now, little giant! One should not be impolite!"

The giant was in front of the newcomer with two steps and…

And, beyond comprehension, along a beautiful arched trajectory, he flew back to his table, knocking to the ground his entire company and a couple of quarts of rum.

The rest of the events followed quickly. Some of the customers jumped to their feet and ran toward the stranger who picked up a chair and knocked the lamp off the ceiling.

A riot erupted. The sound of broken glass, cries, and fisticuffs filled the room. At a convenient moment, Pigeon threw the entire bar counter into the melee, and then the innkeeper with a kitchen knife, the tapster with a fire-poker, and the maitre d' with his son.

By the next evening, the restaurant was restored, music was loud again, and, apart from those regulars who were still in the hospital, the usual evening crowd gathered.

At nine o'clock, the door opened and the cheerful stranger entered.

He waved his straw hat with the grandeur of a lord, and, with a polite smirk, stepped to the center.

The innkeeper, the tapster, the maitre d' and his son froze.

"Ladies and gentlemen!" started Pigeon. "My concert, which was postponed due to yesterday evening's session of Swedish gymnastics,[6] with your kind permission, I will give tonight. The conductor will loan me his harmonica, and the performance will commence."

He then took the musician's harmonica into his hand, stood on a chair, sat on the top of its back, threw his jacket gracefully to the maitre d', and with deep feeling played *"Louis the Stoker Sailed to the New Hebrides."* He sang the second verse. The number was, beyond a doubt, well received. The atmosphere was still chilly, but many had released the grip on their pocketknives, a sure sign of easing tension in this neighborhood. And when Pigeon played the march beginning with *"Hey sailor, hey sailor, what is storm to you, what is danger to you,"* which he completed with a short tap dance, everybody applauded and demanded with wild foot-thumping that the artist continue his concert.

By the closing hour, Harrincourt had established his popularity. Ample small change had fallen into his plate and when, using a piece of silk paper stretched onto a comb, he buzzed the tune of the hit *"Laugh you clown, though tears trickle down your painted face,"* spirits rose so high that Lala, the bicycle thief who had always been known for living large, ordered strawberry punch, and until dawn, many bottles of rum were sold.

2

Harrincourt was the Port's favorite. There were very few whose strength was comparable to his, yet he tried to avoid any conflict and tolerated the worst practical jokes.

For his dovish nature, he earned the nickname "Pigeon."

He performed in pubs every night. He played more than just the harmonica. If it came to it, he played the fiddle and the cittern and could do card tricks. Nobody ever heard him swear. He conducted as polite conversations with the fourteen-year-old cigar seller as if the boy were an equal of the pub's regular scum. He was always clean-shaven, and he sent birthday flowers to Mimi, the *Knife Thrower* pub's barmaid.

Jealous cavaliers of the night attempted to stab him on several occasions and rarely without reason. With fatherly gentleness, he took all these men to the nearest emergency room to get bandages.

Such a chap was Pigeon.

Neither Alec Rags the helmsman, nor the boatswain was aware of the above prelude. That, in itself, would not have been a problem, but the two seamen brought with them to the restaurant the fat Yvette, a lady who pleased them and who, although weighing 180 pounds, had a perfect baby face. Yvette applauded Pigeon constantly during his show. Even this small accolade was not to the liking of the helmsman. But later, the fat Yvette, with unheard of impertinence, took a whole five-frank coin from the palm of the boatswain and threw it to this vagabond comedian.

"Hey! Jester! Give me back my five franks!" said the boatswain, stepping to the center of the pub.

To his astonishment, the performer handed the money over.

"Here you go, pal. Just don't get yourself worked up, because once my cousin suffered a stroke when he did. The poor devil owned a general store in Metz…"

"How dare you mock me?! Take this!"

The rest has been described. The boatswain had gotten such a slap from Pigeon that he had swallowed a quarter pound of chewing tobacco, and Pigeon had continued beating the helmsman until he had begged him in earnest to stop. The helmsman had taken this occasion to introduce himself as Alec Rags.

Now they were all drinking at the corner table and the helmsman was no longer bothered by the fact that the fat Yvette (who had a perfect baby face) could not take her eyes off Pigeon.

"I am surprised," said the helmsman, while immersing his nose, swollen to the size of an eggplant, into a glass of water, "that you have chosen such an ugly trade. Whoever can give a slap this big has the entire world at his feet."

The boatswain nodded with conviction. He was a star witness.

"My trade is beautiful," Pigeon defended himself. "Philharmonics and ballet count as serious professions these days."

"A man like you must take on the high seas! The oceans! Have you ever thought of becoming a sailor?"

Pigeon's face darkened.

"I was a sailor once."

"Splendid! If you qualify, you can join us on the *Brigitta*. Do you have papers?"

"No, I don't."

"Then you qualify. Do you want to come with us?"

Yvette abruptly interrupted them:

"Don't go Mr. Pigeon! The *Brigitta* will sink soon. It is a shabby, rotten sailboat. I will tell you honestly, if the sailor gentlemen will not take it as insult that only the most desperate jailbirds would accept a job on it."

"Don't listen to Yvette. The *Brigitta* is a very good ship," the helmsmen said dubiously. Yvette turned pale from outrage:

"You dare say this to me? You want to tell me tales about ships, after I have been making friends with the world's naval corps for twenty years? I say that the *Brigitta* will perish. Its beams are rotting, and it submerges half an inch deeper than its Plimsoll mark."

"That's true," admitted the boatswain, "but after all, folks don't board ships looking to live restfully to a ripe old age. Are you coming or not, Pigeon?"

"Is that vessel really that dangerous?" Pigeon asked pensively. The helmsman sighed and shrugged his shoulders:

"Since the mother of all ships is present, I must confess that the *Brigitta* could not aspire to a blue ribbon. If you were a family man, I wouldn't invite you."

"Thank you. Since I have a family, I accept the invitation, and I will enlist on the *Brigitta*."

"But are you sure that you don't have papers?"

"Not a single one."

"You will have to provide a certificate to that effect. The captain is an old-fashioned man, and he insists on certain formalities. Let's go."

"Don't go, Mr. Pigeon," cooed Yvette, weeping as if for her spouse while melancholic wrinkles appeared on her perfect baby face. "Don't go, Mr. Pigeon. If you need five or ten franks from time to time, I will happily lend you the money."

"Thank you for your generous credit line offer, but I cannot accept it. Hey! Jeanette! Bring a glass of rum and a bouquet of flowers for the lady and charge it to my account. I kiss your hands, noble lady!"

And they were gone. In the street, Yvette's cooing voice followed him for a second, "Don't go, Mr. Pigeon!"

CHAPTER TWO

1

But Mr. Pigeon went.

It was enough to see the *Brigitta* from a distance to realize that Yvette had not been exaggerating. Even a short coastline trip would have been risky for this steamboat. Yet it went on high-seas voyages that lasted several months.

Pigeon made a deal with the captain within the hour. In four days, they would leave for Havana, then onward through the Panama Canal to the Pacific Ocean. The trip would be concluded in less than a year.

"Tell me," asked the boatswain when they were on shore again, "why did you enlist immediately when you heard that traveling on this ship puts your life at risk? Do you want to die perhaps?"

"No way!" replied Pigeon somewhat frightened. "I just love danger."

Uh-oh! I better watch out, he thought, and went to a coffee shop to write a letter to his mother and sister. His widowed mother and Anette, his fourteen-year old sister lived in the Harrincourts' old family residence in the villa district of Paris. Unfortunately, the house was mortgaged well above its value. Their acquaintances in Parisian high society had no idea that the young Harrincourt was a pub singer in Marseille or that the modest household of this fine, well-respected, aristocratic family was sustained from his income.

Harrincourt used to be a cadet at the naval academy. He was well loved there, too, because some are born to this world to be loved everywhere. But grouchy individuals, such as the Marquee Lauton Tracy, Naval Superintendent, resist any charm with their stone-cold hearts. Lauton Tracy lived all by himself at his vineyard near Lyon. On occasion, he made appearances at the Naval Academy or aboard the training boat for a few days, so that he could deliver grim sermons, waving his bony fingers and pushing his bushy eyebrows together above his skinny, mummy-like face.

Because of him, the cadets were perpetually bitter and desperate. Even the teachers were not fond of him. However, Tracy's family was well connected, seemingly ensuring that instead of retirement, he would die of old age amidst a naval parade. But Harrincourt, whose promotion the Superintendent had denied after a war-game maneuver, made sure that Tracy's future took a different path.

That fateful day, Harrincourt cheerfully showed up in the cadets' sleeping quarters:

"Today that old Tracy lost favor with me. I will make him retire."

"You are out of your mind," commented one of his colleagues, not without foundation.

"You can wager a silver cigarette lighter that Uncle Tracy will be sent to retirement before the next exams."

"I accept the bet."

Harrincourt won the lighter but lost his career. The Naval Superintendent's retirement happened under fairly sad circumstances. During the Great War, the Allied Forces mutually gave decorations to a few officers. The French appointed British cavalry officers as captains of the Senegal infantry, and the British reciprocated by appointing their French comrades to posts with Scottish and Irish troops. Everyone knew Tracy was an honorary captain in a Scottish regiment. The Prince of Wales was visiting in Paris at the time, and on this occasion Tracy was invited to the Naval Academy ball, the patron of which was His Majesty. The cadets were working day and night, and Harrincourt was among those who addressed the invitations. The Undersecretary who signed every card, of course did not read the text of each and every one; if he had, he would have noticed that one of them had a different text. Otherwise it appeared to be the same as the rest. But at the bottom it was written:

"The honorary members of the British Army
are requested to wear the appropriate parade uniform."

It is impossible to describe what kind of a scene it was when the old, bald Tracy appeared at the ball wearing a Scottish captain's uniform, sporting a checkered kilt and baring his nude knees. The event remained the topic of conversation for years. According to the Prime Minister, the sight was unforgettable. Nobody made a scene, and His Majesty the Prince of Wales made a few unbiased remarks to the embarrassed Tracy who was on the verge of passing out, thanking him for his astute thoughtfulness in displaying the traditional French-British friendship donning this uniform.

Those unable to suppress their laugh retreated to an adjacent room. They were soon joined by His Majesty.

Afterward, there was a general movement for retiring the old superintendent. The high-ranking members of his family were unwilling to compromise themselves by defending him, and Harrincourt won his bet. But Tracy's invitation card, even if it did not absolve the old man of the guilt of naïveté, was evidence that there was a prankster involved. Thus ended Harrincourt's naval career.

This was a great disaster for his family, and Harrincourt knew what he had caused with his carelessness. But he decided to make up for his mistake. His mother and sister should not suffer hardship because of him. He would sacrifice himself for them. He bought a ten thousand-dollar life insurance policy that would pay the beneficiaries if "in the course of his professional duties, Jules Manfred Harrincourt should die."

He decided that his mother and sister would get the ten thousand dollars. He would make sure that "in the course of his professional duties" he would suffer a fatal accident.

He sold all his possessions, added his modest paternal

inheritance to it, and paid the premium of the policy for half a year. From that point on, he was very careful in his life outside of work because he had to die in the course of his professional duties – within half a year. If he were to be run down by a car or stabbed to death on the streets, it would be to no avail.

This is how he wound up in Marseille, and why he jumped to accept the job on the *Brigitta*. To be a sailor is a "profession." The ten thousand dollars would be sufficient for his mother and sister to make ends meet.

The guests at the pubs had no clue that the sentimental and cheerful tunes were sung by a man who had condemned himself to death.

2

However, it came to light that although it is hard to live, it is not so easy to die either.

It was eight o'clock in the evening, and the *Brigitta* was to set sail before midnight. The helmsman, the boatswain, and Pigeon had a small farewell party at the *Cheerful Morgue* pub.

Pigeon, for the last time, performed his most beautiful couplet. It was followed by a thundering applause; flowers and small change were thrown at his feet, but, since the helmsman and the boatswain had already gone, Pigeon also waved his straw hat, took his bamboo walking stick under his arm, and left. He cheerfully strolled down the narrow alley leading to the pier. From the shadow of a gate, Yvette stepped up to him:

"Mr. Pigeon," she cooed with her tear-soaked baby face.

Pigeon turned to her with a kind smile.

"I kiss your hand, my lady. The memory of the fact that I can see you no more will live in me forever."

He politely kissed Yvette's hands. He then went on his way.

Rather, he would have gone on his way.

But the 180-pound, perfectly baby-faced wench, amidst pouring tears, gathered all the protective spirit of her gentle heart and banged him on the head with a police baton so hard that Mr. Pigeon did not regain consciousness until dawn. He was lying on the cobblestones of the deserted alley.

And the *Brigitta* was already at sea.

CHAPTER THREE

1

Harrincourt had a mere five months to live. During that time, he had to die unless he wanted his ancestors' house to be auctioned and his relatives to sink among the poor of Paris.

He was contemplating this somberly while chewing the confection of the poor – a couple of sunflower seeds – and sitting on a bench at the old pier.

All of a sudden, his eyes caught Fort St. Jean on the other side: the fort of foreign legionnaire rookies, upon the hill, across from the wonderful cathedral of *Notre Dame de la Garde*.

The Foreign Legion!

After all, it was a profession. One entered a contract with the French government and received a salary. And there it was really not difficult to die.

But why would he have to die?

Yippee!

He rushed downtown. He found the insurance firm's huge palace on *La Canebière*.[8] His elegance may have appeared quite fancy at the piers (especially one of his shoes, which had its buttoned, white insole in an almost perfect condition), but here he was not allowed to see the chief executive officer. After articulating a couple of life-threatening statements, making unusually rude and slanderous attacks on character, and limiting the security guard's personal freedom by grabbing him by the neck, Harrincourt finally stood before a manager.

Harrincourt enthusiastically presented his idea:

"I have a first-class offer. Let's play with open cards. If I choose a profession that will kill me, you pay ten thousand dollars. Give me five thousand, and I will stay alive."

"I think it will be better if you die," the benevolent manager suggested after a brief consideration. "That way business would be more by the book."

"But Sir! The death of a man means nothing to you?"

"Sure it does. It means the liquidation of a policy."

"You would make money on my offer," he explained with conviction. "If you will not make a deal, I will choose a profession that will kill me in the shortest time, and you will have to pay the entire ten thousand dollars."

"Not quite so. We must take certain deductions from the ten thousand for handling the paperwork, and above that our bank will charge 74 cents as a transaction fee." He said this with his mind obviously wandering elsewhere, all the while scribbling with his pencil on a piece of paper. "And besides, today there is no profession not controlled by government regulations to assure the safety of the workers."

"And if I enlist in the Foreign Legion?"

The manager looked up with sudden surprise:

"That's not a profession! Wait!" He lifted the handset, and pushed a button. "Hallo! Legal Affairs? I want to speak with *avocat*[9] Lagarde. Good morning! A gentleman has a life insurance policy for accidental death suffered in the course of professional duties, and he wants to enlist in the Foreign Legion. What? Thank you." He hung up. "You were right. If you die in the Foreign Legion, then we'll fire the guy who issued your policy because he should have stipulated your profession. Because, you see, there are professional career soldiers."

"Are you then willing to pay half of the policy, five thousand dollars? In the Legion I will be sure to die soon."

"Look, mister, let us not alter the plan. This keeps our business practice more solid, even if it costs us somewhat more."

With a disarming smile he stood up and walked the young man

to the door.

Pigeon was very angry:

"On your sleepless nights, I want you to remember the man you spoke with today!" he said fuming. "Struggle with your conscience! Toss and turn all night, weeping on your pillows!"

"I will do that if get the chance," replied the manager with obliging politeness. "Do you wish anything else?"

"No. You think that I am a coward. You are mistaken. You can rest assured that I will die! Good day!"

The manager politely bowed:

"Rest in peace."

Pigeon ran down the stairs in anger. Without a second thought, he reported to the fort right away and enlisted in the Legion's service.

2

Pigeon examined himself nervously. Why was he smiling all the time? A man who must die should at least behave seriously, even if a noble somberness is out of the question.

He did not have a shred of doubt, even for a second, that before the next insurance premium was due he would make sure to become a victim of his profession. Until then, he would do some introspection. Most men, after making such tragic decisions, meditate with their chins raised, or they write a diary, but they certainly do not keep whistling all the time. However, all his efforts to be somber were in vain. His attempt to become a serious man before his fast-approaching passing proved to be hopeless.

The platoon of rookie legionnaires would leave in two days. Space was in short supply at Fort St. Jean, and the newcomers were shipped out quickly.

One morning Harrincourt was in the middle of attempting to walk with a cloudy sadness when one of the corporals yelled to him and summoned him to the warehouse to sort the underwear.

The corporal who ran the warehouse was an old, crippled legionnaire, a tough-as-nails cannibal perfectly suited for the task of giving an idea about order to undisciplined civilians. This man never smiled because there was a machine gun bullet in his head that could not be removed by surgery.

"You throw me the underwear one by one. I will make the inventory."

"Very good."

"Silence! A private doesn't speak!"

Pigeon smiled apologetically and threw the undergarments one by one.

He then sprang to attention. The corporal looked at him questioningly.

"I report to you, Sir, that I would like to whistle, Sir."

The cannibal was astonished. This man must have been in the armed forces before – that much was evident from his poise. And how young he was! In reality, he should have reprimanded him for such a report, but the private had something in his face that reminded him of a nice dog. *What the heck*, he thought.

"Well, you may whistle if you are in the mood, considering you will leave for Africa the day after tomorrow."

"It will work out one way or another. Even there, one does not get eaten but in certain regions." And then he was whistling. Not some contemporary, fancy song, but an old Parisian coachmen's tune. He did not request separate permission to wave the undergarments left and right at the rhythm of the music like some sort of veil dancer throwing them to the corporal in a graceful move. This youngster was out of his mind, that much was certain.

When they were done with the work, the corporal rather morosely said to the rookie:

"You may drink a glass of wine with me if you are thirsty."

Pigeon was a good judge of character. He slammed his heels together so that the whole warehouse trembled:

"Thank you, *mon chef!*[10]"

He could salute properly, that much was certain.

In the canteen, the man-hating corporal with the bullet in his head drew quite a bit of attention when he had the rookie seated at his normally lonely table.

"That thing, that tune, whistle it for me again, you snot-face."

"At your command, buddy," replied Pigeon, and addressing the corporal as "buddy" was compensated for by a click of the heels under the table that made the glasses quiver.

He whistled more songs, and they drank much *Bordeaux* wine. After the fourth bottle, the old corporal confessed to Pigeon that he was still in love with that damned woman. Pigeon put his arms around the corporal's shoulder, rested his head on the corporal's green lapel, and then, in response, he sang in a sentimental tone:

"I love no one else but you,
Beautiful Rue Malesherbes,
Beautiful Rue Malesherbes,
Farewell forever…"

The corporal must have had a cold because he was frequently sniffling, and his pipe didn't have a proper draw, either.

The next morning, Pigeon was summoned again to the warehouse, but instead of sorting underwear, he had to eat homemade sausages. This was a pleasant existence for a rookie who would leave for Oran the next day; and from there, onward to the desert.

The next day, after the roll call and line up, the rookies left the fort marching to the port, where an Africa-bound ship waited for them.

Pigeon stood in the courtyard of the fort incredulously.

His name was not called! The platoon was led away without him. He was about to protest such incomprehensible absentmindedness when the corporal with the bullet in his head stepped up to him and said:

"You can thank me, you snot-face. I arranged that, for the time being, they leave you here to work in the warehouse."

CHAPTER FOUR

1

Pigeon decided that he would never again be a likeable fellow to anyone. He lost a full week of his valuable time in Marseille, where under no circumstances could a legionnaire become the victim of his profession. The veteran soldier also regretted by then to have tried, even if temporarily, to protect this child-faced recruit from the horrors of the desert. Because the rookie, ever since the platoon had left without him, whistled nothing but the most contemporary jazz tunes, and, on top of that, so much off key that the corporal's old head wound started aching again. Thus, after a short time, Pigeon was en route to Oran aboard the steamer *Father of the Legion*.

The small, dirty boat danced restlessly on the waves of the Mediterranean. The legionnaires sat at the bottom of the boat, where they drank coffee from their mess tins as always. The bad-smelling smoke of *Caporal* cigarettes filled the galley like a thick fog.

The trellised lantern kept swinging with a perpetual squeak. The soldiers squatted rigidly in the gloomy room among their bags, crates, and blankets.

From the outside, the constant murmur of the stormy sea blared in their ears. An old legionnaire, who had begun his second five-year term and thus had a two-month vacation in Marseille, was returning to Africa together with the rookies. He had a long, graying, brown moustache and a large Adam's apple. His name was Pilotte. He was now quietly smoking his pipe, and in a subdued voice he was telling the inexperienced rookies what fate awaited them.

"In the beginning, it's pretty bad down there, but later, when you realize that you can never get used to it, you accept everything with resignation."

The soldiers listened to him with anxious and dark looks. Each was a study in character: lean, bloodless adolescent heads with deep, dark rings under their eyes and sun-tanned, determined, strong manly faces. Only one man did not pay attention – a thin legionnaire whose ears were sticking out prominently. Two long parallel wrinkles ran down from his nose to the angles of his mouth. When he smiled, these two wrinkles deepened into grooves, and because he was perpetually smiling, the two peculiar grooves appeared as if they had frozen on his face. His glistening, rapid eyes were constantly on the move in every direction, and his hair, combed down to his forehead, made it even more evident that he was retarded. Because he would draw with anything and everything that he could put in his hand, they called him Chalky. In a short time, Chalky became the prime target of cruel practical jokes. However, so it seemed, he was unaware of this.

"How is the food?" somebody asked.

"It is excellent. Only, during long marches, it is a little simple. If there is no time for cooking, everyone gets a couple of handfuls of flour and onions and eats it the best he can."

Across from Pilotte was seated the most peculiar character in the Legion. He was of average height, but a grotesquely chunky man. He was not obese, just chunky. He had a thick neck, shoulders as wide as planks, big hipbones, a horrific gorilla-jaw, and, on his balding head, a couple of thick, long, entangled black locks of hair. He spoke very little, always looking at his environment with a melancholic sadness, and, from time to time, reading dirty sheets of paper with which he filled all his pockets.

"I have heard," he cut in with his hoarse voice, "that many artists have served in the Foreign Legion."

Pilotte spat:

"Two years ago I served with a Norwegian circus artist, a strongman named Krögmann. The poor devil was bludgeoned to death during an innocent fight in a pub. Then I know an upholsterer who serves with the *sapeurs*[11] stationed in Meknes, and he plays the trumpet beautifully. I have not met any other artist in Africa."

"Are you an artist, by chance?" a rookie asked.

The chunky man, pondering, stroked his gorilla-jaw, on which thick, black stubble gave a dark shadow:

"Yes," he said with a sigh, "I am an artist."

"What kind of an artist?"

"I am Troppauer, the poet," he said as though he were expecting stunned admiration. But these resigned soldiers showed no sign of awe. Rather, they exchanged glances with each other as physicians do when reaching a consensus during a consult in the patient's presence.

"If you will allow me," Troppauer, the poet, announced modestly, "I will read you one of my better known poems."

And before they could reach a decision about his request, he had already pulled out one of his stacks of dirty paper, spread it out with obvious great joy, and to the dismay of his fellow soldiers, started to read aloud:

"*I am a flower*. Written by Hümér Troppauer."

And he read with a calm, self-satisfied smile, from time to time adjusting his long, dark locks of hair.

When he finished the last line, he looked around triumphantly. There was a spine-chilling silence in the bottom of the boat. Pilotte kept his hand on his bayonet.

Only a single voice broke the silence with an exuberant applause:

"Bravo! It was indeed beautiful!"

It was Pigeon. His face was an ear-to-ear smile because of the joy of art. Hümér Troppauer bowed to the audience with a modest and embarrassed smile on his face, pressing down the chin of his gorilla-jaw onto his chest, and his locks of hair dangling:

"I really don't know how I earned your admiration," he said with embarrassment. "Perhaps this poem is so beautiful because I wrote it remembering my sweet mother, may God rest her soul." Incredulously, the soldiers noticed that two fat tears were rolling down from Troppauer's eyes, and his voice cracked. "If you will allow me to describe my mother, I will read you a poetic short novel…"

"Let's hear it! Let's hear it!"

Pigeon exclaimed enthusiastically and clapped his hands.

"Let's hear it! Let's hear it!" squealed a tiny voice. It was Chalky. But he had no clue what was going on.

But the weeping poet could not start reading his opus because a couple of determined soldiers rose from their seats and stepped in front of him.

"You stop this idiotic nonsense at once!" said a Canadian giant.

"But gentlemen! Aren't my poems… beautiful?" he asked, appearing to be on the brink of crying.

"Your poems are boring and stupid!" shouted a Greek wrestler, shaking his fist.

What followed was like a bad dream. The poet punched the Greek wrestler in the face with a vengeance, and the Greek flew across the galley, banged against a beam with his jaw broken, and collapsed unconscious. Troppauer then threw the Canadian lumberman at his cohorts with ease.

There were a few more morose critics rushing against the forceful poet but to no avail. Troppauer threw them on top of each other like tiny wood shavings.

The soldiers watched all this with frightened awe.

The fight was over, and the artist stood all alone at the center of the galley and looked around disapprovingly.

Somebody was moaning; otherwise it was quiet.

The poet sat back into his seat, spread out his dirty bunch of papers, and, in a highbrow, elevated style, chanted:

"*Mother, you are the star of your orphaned son.* Written by Hümér Troppauer. Chapter one…"

The legionnaires then listened to the more than twenty-two-page poem with tense attention all the way.

2

Oran appeared on the distant horizon. The African shore, with its white, box-like, stand-alone houses and palm trees, spread like a smudged canvas in the fog-like light of the morning sun's perpendicular beams.

"All hands on deck!" shouted a sergeant down to the bottom of the boat.

All soldiers appeared on board carrying their gear. A naval officer was watching the shore with his binoculars.

The soldiers' eyes were also fixed on the port they were approaching.

Here comes Africa!

The naval officer looked at the legionnaires indifferently.

And then he was astonished:

"Harrin…court?"

Pigeon was surprised, too:

"Cham…bell?" he stammered.

They had attended the Naval Academy together.

"The sergeant will make an exception and will allow you to step away from the line. I want to have a word with you, Legionnaire," said the officer.

Pigeon stepped out of the line, and followed the officer.

"Harrincourt, are you out of your mind?" he asked anxiously, when they got farther away from the line.

"Lieutenant, Sir…"

"Just call me Jean, as in the old times."

"Well, dear Jean, how can you object to my joining the Foreign Legion?"

"You know very well what the Legion means. The only kind of man that should come here is the one whose death is not a loss when the bullet of a stupid Bedouin kills him in the desert. Listen to me: I am well connected. Field Marshal Cochran, the commander of the city of Oran, is my uncle, and if I spoke with him, perhaps…"

Harrincourt turned pale.

"Don't even think about it! I want to die, and that's the end of it. It's a private matter. I beg you not to interfere with my intentions."

They heard a rattle and a splash as the anchor was lowered. The officer shook hands with his former fellow cadet, and Harrincourt stepped back in line.

A short bridge was rolled out and banged against the pier. The captain's sword flashed, he then marched ashore on the bridge, followed by the thumps of heavy boots.

Chambell sadly followed the platoon with his eyes as they disappeared behind the veil of dust that danced in the sunshine, until the last soldier turned at the corner onto a road that, between a row of ocher houses and green lamp posts, led to Fort St. Thérèse.

Poor Harrincourt, he thought with a sigh.

CHAPTER FIVE

1

A jolly sergeant approached them. His face was covered with pores inflicted by a gunpowder explosion, and one of his eyes was barely visible in its white, bumpy, sponge-like socket. The explosion had left only a few cat-like whiskers of his moustache. Apart from these features, he was a man of jovial disposition. He was waving at the grunts from afar, and then walked by their ranks eyeing them from head to toe.

"I am very pleased with you," he said with honest appreciation. "It would be such a waste if they brought decent men here to bite the dust. Because you will all bite the dust here! *Rompez!*[12]"

He waved again with an encouraging bright smile and hurried away. This was their reception and, to be precise, this was Sergeant Latouret.

A petty officer assigned their sleeping quarters in a long, whitewashed room, and the dead-tired soldiers immediately started to shine their belts and buttons.

Only the idiot Chalky lay down on his bed, and, with a broad smile, fell asleep. Pigeon shook him:

"Hey! Mr. Idiot! Do the *paquetage*[13] because you will be punished if your button is dirty."

"That's alright. I had an uncle in Strasbourg who, on an occasion in the army, when he should have cleaned his buttons…"

"Are you sure you want to tell stories? If in the morning your belts and buttons don't shine, you are going to get it."

"That's alright."

And he lay back. Pigeon got angry. He pulled Chalky's coat off, took the rest of his gear, and cleaned it along with his own. The others had already been fast asleep for hours when Pigeon was still warming a piece of wax on the tip of a matchstick and was shining Chalky's belt with it. Meanwhile he murmured unfriendly things about the idiot who was sleeping calmly.

The Legion must have been involved in a military action because, instead of the usual time of the basic training, they stayed in Oran for only four weeks.

The amount of marching, running, bayonet and shooting practices that filled these four weeks exceeded the expectations of the most pessimistic soldiers.

Sergeant Latouret, in the exhausting noon heat, from time to time ran along the platoon in the direction opposite of their march:

"Come on, boys! Move it, move it! What will you do if it ever comes to some serious marching? Parade march!"

This was the last thing they needed.

They had to march the stretch-kneed, foot-banging parade step of the Legion.

"Come on, my darlings! Bang your feet to the ground! Bang them! This is not a waltz, but a march! One-two! On the double! Corporal! Get a stretcher and take that bloke to the carriage. When he recovers, he will stand guard in front of the Governor's Palace."

Pigeon noted with much self-disgust that he was gaining weight. He was not unaccustomed to the hardships of military life, but under the pressure of the world-renowned training of the Foreign Legion, it would have been expected of him to draw nearer to his passing.

Yet, he was the only one during basic training the dreadful sergeant allowed leave to the city. This grinning, blue-eyed snot-face could do the parade march until the desert crashed under his feet, and he put the rifle on his shoulder like an automaton. How it had happened was anyone's guess, but one day Latouret said:

"You may leave until the evening. Don't you grin or I will have you tied up!"

Pigeon began a long walk along the meandering, dirty, narrow streets, carefully stepping over the Arabs sleeping on the pavement. He entered an adobe shack where coffee was sold. The shack had a single room, four bare walls, and a single opening, the entrance. There was no chair in it, nor any other furniture; only an old bearded Arab who was crouching on the ground in front of an ember-filled pan. He kept boiling water in a small pot, and, when the soldier entered, poured a scoop of coffee in the water. Only after doing so he said:

"Salem."

"The same to you, sonny."

The room was three steps in its width and the same in its length. It was not bigger than a good-sized pigsty. And it didn't smell any better, either. Pigeon just swallowed the coffee and hurried out.

And then Pigeon observed a most peculiar event.

As he came out the door, Pigeon stepped aside to prop his foot on a stone block because a button had come loose on the leg of his pants, and he wanted to sew it tight. Most legionnaires carried needles and thread, for a lost button, a minor parting at a seam was punished so severely that only the riffraff neglected the necessary precautions. He placed his foot on a brick, inserted the thread into the eye of the needle, and tightened the button. He then tightened another one.

Suddenly he pricked his finger.

Just at that moment, a woman hurried out of the adobe shack.

He was certain that while he was sewing his buttons nobody had entered the coffee shack. A moment ago only the old Arab had been inside the narrow, bare-walled room. There was no opening through which someone could have entered the shack from the other side, and there was no furniture that could have hidden anyone else present in the room. The old Arab could not have transformed into a young maiden, and the lady could not have popped out from the bare, compacted clay floor.

How could a woman leave the shack, if she had not been in there?

He decided to return to the coffee-shack.

The door was locked! Either the woman locked it from the

outside or, more likely, the Arab locked the deadbolt from the inside.

What was this? A miracle? A ghost?

The woman did not see the soldier because she immediately turned in the other direction and hurried away. Her white breeches and shiny black riding boots just then disappeared at the corner as she turned.

Pigeon followed her quickly. The woman was headed from the suburb that spread near Fort St. Thérèse toward the European quarter along the rows of plank houses flanking the long *Avenue Magenta*. She must have been used to the tropical climate because there was no neck-protecting back flap dangling from her cap.

On the back of her right hand there was an unusual birthmark of almost perfect geometry. The legionnaire could see it well because he was separated from the woman by less than two steps. She was walking ahead of him, and on the back of her hand there was a dark, triangle-shaped spot on the beautiful, smooth skin. Most peculiar!

Pigeon did not know why he was following her. A woman that had sprung from the ground was certainly interesting. Especially so, if there was a dark, triangle-shaped birthmark on her hand.

They reached the villas of the European quarter. The woman proceeded with ever faster steps. Pigeon dropped behind and snuck from palm to palm to follow her cautiously.

She stopped at the backdoor of a building that was surrounded by a garden with thick vegetation. She looked around. She did not see him because he had hidden behind a tree just in time.

She rang the bell hurriedly. The small gate opened. Pigeon saw that an old butler opened it and bowed deeply. The woman entered.

The soldier waited awhile, and then he returned to the main road toward the front entrance. He took good a look at the villa from the front as well. It was a huge, old-fashioned, two-story building. It had a forbidding quietness about it. Every shutter was closed, the gate was locked, the garden was silent; there was no sound; nor was a man or an animal about.

There was a policeman walking nearby, and he waved at the

legionnaire in a friendly manner.

Pigeon was piqued by a childish curiosity.

"Tell me, Mr. Colleague," he asked the policeman, "who lives in this beautiful villa?"

"Nobody. It is uninhabited."

Hmm… this case was becoming quite a mystery.

"It's such a nice house."

"Yes, but no one wants to rent it. It has been uninhabited for more than half a year, ever since Dr. André Bretail shot his wife, a spahi[14] captain, and finally himself. Do you have a cigarette?"

"A what? Oh, yes, of course. Please."

"Put your pencil away. I was asking for a cigarette!" He formed a horn with his hands and shouted every syllable separately because he presumed that the poor devil was hard of hearing: "Ci-ga-rette!"

"No, thanks, I don't wish to smoke right now," Pigeon replied, reaching for his forehead, and nervously lighting up a *Caporal*. "Are you sure that no one lives here?"

"Absolutely," shouted the policeman. "I have been at this post for a year. There is a night guard who has a key, and he goes through each uninhabited villa from room to room every third day."

"Don't you yell at me or I'll stab you! Do you know by chance a lady who has a triangle-shaped spot or birthmark on her right hand? I saw a lady like that in the neighborhood."

The policeman drew a cross at his chest.

"What was that for?" Pigeon urged him to answer. "Don't waste my time with liturgy! Just answer the question. Do you know such a lady?"

"I knew only one lady with such a peculiar mark," he replied. "It was the poor Mrs. Bretail – who was shot to death by her husband in this house."

2

Pigeon had no further questions. He turned around and hurried back to the Fort.

Please, please! Let's leave these things alone, thought Pigeon. He had nothing to do with strange horror dramas and haunting souls. He himself had an urgent need to get started in the haunting business.

Pigeon liked good food, to have hearty laughs, to whistle melodious tunes, and, from time to time, to get into a fistfight or to practice another form of bodily exercise, but he honestly hated mysteries, secrets, and exciting adventures. He decided against pursuing the case and returned to the Fort.

"Go to the office and see Captain Raffles," said the corporal when Pigeon arrived.

The commander of the Fort, Captain Raffles, was a popular, benevolent officer. He received the private with a friendly smile:

"I hear that you are a decent man. Sergeant Latouret gave an outstanding report about you. In the past ten years, this is the first time that this man-skinner has found anyone likeable. We are currently in need of petty officers, thus a few chosen men, and you among them, are assigned to our military school program. Therefore, you will stay at Fort St. Thérèse for the next three months.

Pigeon was shocked. To hell with his damned likeable personality!

"*Mon commandant*, I respectfully request to be sent to the Sahara."

The Captain looked at him with much wonderment in his eyes; he then slammed his hand on the desk:

"Private! I have assigned you to military school for the period of three months. About face! *En avant! Marche!*[15]"

When he reached the courtyard, he bit his knuckles in anger for a few seconds. It was a curse, a misfortune that, like a vicious bloodhound, luck was chasing him and did not let him live, or rather, did not let him die.

"Well, you slobber-face!" the roasted-faced sergeant stepped to him with all of his three bobcat whiskers. "Your future depended on me. Admiral Cochran came to visit the Captain about you because one of his relatives was a good friend of yours. But the Legion gives no privileges based on connections. The Captain said to the Admiral: 'It depends on Sergeant Latouret whether or not I can do something for this man.' You can thank your parade march that I recommended you to military school…"

The sergeant would have been greatly surprised if he had even the remotest idea what the private was thinking about him, about parade march, and in general about the entire Latouret family.

CHAPTER SIX

1

From the window of the military school, Pigeon watched the preparations of the company that was about to leave for the desert. What could he do? *Oh God!* he thought, *The poor widow and the kind, delicate young lady on Faubourg-Montmartre, whom I love most in this world, would get ten thousand dollars. And for that, all that needs to happen is for a lazy, undependable character like me to die. How is it that I am not allowed to die?*

Then he got lucky. The lesson was about military law and court-martial procedures. At the end of the lecture Pigeon sighed with relief.

The lecturer, among other paragraphs of the law, recited the following:

"An attempt at deserting the Legion results in the withdrawal of all privileges and preferences. Candidates for the rank of petty officer are returned to the enlisted status, to their prior assignment."

The problem was solved! He would desert the Legion that very day – maybe go to the swimming pool – and two days later, as prescribed by the law, he would leave for the desert together with the rest as per his prior assignment.

An hour later, he climbed the gutter of a building in the backyard of the Fort, and when the sentinel moved in the opposite direction, he jumped to the other side of the wall. And then he was running!

After the taps, eight patrols took off in search of Pigeon, and a mournful Sergeant Latouret plucked his whiskers.

2

Pigeon took a relaxing walk under the palm trees of the pier, listened to the noise of loading and horns of ships and automobiles, enjoyed breathing in the fresh, salty, evening sea-breeze that came with the high tide, and watched the glittering reflections of the lamps along the shore on the calm mirror of water. He was waiting to be captured. One quarter of an hour passed after another.

Well, what was going on?

What kind of monkey business was this? Where was the patrol? Did they just let deserters enjoy the promenade? Either there was discipline and order in the Legion, or there was not!

He looked around, but there was no sign of a patrol. What a fine kettle of fish, this army! Deserting individuals could relax and smoke cigarettes in the heart of the city, and the honorable Legion would not lift a finger. In his anger, Pigeon did not know what to do. He simply walked to Main Square, under the bright streetlights of the Governor's Palace. There must have been some sort of a reception by the city's military commander because a steady stream of elegant automobiles arrived at the front entrance, and extravagant uniforms, exclusive ermine robes, and white coattails paraded through the gate.

There, he idled another half hour or so.

What the heck was happening? Why was he not captured?

The explanation was quite simple. Every patrol had headed to the old town, the fishermen's pier, the nearby forests, and other places where a deserting legionnaire in his right mind might hide. Nobody was searching for him at the Governor's Palace.

Actually, there was such a person after all. The poet. Hümér Troppauer. He liked Pigeon who had always been an understanding audience. He would do anything but capture this kind, gold-hearted guy. As the leader of the patrol, he commanded loudly:

"To Main Square!"

That was a place where he would not bump into the fugitive.

However, soon after reaching the elegant district, one of the lads poked Troppauer's side:

"Look! There is the fugitive!"

The poet jerked his head in disbelief:

"This is impossible…"

Yet it was indeed possible. Pigeon waved at them with a friendly smile, then walked up to Troppauer, and impatiently said:

"Where have you been wandering this long? I have never seen such a lousy military."

What could they have done? The somber soldiers surrounded him and started to march back to the Fort.

"Why did you flee the Fort and come to the Main Square?" Troppauer asked.

"I was bored," he replied. He then posed the question: "Was there a big uproar?"

"Pretty big. Sergeant Latouret is taking various medications."

They reached a suburb. Pigeon was whistling in a jolly mood. The aimlessly roaming Arabs huddled to the walls of the houses of the narrow street and looked after the patrol with dark glances.

"You are lucky after all," Troppauer said. "We, at the latest the day after tomorrow, will leave for hell, and you will stay in Oran."

"I will not stay in Oran either. I deserted the Legion."

"As I just said, you are lucky. Whoever is captured within twenty-four hours is not considered a deserter. You will get a couple of *pelotes*[16] for absence without leave, and that's the end of it."

Good God! He was lucky again! Luck, like a wretched bloodhound, was chasing him, but he would not give up!

With a skillful move he hooked Troppauer's ankle from behind. The poet fell with a thump that shook the peace of the night. At first, the soldiers did not know what had happened, and by the time they had gathered themselves the detainee was already running away.

Troppauer, as per regulation, ordered to open fire:

"*En joue! Feu!*[17]"

Six rifles took aim at the moon and fired a round at the heavenly object.

"*Pas de gymnastique! En avant! Marche!*[18]"

They did not want to shoot him dead, but now they really wanted to capture him.

Pigeon ran. The thumps of heavy boots followed his trail. He then suddenly realized that he was running among the villas of the European quarter. He reached the villa of the unfortunate Dr. Bretail. What luck! This was supposed to be vacant. He jumped the garden fence from the dark street.

The patrol reached the spot within a few seconds. They shouted back and forth and beamed their flashlights in every direction. They did not see Pigeon jump and knew only that they had lost track of him in this area. He must have run into one of the alleys, or he was hiding in the garden of one of the empty lots. Pretty soon two or three policemen joined the soldiers in disturbing the peace of the night.

Pigeon tiptoed to the house. The house, with its windows covered by dark shutters, was as silent, forbidding and deserted as ever. One of the windows on the ground floor was without a shutter. It must have been a maid's room or a lavatory.

The noise and shooting on the streets had frightened one of the residents in the neighborhood, and he had called police headquarters. Suddenly, a loud siren shrieked. Pigeon did not miss the opportunity. While the siren overpowered every other sound, he stepped back and threw his bayonet through the window. The sidearm flew into the room and broke the glass in its path. Compared to the siren, the sound of cracking glass was like the buzz of a fly next to the roar of a lion. He stepped across the windowsill.

Pigeon found himself in the kitchen. He felt his way in the dark until he reached a door. He kept listening. He then slowly turned the doorknob to proceed.

He didn't know why, but he was startled by the long, sharp

creaking noise of the dried door hinges reverberating in the huge, dark hall into which the door had led. High up, the moon was shining through a ventilation opening.

And there was deep silence.

He started strolling down the corridor that meandered left and right and led to the very door where he had earlier seen the ghostly lady enter the house. This was the rear entrance. He turned the doorknob. It was locked.

For a while, he wandered aimlessly in a maze of corridors that branched in several directions. He was looking for an exit, but the house proved to be a real labyrinth. He sat down on the stairs that led to the servants' quarters and smoked a cigarette. He might hide here until tomorrow, he thought. He threw his cigarette away and went ahead. All of a sudden, he found himself again in the silent, dark hall. The silence dolefully weighed in on the room. However, Pigeon had nerves of steel. He decided to find a bed where he could sleep through the couple of hours necessary to make his desertion indisputable.

He started walking up the wooden staircase that led from the hall to a gallery. Presumably, the bedrooms opened from there.

The wooden staircase gave an ear-piercing creak and exhaled large puffs of dust clouds. This was indeed a place for ghosts.

He reached a hallway upstairs. He opened the first door across the staircase. It was pitch dark. No problem. The main thing was to find some sort of a bed; to have a good sleep required darkness anyway, and he hoped that the ghosts would not bother him.

He groped carefully along the wall. His hands felt the light switch next to a wardrobe. He turned it on. The room filled with light.

He exclaimed in astonishment.

In the middle of the room, in a large pool of blood, a man dressed in pajamas was lying on the floor, face down, and dead.

CHAPTER SEVEN

1

"Uh-oh," Harrincourt uttered under his breath after shrinking back from the sight.

Uh-oh. Keep your cool, Harrincourt. It appears that fate irresistibly propels you towards some sort of horror. Be on your guard, Sir! You must not lose your marbles!

He bent down to the corpse. How long could this man have been lying here?

What kind of a silly question was this? Good God! The blood had not even clotted yet, and a line of it was slowly flowing from the pool and had just reached the edge of the rug. Harrincourt touched the man's hand. It had not yet turned entirely cold. He kneeled down next to the corpse and turned him on his back. The blank stare in the man's eyes made it obvious that he was already dead.

The victim was a man around forty years of age. The dagger used for stabbing him in the heart was lying on the floor about two feet from the corpse. But look! This was no dagger! This was an *éguille*, the thin bayonet of legionnaires. He picked it up.

If he were a detective, he would start with this clue. A legionnaire scratches a mark in every piece of his hardware, so that soldiers could not replace their lost items by stealing from another one.

He held the handle of the bayonet close to his face to search for the scratched name on the wooden insert.

He dropped the weapon in his astonishment.

It was his own *éguille!*

"Uh-oh."

You must not lose your marbles, Harrincourt. Pull yourself together. What could have happened here? But of course!

He had thrown this bayonet through the window when the siren of the police van sounded.

Therefore?

Therefore, while he was wandering in the maze of corridors, searching for the backdoor, somebody had jumped into the house from the garden, picked up his bayonet in the kitchen, ran up here, killed this man, and…

And?

With a jump he was out of the room, running down the stairs. The murderer could still be inside the house.

He turned on the light in the hall. Nothing moved; dust-covered furniture sat in deafening silence. The echo of his own footsteps and the crackling of the dry parquet under his feet filled the room.

Then, from a distance, he heard a woman's voice softly humming a tune. He froze in his steps. Was it possible that, after all, ghosts actually exist?

That's nonsense.

He listened. Somewhere very softly a woman was singing.

"*Si l'on savait… Si l'on savait…*[19]"

The song then continued in a hum, without words, like a lullaby.

He proceeded up the stairs toward the source of the sound.

He went by the open door and saw the corpse lying on the floor in the same rigid position as before. He hurried ahead.

He could clearly make out that someone was humming in the room next to the scene of the murder. He pressed his ear against the door.

Beyond a doubt, someone was softly humming inside. Was there a crazy woman in there or what?

Uh-oh.

Uh-oh, Harrincourt. What is this feeling in your throat? Someone is humming in that room. That's for sure. And you are standing out here, with hands somewhat cold and sweaty. Open the door, private. Open it, or else I will have you tied up, you high society lowlife! he chastised himself.

He shoved the door in, and...

At the same moment, everything fell dead silent in the room. He heard the last cord of the song dying mid-air just next to him.

And the room was empty.

The room, in which someone had been singing when he had gripped the doorknob, was now empty; the floor was thickly covered with dust; and there was not a single visible footprint on it.

But who, then, was singing?

It doesn't matter. I won't pry. Let's leave it at that. Is it any of my business? He stepped out of the room and closed the door. He had to recover his bayonet to eliminate the incriminating evidence, and then he would leave.

"*Si l'on savait... Si l'on savait...*"

The woman was again singing in that room.

What?!

God damn it, I will get to the bottom of this! He opened the door as fast as lightning. And as he opened it, the last note was clearly audible, but there was no one in the room, and the song stopped.

He turned around. In the brightly lit, huge hall everything was quiet and motionless. He closed the door and leaned against the gallery banister. The nerves of a man who had attended the Naval Academy would not crush that easily. And after all...

"*Si l'on savait... Si l'on savait...*"

The song broke out again in the room.

He folded his arms and kept his eyes fixed on the closed door. *You, door! You are mistaken if you believe that I will open you. I do not believe in ghosts. I do not understand this entire thing, but I acknowledge a certain pressure on the left side of my chest.*

He returned to the room where the victim's body lay. The humming now continued unceasingly.

From behind a small, half opened, wallpapered door, he heard the quiet splashing of water.

He entered. It was the bathroom. Water was running from the

faucet and was already overflowing the rim of the tub. He quickly closed the tap and looked around. A white tailcoat outfit with all the accessories was laid out on a chair. In front of the mirror, on a sheet of glass, there was a shaving brush and a Gillette blade. It must have been used just recently because the soap was still wet. There were a number of small items on a vanity table: watch, handkerchief, fountain pen, and such.

I have had enough, thank you. Let's get out of here nice and quiet. I am fed up with this. He stepped out of the bathroom.

A lieutenant wearing his parade uniform stepped in front of him, slammed his heels together, and saluted him:

"I am reporting to you, Sir, that the time is half past eleven."

The corpse was at his feet. Someone was humming in the next room. And here was a lieutenant reporting to a private that the time was half past eleven.

He instinctively felt that there was some confusion, and, if he cleared it up, he would be in deep trouble.

He cleared his throat.

"Is it really as late as half past eleven?"

"Exactly, Major, Sir!"

He wanted to turn around because he had the feeling that a major was standing behind him. He gathered all his nerves in an effort to remain indifferent and calm.

"Yes, yes," he said, and he had to clear his throat again.

"The car is waiting at the backdoor. Please get dressed, Sir; meanwhile, I will turn off the lights everywhere. This is now the most important."

Is that so? He shrugged his shoulders indifferently, although deep in his soul he felt that the lieutenant's behavior was beyond reason since, standing next to the corpse of a freshly murdered man, he found that turning off the lights everywhere was the most important of his duties.

While the lieutenant was away tuning off the lights, Harrincourt rubbed his forehead with both hands. One needed nerves of steel here. But what could a man do if he got cramps during swimming? A stupid man would struggle and drown. The smart one would stretch out on the surface of the water without moving, knowing that as long as he did not move, he would stay afloat.

Thus, he entered the bathroom and calmly started to get dressed. He put on the white tailcoat. It was somewhat loose at the waist albeit not too conspicuously.

He had the same luck with the shoes. The pair was only one size larger than his feet. He took his own belongings from his pockets and then looked around. A tropical hat hung on a hook. He put it on. There were a large gold pocket cigarette case, a folding pocketknife, a pocket watch with an officer's chain, a wallet, and other small items scattered on the vanity table. He pocketed put all this stuff, feeling the moral disgust of a gentleman. This was someone else's property. But what could he do?

There was a second watch under the silk handkerchief. A wristwatch. Whoever heard of such a thing as wearing two watches? It appeared that time played a particularly important role in this half-witted story.

Swim with the current, swim with the current, he said to himself repeatedly as he buckled the strap of the watch around his wrist. It was a baroque-style piece made in poor taste. The watch had an over-decorated silver lid with a crocodile head. The wind-up knob poked out from the mouth of the animal. Only idiots would wear such a corny timepiece to an elegant soirée. But what could he do?

He stepped out of the bathroom.

By then, the lieutenant was already standing by the body. He straightened up in formal salute.

"May we get going, Sir?" he asked. Pigeon made a hesitant gesture toward the corpse.

The lieutenant waved his hand indifferently.

"We should not be held up on this account."

Alright then. He must have overblown the importance of the dead body, so it seemed. He walked down the squeaky staircase. They hurried across the hall toward the corridor and headed to the backdoor.

It was now unlocked.

It opened to an alley. In the shadow of the lush foliage of some trees, an impossibly small car was waiting for them. The officer opened its door.

"If you please, Major, Sir; it is just past midnight."

He sat in the car. The officer sat behind the wheel, slammed the door, and they took off.

The car drove down the *Avenue Magenta*, and after a brief detour, it coasted to a stop directly in front of a brightly lit gate.

Oh my!

The Governor's Palace! The outlook was grim.

But the door of the car was already open, and the doorman stood by respectfully while the lieutenant, with Harrincourt right behind him, entered the lobby. In the dazzling hall they were greeted by butlers wearing uniforms heavily decorated with golden embroidery.

This is a certain ten-year imprisonment in a fort's dungeon, at the very least, Pigeon thought while passing his eyes over the huge black marble columns with feigned indifference.

A colonel hurried down a long flight of marble stairs that reminded Pigeon of Jacob's ladder. Pigeon's heels trembled. Only a second separated him from slamming his heels together and assuming the rigid posture of formal military salute.

"Welcome my dear friend," the colonel greeted Pigeon jovially.

Pigeon's heart was pounding as he grabbed the extended hand, and he smiled like someone who had to force himself to put on a happy face even though being poked from behind with a long needle.

The colonel quickly led him up the Jacob's ladder covered with red carpet.

This is now as certain to be a life sentence as the sun will rise tomorrow – and in chains from top to bottom.

A dark-faced gentleman wearing numerous medals on his white tailcoat came towards them with a red fez on his head. He must have been some sort of pasha.

The colonel casually introduced Pigeon to him: "Marquis Francois Verbier."

What was happening here? This was total madness!

They reached a large ballroom where only a handful of elderly ladies and a couple of high-ranking officers were sauntering on the glistening parquet. A white-haired giant approached them wearing a uniform covered with medals worthy of an emperor.

A field marshal!

"Your Excellency," the colonel said, "let me introduce to you Marquis Francois Verbier, an old friend of mine."

"It is a pleasure to meet you. I am Field Marshal Cochran, the military governor of this beautiful city."

Tomorrow morning I will be executed. They will shoot me in the head, Pigeon thought.

The colonel then took him to a short, fat general sporting a catfish moustache, and on the way whispered to Pigeon:

"At least here you will have no need for introduction."

What? Why was it unnecessary to be introduced to the general? At this point it didn't matter. If it was unnecessary, well, so be it. He would not insist on getting introduced. After a meaningful nod toward Pigeon, the colonel left the two of them alone. What was this? Where was he going? The general patted his shoulder with a smile and said in a low voice:

"You are looking good, my friend." He then gently folded his arm into Pigeon's and strolled along.

I will be executed tomorrow. It is now beyond a doubt, Pigeon thought.

They reached a huge balcony from which a marble staircase led down to a park behind the palace. The park was rich with the continent's rarest and most beautiful flowers, and palm trees decorated with a myriad of colorful tiny light bulbs. On each step of the staircase, a soldier stood guard in parade uniform. On each and every step, all the way down to the park.

"Check out the fountain," the general whispered quickly. "It is possible that Macquart has not come, but it doesn't matter. You should be concerned with only one thing: to ask Madame Colette for a dance; you can clear up the rest at the fountain. Vicomte Lambertier will accost you. Just go. But as I said, it is possible that Macquart has not come."

"It doesn't matter. I already know that…"

He was headed to the fountain. The general was probably watching, therefore he had to go there.

Thousand-watt bulbs poured their bright light from above the wet, glistening marble statues that surrounded the fountain's vast reflecting pool. Jet streams of water were dancing and glittering, and soft music filled the sultry air, thick with the heavy scent of flowers. Somebody placed a hand on his shoulder:

"I am happy to see you!"

Pigeon replied with convincing indifference:

"The pleasure is mine, Vicomte Lambertier."

The man turned dead pale and his knees trembled.

"For God's sake! Are you out of your mind calling me by name?!"

Alright. Let's put a stop to this nonsense. This must be a premeditated and horrifying practical joke. They want to drive me crazy, Pigeon thought. Yet, this man turned so white, and his teeth were chattering in such absolute fear. However, he was smiling now and, pointing toward one of the nymphs of the fountain, he cheerfully said:

"Did you bring the sketch? Is it with you?"

Pigeon pointed at another nymph of the fountain:

"It is not with me."

"You were wise not to bring it with you. It is absolutely certain that we are being watched. See you tomorrow. Macquart has not come."

Pigeon waved his hand superciliously:

"It doesn't matter."

The Vicomte was gone. *Now, let's go. It is high time to get going,* Pigeon thought. He strolled along leisurely. A servant stopped in front of him and offered sandwiches. Wait a minute! He realized he was hungry. Hungry as a wolf.

He ate two sandwiches. He ate a couple of pieces of torte cake from another servant. He now sought out the servants. After having eaten his way through a few promenades, he became thirsty as hell. They were also offering refreshments. Pigeon did not dare to stop anywhere because he had forgotten his name and so had to avoid introducing himself. He therefore had a quick drink from every servant he bumped into, and then moved on promptly. He collected a most peculiar cocktail in his stomach. It consisted of champagne, raspberry soda, vermouth, almond milk, red *chablis*, and a small glass of ammonia solution that was served for soothing mosquito bites.

Look! The park was slowly spinning!

Later, when the applauding guests made him repeat the song *"Louis the Stoker Sailed to the New Hebrides[20]"* for the third time, Pigeon was surprised to notice that he was playing the piano and the musicians, with their instruments in their hands, were standing by on the dance floor opposite the stage. Why weren't they playing?

Of course, he did not remember that he himself had chased them off the stage. Good God! He was at an elegant place! *Major, Sir*, Pigeon said to himself, *Let's have that etude in C-minor. How does it go from here? To hell with this Chopin! I always had trouble with him!* "Well, until I remember the tune, if the ladies and gentlemen would be kind enough to permit me, I will play the '*Song of the Jolly Miners…*'"

Marquis Verbier conquered the crowd. The only charm at balls like this was if there was a gregarious, cheerful, tipsy young man among the guests.

Pigeon wanted to leave, but he got mixed up with one group of people after another, and he was humming under his breath:

"Let's go my boy, let's get out of here! This spells trouble. Go home!"

His stomach, as if it had imagined itself to be a cocktail mixer at a bar, was swirling the drinks. Suddenly, he spotted some sort of a side door. *Let's check it out.*

From behind a bed of flowers, someone stepped up to him and grabbed his arm.

"I am Macquart."

"I was told that you hadn't come," he stuttered taken off guard.

"They were mistaken. Three men will be on their way to the field. Lorsakoff sent me to contact you. Tell me, please, what time is it?"

Pigeon pulled out the gold pocket watch.

"It is past one o'clock."

Macquart glanced around, then, without a word, he took the watch and pocketed it.

"We are settled," he whispered.

"Do you think so?" replied Pigeon with resignation.

"Here you go," said the other. "Here is a box of *Simon Arzt.*"

And he pushed a box into his hand.

Not much of a business deal. Twenty *Simon Arzt* cigarettes for a gold watch? At the very least they could have been *Caporal.*

"Good bye," he said, and quietly, quickly added: "The box contains fifteen thousand franks."

And then he left. *Hey! You Sir! Come back,* Pigeon wanted to shout. But Macquart was gone.

"It doesn't matter..."

How on earth did he arrive here at the fountain amidst the crowd, again? And who was the short, fat general with the big mustache? He had seen this one watching him during the course of the evening.

Someone touched his shoulder.

"It is half past one, Sir."

He turned around. It was the officer who turns off the lights if there is a dead person in the house. This guy always announced the precise time. Pigeon followed him without a word.

In front of the gate sat the same incredibly small car as before. A motorized baby stroller!

The officer started the engine.

They drove along meandering roads without saying a word. First, they proceeded on broad roads bordered by bright electric streetlights, then in the deserted alleys of the poverty-ridden periphery. They stopped. Stray dogs fled from their arriving car. As he stepped on the brakes, the officer quietly said:

"It is two o'clock, Sir."

This guy was like the radio. He kept announcing the precise time of the day.

Pigeon got out of the car and stepped into the uninviting, deserted night, waiting for the officer to join him. But the officer slammed the door, put the car in gear, and drove off, leaving Pigeon behind.

In a white tailcoat. On a farm field.

He was in trouble again. There was not a soul around. The stray dogs had slowly returned and were curiously circling him. *It was quite a fine prank by the lieutenant, I say,* he thought helplessly.

A few steps from him stood a small lonely shack that probably belonged to a field guard. Ah! There might be some sort of a rag in the shack that he could put on.

But what would he do if he returned to the Legion without his uniform and weapon? He wanted only to return to his company headed for the Sahara, but if his government-issue gear was missing, it meant several years of hard labor.

What a big mess he had gotten himself into!

With a heavy heart and a bad taste in his mouth, he opened the door of the shack.

He entered the musty room and lit a match. And then he exclaimed in astonishment.

On a bench, neatly folded, he found his uniform, his hat, his sidearm, and under the bench was his pair of boots.

CHAPTER EIGHT

1

Lorsakoff paced his room like a beast locked up in a cage. His window looked out on the dust-covered palm trees of the fishermen's harbor. It was dawn. The dirty, little, old house on the outskirts of the city was mute and quiet. The Arab coffee brewer on the ground floor had closed for the day hours earlier and was now sleeping on a rug in front of his shop.

The wooden staircase squeaked outside. The Russian reached into his back pocket. Someone was knocking on the door. He opened the door slightly.

"What took you so long?" he said, letting his visitor in and closing the door behind him. "Did you bring the watch?"

"Here you go," replied Macquart, the visitor. Those who had seen him at the soiree would not have recognized him now. He was wearing a docker's light blue overalls and a pair of dirty, laceless tennis shoes through which his bare feet peeped out.

He handed the watch over. Lorsakoff reached for it with impatient greed.

"But this is… Yves said it was a wristwatch."

"He gave me this."

"Turn the lights off."

Macquart followed instruction. A moment later the Russian spoke again:

"Turn the lights on."

After the switch clicked and the room became light, the barrel of a revolver pressed against Macquart's stomach, and a dead-pale Lorsakoff said in an angry hiss:

"Give me the wristwatch. Don't try to argue with me. I am aware of your record, Macquart. I have known for over a year that you sold out the Junghans brothers the same way. But you'll fail this time."

"Are you out of your mind?" the other asked calmly. "I asked him for the time, and, as agreed, he opened the lid of the watch. I took the watch from him and gave him the cigarette pack."

"Yves specifically said on the phone that it was a wristwatch. Dr. Bretail's watch."

"And what kind of a watch is this? At least you should look at it more thoroughly."

"Pick up the watch," said Lorsakoff, still pointing his revolver at Macquart. "Stay there, standing, and hand it over. Don't poke into your pocket or I will shoot."

He looked at the watch and murmured with surprise:

"B.Y. Beyond a doubt, it belongs to the Major. Bertram Yves."

Lorsakoff held his revolver with less conviction. The other looked back at him with a sarcastic smirk.

"Look, Lorsakoff, I am not afraid of you. I could have done away with you by now." And as he said these words, he pressed his thumb in his palm. From his large birthstone ring some sort of liquid ejected in a long, thin stream that foamed and sizzled on the tablecloth, burning a large hole in it in seconds. "Sulfuric acid. While you were inspecting the watch, I could have killed you. But we need each other. Especially now, when it has become obvious that Yves has double-crossed and used both of us as mere tools in pursuing his own agenda."

"Then why did he explain to me on the phone in meticulous detail about an unusual wristwatch having a lid that can be popped open and the shape of a crocodile head?"

"Because he needed time to cover his tracks."

Lorsakoff lowered his pistol:

"Murky, but I admit that I was probably wrong about you. The biggest problem is that neither of us knows the Major personally."

"I saw him today."

"How do you know that it was he?"

"General Aubert walked with him arm in arm down the staircase, and later at the fountain, the previously agreed upon place, he met Vicomte Lambertier."

"What kind of man is he?"

"His fame does not give him enough credit. I could have sworn that he was a twenty-two-year-old, flighty lad. He is handsome, has a few freckles, smiles all the time, and pretends to be an idiot. He plays a drunk so well that any actor would envy him."

"But why did he say on the phone that the plan was hidden in the crocodile-ornamented watch, if his intention was double-crossing us?"

"His intentions changed after he phoned. Something must have happened since then."

Lorsakoff cursed.

"If that is the case, he will bitterly regret it. I will have his neck in my hands soon enough."

"How so?"

"Don't be an idiot! Don't you remember our conclusion? That Dr. Bretail's draft needs to be verified on site? He must go there. And then he will be in my hands. You must inform Laporter and Hildebrandt sometime today."

"In my opinion, we must first and foremost speak with Grison. Only he was in personal contact with the Major."

"You are right. Let's go to Grison's right now."

He put the watch in his pocket and turned the light off, then Lorsakoff and Macquart left the place together. At the gate, the Russian stopped for a moment:

"Hmm… A few minutes ago the old Arab coffee-brewer was sleeping here. Where the heck did he go?"

For a few seconds they looked left and right with suspicion, but their business was pressing, and they hurried away.

After their departure, the Arab coffee-brewer carefully walked down the staircase.

For he had been listening at the door all along.

2

A humid, gray dawn slowly disrupted the shadows of the night among the trees and the houses.

They were in a hurry.

The long alley leading down to the seashore was deserted. Unexpectedly, someone came toward them from the opposite direction. It was a soldier. He was dreadfully drunk. He was singing and bumped into the wall of every other house. Then, with wild and ugly cussing, he swore at the Arabs and called them into the street so that he could crush all of them. He leaned against the wall of a house and dug out a cigarette from his pocket. He waved with a friendly gesture at the two approaching men:

"Come, gentlemen, come. Please, give a light to a poor soldier who will perhaps die for civilization tomorrow, in the name of patriotism! *Vive la France!*"

Lorsakoff and Macquart were headed to the very house against which the legionnaire was leaning. The Russian laughed, pulled out his lighter, and tried to light it repeatedly because, apparently, it was low on kerosene. The soldier, like the typical drunk, leaned very close to Lorsakoff's face with his cigarette.

"Don't go upstairs."

"Isn't Grison at home?"

"He is at home alright. Dead. He was murdered."

"Come to the fish market."

The lighter finally caught fire, and the soldier, after a few puffs, put his hat on crookedly and wobbled along, howling inarticulate songs.

"Poor Grison," Macquart said. "You were right, Lorsakoff. A new player must have entered the game, messing up our arrangements, and Yves has turned against us."

"You must be careful, Macquart, because among us no one but you knows him personally, and he is aware of it."

"You don't need to worry about me, after all..."

A gunshot thundered. The bullet whistled by Macquart's head.

They both jumped in the vault of a gate. They waited.

There was absolute silence.

Macquart looked out carefully. The street was silent and deserted. No one was in sight.

"*Nom du nom!*[21]" Macquart gnashed his teeth. "It seems that the bastards have started to play the game for life or death."

They met the soldier again in the crowd of the bustling early-morning fish market. He approached them, asking them to pay for a drink of brandy because the next day he would leave for the desert. They sat down in a pub.

"Speak up, Hildebrandt," the Russian whispered.

"I had an appointment with Grison last night," the soldier said. "When I knocked on his door, there was no answer. I turned the knob. The door wasn't locked. The apartment was turned upside down, everything was scattered on the floor, the bed sheets were shredded, and I found Grison lying dead on the floor in the middle of the room, stabbed and with his head crushed."

They fell silent.

"Are you leaving tomorrow morning?[22]"

"Yes. We are going to Aut-Taurirt.[23] Grison did an excellent job sniffing that out."

"Listen," Lorsakoff said. "Until further notice, remember this: A wristwatch that depicts a crocodile, if you can get it, means fifty thousand franks to you. I want to speak with Laporter. You will be hearing from me later today. Until then, proceed with everything as agreed."

The soldier returned to the fort. He was on leave until the morning before their departure. While he was reporting to the watch commander, a patrol arrived escorting Pigeon. Pigeon was all smiles when he extended his arm to be handcuffed.

Hildebrandt turned pale.

On the fugitive's wrist, he saw a watch that depicted a crocodile.

3

Sergeant Latouret, who was devastated over the incident, did not say a single word to his ungrateful, wicked protégé. He just stroked his singed cat whiskers from time to time and stared with bulging eyes at the young man. *Nom du nom* was the expression held by his eyes.

"Are you out of your mind?" scolded Troppauer the poet.[24] "You had as classy a comfort here as my colleague Dante had in Paradise, and you squandered it!"

Pigeon shrugged his shoulders.

"I didn't join the Legion to be bored. I have become hooked on your poems, and I want to listen to them from now on, through rain or shine!"

"Honest?" the poet was visibly moved.

"Absolutely! I have been devoted to poetry since my childhood, and I have the feeling that one day I will be proud of the fact that I was among the first fans of the great Troppauer."

The masticator muscles around the gorilla jaws moved, and tears fogged the big, vacant eyes.

"I assure you that when I become a great poet I will spread the word about this fact. I understand your admiration, but that you are ready to follow me to the desert, this is a really moving gesture on your part."

"Through rain or shine for your poetry!" Pigeon exclaimed enthusiastically. "I have grown used to and love these poems, and I don't want to live without them."

Troppauer blushed and looked down:

"I am glad that I could present you with the gift of a universe," he stammered and, with his large, trembling hands, he self-consciously pulled out a down and dirty epos from his pocket. He smoothed out the paper, swallowed joyfully, and in a dramatic voice presented: "*The regiment will start marching tomorrow, yahoo!* Written by Hümér Troppauer."

Pigeon could give himself to his own thoughts with much joy

during Troppauer's long poems. He grew used to the hum of the hoarse voice providing the background for his meditation, and, if the poet paused with an exhilarated face, he hugged him and came up with a line at random:

"Beautiful! Wonderful! Unforgettable! Don't you have another one?"

"I wrote four more chants of this."

"It's not enough! Read it, but quick! You… you Pushkin!"

The poet joyfully licked the lips of his wide mouth, embarrassedly stroked his stubby blue chin, and continued reading. Pigeon, on the other hand, continued contemplating what to do with the fifteen thousand franks. It was clear that the money was not his. He could not pocket another man's money simply because it wound up in his hands due to a mix-up. First and foremost, he had to check out the contents of the wallet he had had to pocket in the bathroom together with the other belongings of the man who had been murdered. When he had changed clothes in the shack, he had retained these items. He had everything in the pocket of his jacket, but to look at them, one needed an "airtight" secure place. But such a place was hard to come by in a fort. For instance, the lavatories had no doors. It was impossible to remain unsupervised for even one second. Where could he look into that wallet? It was an impossible situation after all. Here it was, in his pocket, but he had no opportunity to look into it. There were always people around in the sleeping quarters, so that place was out of the question; the canteen was even less suitable, and he was not allowed to go to the city. Damned situation!

"Well?" asked the triumphant Troppauer.

"I can't find words to describe… Man! With your genius, why are you here, and not resting on your Nobel Laurels in Sweden?"

"What can a poet expect from his contemporary audience these days?" he asked with tragic resignation, and he raked his fingers among his thinning but long locks of hair. "So, you liked it?"

"It was grand! Only the last two lines, as if, God only knows…"

"Yes! You got it!" The poet's enthusiasm spilled over. "You perfectly captured the essence! I have felt myself, too, that my mood was on the decline at this passage, and I should have stopped at the part where I remain all alone in the universe as a single star."

He pulled out an indigo pencil, moistened it in his mouth, and struck out the two lines right away.

"Now comes the third chant, which is somewhat long but superior to the ones thus far."

"It cannot be too long if it is a Troppauer poem! Read it or I will stab you! You, you immortal!"

Two officers hurriedly crossed the courtyard of the fort. There was a big turmoil. A hand-grenade had exploded in the laundry that afternoon, and, of the nine soldiers present, only one survived, albeit seriously wounded.[25] They were now nervously waiting for the Inspection Committee led by an expert from Headquarters. However, they received a phone message that the committee would not do the sight visit until the next morning, and until then the area should be secured. They were responsible for ensuring that until the arrival of the Committee, nothing should be moved from its current position.

The curious soldiers were immediately dismissed from around the laundry, and a lieutenant ordered loudly:

"Sergeant Latouret!"

"*Oui, mon commandant.*[26]"

"Until the arrival of the Committee, you will arrange for guarding the laundry. Everything must remain as is. No one must enter the room."

Pigeon's train of thought had reached the point where he was fed up with every mystery. He would never develop the skill to sort out the clues. At that moment, Troppauer reached the passage of his poem that said, "*If the universe will be shaken, and from somewhere a chime of curse will sound...*"

And it did sound!

"Troppauer, you imbecile eight-humped camel, what the...?!"

To say the least, the chime of curse sounded. From the lips of Sergeant Latouret came words packed with such vehemence that the universe was shaken indeed, and even the most distant members of the Troppauer family would have felt deeply ashamed if only half of Latouret's statements were true.

The poet, humiliated to dust, left to have dinner with his writing and his disheveled locks of hair in tow. Pigeon stood as erect as a pole. Latouret pulled at his mustache and stared at Pigeon. The old wounds on his face flared up.

"Private!"

"*Oui, mon chef!*"

He paused theatrically.

"Eight corpses are lying in the laundry, or what is left of them. You will stand guard for six hours. You will report to the watch commander in full convoy gear in five minutes."

It was brutal. It never occurred to the lieutenant to send a single post to that horrible place for the night. Especially a man who would leave for the desert the very next morning.

"Understood?"

"Yes, Sir!"

"What are you grinning about?" he yelled, losing his temper because he expected Pigeon to turn green with horror and anger. "Are you perhaps happy about your assignment?"

"I am happy, Sir!" he said honestly because he was glad indeed. At this lonely place he would have a chance to inspect the wallet that he kept in his pocket. They would certainly not disturb him there.

In his anger, the Sergeant turned as red as a lobster.

"You are happy? You dare to be happy? I will teach you to be sorry, you can rest assured of that! You... You... *Rompez! Rompez!* Or I will cut you in half!"

Poor man, how worked up he became, Pigeon thought on his way to the barracks. Pilotte was sitting on his bed and was occupied with thoroughly rubbing his feet with tallow. He was keenly aware what it meant if the company commenced marching. Hildebrandt was writing a letter, although he secretly watched Pigeon and furtively glanced at one of his comrades who appeared to be asleep.

That comrade was Pencroft. He was a thin man with a large nose, and he had broad shoulders. He had come from America. Had the steamboat departed just five minutes later, he would have wound up in the electric chair. But this way he escaped and nothing could be done about it. He was involved in a political murder, and they let him escape in Cherbourg. He was practically never seen hanging out with Hildebrandt. The American fraternized with a Greek, freestyle-wrestling prizefighter named Adrogopoulos. It was a sports friendship. At one time Pencroft was a professional boxer who made a living by instructing policemen in self-defense in various European countries. Hildebrandt spent most of his time with the "Count." The Count was a serious, somewhat tart man with a tall forehead. His looks made clear that he came from one of the higher social classes. He never spoke of his civilian past.

Pigeon fraternized with everyone. He was popular among the soldiers, and, because of a waiter from Marseille, the name "Pigeon" followed him to Africa. When the waiter, who had joined the Legion, called him by that name for the first time, the soldiers laughed. Later they grew used to it, and Harrincourt kept his epithet. Nevertheless, his number one friend was Troppauer the poet. They were close friends with Chalky as well, if aiding a hapless half-wit counts as friendship. Whenever Chalky smiled, the deep, precocious creases of congenital mental retardation wrinkled his face. He was asleep now, his hat pulled over his eyes, his clothes on, his hands clamped together under the back of his neck, and his belongings scattered around him. Pigeon shook him:

"Hey, pal! The company will leave at dawn! Gather your stuff! You can sleep afterwards."

"One can sleep anytime," and he smiled. "Please, what do you want now, Pigeon? We are not leaving yet!"

"But when the bugle calls you to line up, there will be no time."

"Then we won't need it anyway because we are already leaving." Having said that, he pulled his cap over his eyes again and continued sleeping.

What should he do?

"Hildebrandt. Pack the stuff of this hapless mate. I have to report for duty to stand guard at the laundry."

All eyes turned to him.

"With the eight dead bodies?" Adrogopoulos asked with a shiver.

"Yes, of course. And I have no time to pack Chalky's clobber."

Pilotte rose from his seat and started packing the idiot's

backpack, all the while murmuring something with a grim face.

"Listen, Pigeon. This is the Foreign Legion and not the Salvation Army!"

Nevertheless, he kept packing the stuff and voicing his indignation.

Pigeon ran to report to the Sergeant. Latouret eyed him from head to toe. Had they not needed a guard at the laundry in a hurry, he probably would have found something objectionable. But under the circumstances, he said only this as a warning:

"This duty is as rigorous as if you were on post at the Governor's Palace. Three steps, followed by an orderly turn, then another three steps. If you sit down or light up a cigarette, I will have you court-martialed. Is that understood?"

"Yes, Sir!"

This man, this man! He says this 'yes, sir,' as if I had just given him praise. He is radiant, thought the Sergeant.

He now didn't care if his course of action was not in line with regulations, and with a menacing smile he added:

"Of course, electricity should not be wasted on lights, and you will stand guard in the dark. A legionnaire is not frightened of eight corpses and not afraid of ghosts. What? What are you happy about?! Why are you smiling?! *Rompez! Rompez!* Or I will cut your stomach open!"

And he had to loosen his collar because he felt that he would suffer a stroke at once.

In spite of the expectations to the contrary, Pigeon was indeed happy. Because at the first light of dawn, he could check the contents of the wallet without fear of surprise; because, since it was dark in the laundry, people could not peek in from the outside, yet he could notice anyone approaching.

The laundry was separated from the other buildings of the fort by a good ten-minute walk. Even during the daytime, there was rarely a soldier around the place unless he really needed to wash some clothes, like the victims of the exploded grenade had. The little house stood in the night at the far end of the vast, deserted practice field.

Eight dead men were in this building. *It appears that fate has specialized in trying to frighten poor old Pigeon*, he thought with a chuckle. Well, fate can eat its heart out. He stepped into the abandoned laundry from the dark field calmly, almost cheerfully.

In the distance, he heard the bugle signaling taps, and soon the yellow glow of the sleeping quarters' windows went dark. At the end of the gigantic field stood the lonely little house surrounded by a few still palm trees.

He closed the door. He started pacing back and forth with slow measured steps, as instructed by the Sergeant.

4

It was ten o'clock.

Through a window that lacked its mosquito net, the moon was shining in and its narrow circle of light crept slowly on the floor.

One, two, three… thump, about face… one, two, three…

It was quite a boring assignment with this pacing back and forth – that much was sure. If only he could smoke a cigarette. Or at least he could get an idea of what the world around him looked like.

He heard the muffled sound of bells in the distance. In the dead silence the floor creaked under his steps. It was not a pleasant duty for those with weak nerves. It was his good luck that such things were unheard of in the Harrincourt family. He was as laid back as if he were in the canteen. From time to time he caught himself silently whistling.

Something creaked in the corner. Twice. Then it was quiet. Of course, it was an old hardwood floor, and as the temperature was slowly dropping during the night, the planks that had expanded in the heat of the day were now shrinking. That was the cause of the creaking.

If someone never learned his physics in school, he would be scared out of his wits now.

The prolonged whistle of a train sounded from afar. He could see through the window that a stray dog was running across the field. Everything was quiet, except that he heard water slowly dripping somewhere. Probably a faucet was leaking. Now he heard another creak. Hmm, why does the cooling down make the floor creak always in the same single spot?

The moonlight glided ahead on the floor and illuminated the head of a man lying on his back. The dead face was white as chalk, with blue lips and eyes wide open.

You are ugly, my friend, beyond a doubt. But don't be afraid. Pigeon won't hurt you; he only stands guard. And tomorrow they will bury all eight of you, and then you can relax and dedicate yourselves to decay. A day plus or minus makes no difference in eternity. Poor blessed Sergeant Latouret, may he rest in peace if the will of unpredictable fate would inflict him with a stroke. He would now get worked up because he thought that a duty like this would bring on epilepsy in the average man! And as the moonlight glided forward, a brown spot became visible: a bloodstained jacket that was used for covering the body.

One, two, three… thump, about face… one, two, three…

Please, this perpetual creaking is too much. Not that I am afraid, but somebody is here, and that is forbidden. What kind of stupidity is it to hide in such a place? Although it is possible that a rodent is under the floor.

Creak…

As the circle of its light glided over a head, the moon now lit a snow-white hand making a tight fist. The church bell in the distance signaled the passage of another quarter of an hour, and the loud squawk of a bird disturbed the night for a moment. The moon now cast the shadows of a couple of long palm leaves on the floor.

It creaked again, then twice more, and sharp.

Son of a haunting grandpa!

Let's do it by the rules, he thought. A quick move, and his bayonet-fitted rifle was in attack position; as the loading chamber clicked, Pigeon shouted:

"*Halte! Qui va là?*[27]"

Dead silence followed.

He pulled out his flashlight. He did not want to turn the lights on. If it were nothing more than a rodent chewing under the rotten wood floor, he would get himself in trouble for turning the lights on in violation of his orders. And old cat-whiskers would think that he was yellow, when he had no reason to be afraid. How could he be afraid when he had a bayonet rifle in hand?

The circle of his flashlight danced along the floor, the walls, and the ceiling of the room. There was nothing suspicious anywhere. The explosion had damaged a barrel that stood next to the door and contained rust-proofing minium paint that was used for protecting tin roofs. The orange-red gooey stuff poured out from the barrel and spread on the floor from one wall to the other like a prehistoric creepy-crawly life form. In the corner from which the repeated creaking came, a bloke was lying with his face down in a large pool of blood and was covered with a jacket over the top of his head. This poor man could cause creaking no more. The other one on the left, whose knees were pulled up, seemed to have sustained little damage. But where was his head? The stucco was splashed with plenty of tiny shrapnel and blood; torn and shredded pieces of clothing were scattered everywhere; and rigid bodies were thrown on the floor in almost natural positions. Eight of them.

No, nine! Didn't they say eight? Hmm, this much was certain, there were nine of them here. Incredible! Most peculiar.

God only knows how this had happened. No matter how Pigeon counted, there were nine men plus a leg. He turned off his flashlight. He hung the rifle back on his shoulder and continued pacing. He decided that he was not interested in taking inventory of corpses. Eight or nine, what's the difference? It could not have become more since the explosion, and it could not be fewer either, because it was unlikely that someone was stealing corpses around here.

What the heck was going on with this floor?!

Two sudden creaking noises, a soft sound, and then there was silence.

The moon lit a good portion of the room now, and it shone on the soldier who was face down in the corner. The floor was always creaking there, that was certain, and...

To be sure, he needed nerves of steel for this. For example, he could have sworn that the soldier, as he was lying on his face just a minute ago, had both arms extended. And now, one of his arms... Well, it must be hallucination.

He was not ready to be bogged down with such details. Every dead man may lie in the position of his choosing. The clock tower's twelve strokes signaled midnight. Rigid bodies, illuminated by moonlight, were scattered on the floor. The rest of the room was in gloomy half-shadow; the dripping of the faucet could be heard time to time; and the deserted field outside the building was in clear view.

One, two, three... thump, about face... one, two, three...

What is Colette doing now? wondered Pigeon, with some really sleazy mental association regarding the Parisian dancer. Pigeon had even talked with that one before leaving Paris.

Suddenly, there was the loud creaking again!

He grabbed his rifle again and turned towards the corner. He then stopped mid-movement in astonishment.

A dark object was falling toward him. A tremendous wallop landed on his shoulder, although it was meant for his head. He thrust his rifle ahead, but the bayonet missed the target. At the same time, Pigeon fell outside the path of the moonlight, so the second blow inflicted by the ninth corpse again missed his head and hit his shoulder. Intense pain cut into his arm; he dropped his weapon, and he knew that he was defenseless against the third blow. But no!

The third blow did not come because...

Somewhere from behind Pigeon, two rounds were fired. The door of the laundry opened; the ninth corpse bolted from the room and fled. One could see his shadow running across the field.

Pigeon, although his shoulder and right arm were numb and useless, held his weapon with his left hand, and ran after the attacker.

"Trarah! Trarah!"

Upon hearing the gunshots, the guard at the main building of the fort signaled alarm with his bugle. Immediately after that, the loud voice of a petty officer was heard in the darkness, commanding:

"*Aux armes!*[28]"

The attacker was running on the dark field about thirty paces ahead of Pigeon. Only his silhouette was visible. As he reached the wall of the fort, he climbed and jumped over it without hesitation.

The ninth corpse disappeared into the night.

By the time Pigeon returned from the wall, the field was no longer deserted. The guards came jogging double-quick, with bright carbide lamps, holding their weapons, and ready to fire. A number of petty officers showed up, buckling their belts while running to the site. The Captain also came running in the company of a few other officers.

Sergeant Latouret was leading the line of runners, and at the moment he felt worse than he would in the bloodiest of battles.

The watch commander shouted loudly:

"*Halte! Fixe!*[29]"

They reached the post assigned to the laundry that stood there without his cap and held his rifle in his left hand.

"Private!"

"Sir! I am dutifully reporting: About fifteen minutes ago someone attacked me in the dark, hit me repeatedly with a hard object, and ran away."

"Did you hit him when you fired at him?"

"I did not fire at him."

"Then who did?"

"Someone else must have been hiding in the laundry."

"*Nom de Dieu!*[30]" the Captain hissed between his teeth because this much scandalous mystery and villainy was unprecedented in a fort.

"I am humbly reporting, *mon commandant,* that the man on the post was afraid and made this scene all by himself by shooting with his rifle. This character became a deserter in spite of my prior support of him. He is shadowy, cowardly, and pretentious!"

Your godmother is, Pigeon thought. One of the officers was leaning toward Latouret's opinion. However, before they could have continued with their probe, something happened that frightened the Captain more than the eight corpses would have if they all had gotten up to smoke a final portion of pipe tobacco in this world. For the voice of the petty officer of the watch guard at the gate again shouted into the night:

"*Aux armes! Aux armes!*"

Then the bugle's sound abruptly filled the air, but instead of signaling alarm, it signaled for line-up. Good Lord! This meant the arrival of a superior.

It was the city's military commander.

5

Field Marshal Cochran, when he heard the alarm coming from the fort, had jumped out of bed yelling a thousand curses, saying, "this mound of trash, this is the most shameful spot of the colonial army. What kind of place is this, I ask?! Is this a frontier garrison in the desert?! Isn't this Oran, the seat of the Martial Supreme Court, and of the Central Headquarters of the entire Colonial Army? Just wait! Just wait, you rollicking civilians disguised in military uniforms!" He panted sentences like these while he hastily put on his uniform, and his wife tearfully begged him not to get worked up.

"Shut up, Josephine!" he shouted grimly at his wife. "You are the cause of everything. Because the perpetual soirees, balls, receptions, and other social commitments take up all my time, I could not get around keeping an eye on these fattened, lazy boys who call themselves soldiers![31] They seem to do whatever they please! But this will end here, Josephine! Where is my sword?!"

"Gracious goodness! How have I sinned?"

"Don't you upset me any further! I don't need my sword to use on you! Antoine! Antoine! Summon the driver! Let's go!"

When the car blowing its horn drove up to the gate of the fort, the "to arms" yell sounded, the bugle signaled, both wings of the wide gate opened, and all the officers felt the gloomy and imminent doom of being sent to distant garrisons.

"*Mon excellence,*[32] I report that the number of personnel at the fort…"

Panting, he interrupted the lieutenant with a wave of his hand:

"Keep your numbers. Let's go! Get me a lamp, and let's go ahead to the place where all those small lights are moving around. I will… A different era will commence here! Rather, I will let you gentlemen know the details by a picture postcard sent to Congo! Petty officer! Petty officer! Cancel it, you idiot! Why are you having all the legionnaires of the world line up for me? *Rompez! Rompez!*"

He swept though the courtyard of the fort like a simoom,[33] rattling, huffing and puffing, squeezing his sword in his elbow. A group of pale, scared officers followed him.

The members of the watch guard stood in front of the laundry with Pigeon surrounded in the middle. When the high-ranking officer was within twenty paces, the Captain pulled out his sword:

"Garde à vous![34]"

All heels clacked in unison, and the swords of all officers flashed in a synchronous whoosh. Cochran, panting, without saying a word, looked at them from head to toe, he then paced back and forth for a while.

He stopped in front of an officer. The officer immediately reported:

"The number of…"

"It doesn't matter! The number of personnel will change! We are going to replace the entire garrison! Now, tell me, please," Cochran turned toward the Captain, "what was the story on that grenade; what led to the alarm command; and how did this shooting happen? You know, I have been under the impression for several years that the northern part of Africa, ever since the leadership of my good friend, the late Marshall Lyautey,[35] has been pacified. However, I see that alarms and shootouts still occur nightly in Oran. So, I would like you, if you would be so kind, I would like you to… *Rompez!* You honorable officers should put your swords back in their scabbards; you will draw your swords soon enough and quite often for the defense of France! At ease! All of you! Well, proceed, please."

The Captain replied respectfully yet with a certain degree of coldness in his voice:

"Your Excellency! It is most likely that this man gave a false alarm because he was afraid at his post."

"Sentinel!" Cochran said. "Come here! Why did you shoot?!"

Pigeon's blood froze for a moment. *He'll recognize me!*

"Your Excellency, I report to you, Sir, that I did not fire my weapon. In the darkness, I received such a strong blow on my shoulder that I dropped my rifle."

"Give me a lamp!" the Field Marshal rasped. He grabbed the lamp and held it to Pigeon's face. For a second he looked at him with a blank stare. He recognized him. But his astonishment was evident only for a passing second. He then yelled at him with a sharp voice: "Give me your weapon! Someone fetch me a sheet of white paper!" He rolled up the paper and pushed it into the barrel of the rifle. He then sniffed at the paper. "This weapon was not fired. Show me your shoulder!"

What's going on? Cochran certainly must have recognized him. Was it completely irrelevant whether he showed up once as a gentleman in a white tailcoat and another time as a private in the Legion? How could this be? Not the slightest gesture by the Field Marshal indicated now that he had recognized Pigeon. Now he turned the light towards Pigeon's shoulder to reveal a huge bruise.

"*Mon capitaine,* do you think it is likely that this fresh injury that indicates a very serious blow was self-inflicted by this youngster, and he then fired his weapon?"

The Captain gave Sergeant Latouret a somewhat wondering and gloomy look, but nevertheless, in such a way that even the Sergeant's kidneys started to tremble. A few fast-paced questions followed:

"When were you sent here?"

"Precisely at eight o'clock."

"And why in full convoy gear?"

"Because my company will leave in the morning."

"Is that so? Interesting! Most interesting!" exclaimed Cochran. "That must mean that there is a single company in Fort St. Thérèse, otherwise I could not even contemplate the idea that a man would be chosen for a ten-hour duty from the very company that is scheduled for leaving! Watch Commander!"

"I am reporting, Sir," Latouret stepped forth, "that this man is under punishment because he attempted desertion yesterday."

His Excellency knows it the best,[36] Pigeon thought.

"Aha! Aha!" Cochran kept nodding. "He is under punishment! And the court martial's verdict included this assignment, or there is another possible scenario: This unusual punishment was in the daily order. Or is it perhaps the so-called sergeant's revenge?! Personal ill feelings against a private? And the Sergeant is unaware of the routine that a lone post is not assigned at places like this? Private! What did your attacker look like?"

"I couldn't see him. It was dark."

"Isn't there electricity in the laundry? Why was it dark?"

"Sir, my instructions specified not to waste electricity."

"What?!"

Cochran swallowed deeply so that his Adam's apple scaled four inches up and down his neck, and his eyes bulged as if two buttons were protruding from his skull.

"What?! What was that?! Repeat that! You know what? Don't repeat it. A petty officer that is this thrifty must be sent to the front, where battles are raging. The greatest waste is happening there. He is needed there the most. My dear Captain, this watch commander will replace one of the petty officers at the company that leaves tomorrow. Now I understand everything. The Sergeant's revenge! To assign a grunt whom he hates to a lone post in the dark the night before he starts marching with his company. And for this he managed to turn Oran upside down, and the Legion will make front-page headlines in tomorrow's paper! Well, my dear Captain, during the march, the Sergeant will constantly serve by scouting the road ahead of the company. His order is as follows: Before each stage, he will go on a reconnaissance mission with eight men until reaching the next stop. The eight men are to be replaced at each stage, but not the Sergeant. This lad, whom he assigned here as a sentinel, will travel with the Red Cross medical wagon as a wounded soldier. I will teach their lordships the sergeants a lesson! And if it is possible, don't have any more alarms tonight. Good night! Congratulations!"

"*Garde à vous!*"

The whoosh of swords, banging of boots, and the slow thumps of the Field Marshal's riding boots sounded as he rattled off the scene escorted by a few pale officers.

6

Hildebrandt and Pencroft sat next to each other on the dark staircase leading to the sleeping quarters and whispered:

"How the hell did it happen?" Pencroft asked.

"First of all," Hildebrandt said still panting, for he had run a good hour and a half until he had entered through the fort's main gate, pretending to be drunk. "First of all, that milk-faced chap is either an idiot, or extremely smart and has nerves of steel. I wanted him to be scared out of his wits by the time I attacked him. It was a futile effort. Nevertheless, I would have knocked him out because I sneaked up on him unnoticed. But hell! From somewhere nearby two rounds were fired."

"How could that be?"

"The only explanation is that there were not the two of us in the laundry, but three of us. I was hiding there while the youngster reported for duty with the Sergeant. It appears that someone went there earlier, and because the shots came from the direction of the furnace, he must have been hiding behind it. This means that there must be someone else who is interested in the affair. And this person already knows me because he was already in the dark and must have seen me in the moonlight when I entered the room to hide."

"But who is the milk-face?"

"Lorsakoff didn't say. He just promised a fortune for the crocodile watch. It must somehow be connected with the affair. We'll learn more tomorrow. We'll speak with Lorsakoff at the railway station before our train leaves."

"We must learn who else is here hunting for that watch. It could be the lad's accomplice."

"I have an idea. Take into account all those who were present in the room when Pigeon told us about his assignment at the laundry. I saw the opportunity immediately to attack him there easily and that I could hide there while he was reporting for duty at the watch commander. Someone else in the room must have come up with the same idea. Let's see who was in the room. You, Adrogopoulos, the Count, Troppauer, Pilotte, Yazmirovich, the imbecile Chalky, Lindman, and myself."

Pencroft replied quickly:

"We could perhaps learn which of these left the sleeping quarters."

"I have a better idea. The explosion blasted a large barrel of rust-proofing minium paint, and the stuff leaked out. My boots were covered with the red, gooey stuff. I hope that the man who shot at me did not notice the red paint marks on his boots, and so we can identify him."

"This man has to be put away first!"

A couple of shuffling, mumbling legionnaires approached from the garden path. Hildebrandt and Pencroft fell silent. By the time one of the soldiers turned the lights on, Pencroft the American was fast asleep, lying on his back with his longs legs stretched down several steps on the staircase; slobber was foaming at the corner of his mouth, and he was snoring. Hildebrandt was sitting with his jacket open, his belt hanging from his neck, his cap pulled down to the tip of his nose. With slurred speech, he was explaining something to a highly esteemed cashier lady; meanwhile he had hiccups that almost flipped him over. The arriving soldiers themselves were not much more sober either, except for the petty officer who spat in disgust at the sight of these two characters.

Troppauer was last to arrive, with a wreath on his head in lieu of his cap; he extended his arms and proclaimed a horrific danger that, in the poet's person, starting tomorrow, would threaten every rebellious Arab. He passed by the two distinguished individuals, and with his unshapely, thick legs, he almost stepped on Hildebrandt, then finally staggered into the sleeping quarter.

Both of his boots were covered with a conspicuously thick layer of orange-red rust-proofing minium paint.

CHAPTER NINE

1

Line up!

Most of the soldiers had returned dead drunk last night and had slept but a few hours at the most; nevertheless, they put their clothes on in seconds, cleaned their dirty, muddy shoes quickly, and, by the time the corporal kicked the door in to share his usual opinion with the entire lazy-trash outfit, most of them were already buckling their belts.

The bugle fell silent, the company stood in the courtyard, and the captain, after a few words of farewell, commanded, "March!" After the command "Right turn!" the officer, riding his horse, took the lead; his sword flashed high in the air, the band started playing a march, and the *peloton*[37] turned to the street, singing a loud song.

In the meantime, the official order was received according to which, "Sergeant Latouret is to replace Petty Officer Larnac in the convoy and, on the way to the destination, to serve as constant reconnaissance commander."

Sergeant Latouret liked the red *Pinard* wine that was bountiful produce of the area around Oran, he had grown attached to Fort St. Thérèse, and he loved the peaceful existence of old veterans; yet he now gladly went to the hell-of-a-distant garrison because Pigeon would be in his hands there. This man was a shameful blemish on his otherwise immaculate military career. He would teach this ever-grinning youngster, this shameless pretender a lesson for

69

having destroyed his authority as a petty officer. *Nom du nom!*

For the moment, however, the "ever-grinning youngster" was sleeping in the shade of the canvas-covered carriage that was decorated with a red cross, as fit as a fiddle, yet enjoying all the privileges of convalescent soldiers. His heart went out to poor Latouret. He was an old soldier set in his ways, but he wasn't a bad boy.

The company marched along. Then the evening came, then morning again. They just kept marching.

Pigeon looked out at the rear through the slit of the canvas. Behind him, at a good distance, the rear defense marched with mules laden with machine guns. Farther away, Arab guerillas kept appearing and disappearing behind the sand dunes. They were a disgusting breed.

Legionnaires did not like these marauders who roamed the desert along with the regular troops and set up their camps near the garrisons. They were a disorderly horde: they were stealing and looting, and the booty was their only interest in battle.

The long serpentine column of the company marching in the desert was visible through the front opening of the carriage. There was not a single spot of shade in the unbearable heat on the endless yellow mounds, only the cream-colored, dusty surface of the blinding Sahara and gently curving waves... and waves. As far as the eye could see, yellow waves were everywhere.

The physician had rolled out a blanket on the pile of sacks that contained quinine and was asleep now. This could perhaps be an opportunity to examine the wallet.

No, until he learned what was in it, Pigeon had to be extra cautious. There you have it! As he had just been contemplating to open the wallet, they brought a soldier in who was convulsing. His mouth was foaming, and bloody froth splattered with every growl. They laid him down. The sleepy physician jumped to his feet. "Cold water bottle for his head!" he shouted. But it was over regardless. Probably pulmonary embolism. Or a vessel ruptured. His face and hands were covered with gray dust.

"*Fini,*[38]" mumbled the pudgy physician, and he wiped his short, bristled neck with a handkerchief.

They reached the first oasis by four o'clock in the afternoon. A long whistle sounded. The physician cast an oblique, disapproving glance at the soldier in the wagon who was rosy with good health.

"Doctor, Sir," Pigeon reported unexpectedly, "I would like to get in line with the others, but it is my order to travel this way. Would it be possible for me to trade places with someone more in need, please? My shoulder injury does not incapacitate me in any way."

"I will make arrangements," the physician replied amiably. "It's an honorable decision. I believe the lieutenant will readily approve your changing places with an invalid."

The lieutenant issued the order that the place of the fully recovered private number 40 on the hospital's wagon was to be taken by an ailing soldier, and that private number 40 was reassigned for duty to his platoon marching with the convoy.

2

At last!

In the rapidly cooling night everyone wrapped himself in his robe, and the red-hot stones that were used for baking kesra[39] were glowing in the distant guerilla camp. The bugler called for taps.

At last!

Pigeon went on a walk by himself among the sparse palm trees to find a peaceful spot where he could look at the wallet. Monkeys were screaming in the palm trees, and countless cicadas were chirping all around.

"Stop for a second, comrade!" somebody shouted after him.

It was the Count. Would this become yet another obstacle?

"What's up, Your Excellency?"

"Don't mock me! I don't expect this from you. This, this… This is befitting of the others."

"I am dead serious. Your nickname is no mockery. You are so dignified, pal, that sometimes I myself am convinced that you must have born into an aristocratic family."

"Well, my ancestry…" The oval, refined face turned somber. His vaulted forehead, which was losing its hair in an interesting pattern above the temples, now folded into peculiar wrinkles, and his large, clear blue eyes looked at the distant horizon.

"I would like to tell you something. You are different from the rest. You can even understand the poet; so I can perhaps be frank with you also."

Pigeon said, contrary to his feelings:

"Please, by all means. Be so talkative as to tell me everything. Although, at the moment…"

"I am Polish, and I am from Lukewitz. I was fifteen when I invented a machine…"

With a sigh, Pigeon sat down next to him on a large rock. No matter what, he would just have to listen to this gentleman's drama.

"My real name is Spoliansky and… Can you guess who my father was?"

"Hero of the freedom fight. He was executed by Tsar Pavel the First."

"You are close, but you are not quite right."

"Look, anyone can see that noble blood flows in your veins. Confess that you killed that woman, or admit candidly that you were the officer in the army who lost the money from the regiment's treasury in a card game. In other words, recite your talking picture, and then let us both get some sleep."

The Count sighed. He shook his head sadly and stood up.

"No. I will not tell it after all. Not even to you. I am sorry."

"You have not offended me a bit," Pigeon replied without much effort to cover up his relief, and Spoliansky, with a big sigh, doddered away in the direction of the camp. He was sort of dragging one of his legs after himself.

Is he limping or something? Ah, it doesn't matter, Pigeon thought.

He walked to the edge of the oasis where the bushes were covered with thick dust. The endless sea of sand spread out in a silvery white color in the moonlight as if it were a real ocean.

He looked around. He was far away from everyone. A late-retiring cockatoo cried out, a few frogs croaked in the silence, and the humming of a chorus in the Arab camp filtered to him from afar.

A sliver of moonlight beamed through the crowns of the slender palms. This would be good enough for reading.

He took out the wallet. It was a simple leather wallet available by the millions anywhere. It contained miscellaneous items, but first and foremost, fifteen thousand francs in paper banknotes. There were a couple of receipts and many name cards. He then found a newspaper clipping. It was a half-page story, with its margins marked with red pencil:

"Shocking family tragedy in the house of the recently returned Dr. Bretail

"*In the illustrious villa district of Oran, the Boulevard Bonaparte was the site of a bloody event yesterday evening. Dr. Bretail shot his wife, Captain Corot, and himself leaving no survivors. Not too long ago, Dr. Bretail returned from the Niger where he had served as secretary to the late, great explorer, Russel.[40] Upon his return home, Dr. Bretail married the widow of the tragically departed scientist. The extraordinarily beautiful lady was once a singer who abandoned the stage only for the sake of Russel. However, in Oran, where the Russels had an active social life, the formerly celebrated actress sometimes performed at charity balls. On these occasions, she would sing her famous hit 'Si l'on savait...'*"

Si l'on savait...!

This was the song that Pigeon had heard from the room next to the corpse – the tune that was continually sung, though there was no one there to sing it.

He continued reading.

"*Dr. Bretail and Russel's widow appeared to have a happy marriage until the bloody family tragedy last night.*

"*Only the two butlers were present in the house at the time, and both described the events consistently. Dr. Bretail was away on a trip, probably to Algiers, and Mme Bretail was entertaining Corot, a spahi captain and popular gentleman horseman, as a guest.*

According to the butlers, Captain Corot had visited the Bretail home at other times in the doctor's absence. The tragic events took place at eleven o'clock in the evening. One of the butlers served up tea in the salon. Mme Bretail sat at the piano and sang 'Si l'on savait.' Then, unexpectedly, Dr. Bretail appeared at the door. The butler heard two gunshots, a scream, and a thump: Captain Corot and the lady collapsed, both shot in the head. Before the servant could prevent it, Dr. Bretail shot himself in the head at the temple. By the time the ambulance arrived, no one was alive."

Pigeon lit up a cigarette. He remembered the house. He remembered the dust-covered rooms and that strange woman with the birthmark.

"Was the jealousy well founded or without merit? No one can be certain," the article continued. *"Is it possible that the horrors Dr. Bretail experienced during Russel's expedition took a toll on his nerves? Or perhaps the interesting lady, with the mark of a triangle on her hand and heart, burned first for her late husband's secretary Dr. Bretail and then Captain Corot? We do not know the precise answer to these questions. One thing is certain: Oran's society suffered a painful loss, and this horrible tragedy..."*

From the middle of the article, a photograph stared out at Pigeon. The beautiful woman had an unusual, intriguing face: her thick eyebrows grew together, and her sad eyes were wonderfully expressive.

All of a sudden, from not too far away, the humming of a familiar female voice sounded:

"Si l'on savait..."

For a few seconds he sat there without moving.

The evening breeze brushed the branches of the palm trees against each other with a gentle rustle. And the lyrics turned into humming. Beyond a doubt, this was the same voice.

He jumped to his feet. He started walking towards the source of the voice, yet the distance between him and the hum of the singing was strangely growing. The devil was playing games with him! Now he heard again clearly: *"Si l'on savait..."*

After passing a few trees, he reached the edge of the desert.

He froze.

My God!

The woman was sitting at the foot of a sand dune in the Sahara. It was the same face he had seen staring at him from the newspaper just a moment earlier. The moonlight was shining down on her. She was wearing a white horseback-riding outfit and a cork hat, and everything on her was immaculately clean. Her big, sad eyes and her rather thick, fused eyebrows were clearly visible. She was looking straight at Pigeon, smiling and humming:

"Si l'on savait.... Si l'on savait..."

He started to walk toward the woman with deliberate and determined steps but without running.

She stood up slowly. She cracked the riding whip against her boot and started walking away.

Son of a gun! What if she disappeared behind the sand dunes?! He started to run. He had to clear up the mystery about these perpetual ghosts sooner or later. Would they ever leave him alone?

He circled the mound.

Nothing!

However, as if from very far, perhaps from beyond the fiftieth dune, the melody sounded again, like an alto singing a quiet, gentle lullaby.

Pigeon sat down and nervously started whistling the way one does to gather courage in a lonely, dark alley. Let's face it – this would be too much for anyone.

He gave up pursuing the apparition. Miraculously, the lady sang from a very far distance.

Only she was mistaken if she believed that for her sake Harrincourt would die of a nervous breakdown.

Nevertheless, this humming was getting under his skin.

He nervously lit up a cigarette.

How does a woman in such city clothing wind up in the desert? The company certainly would have noticed her traveling in the open, endless plane. How could she walk about with such ease in the middle of the 113-degree[41] heat, in the middle of the Sahara? Who could she be? She could not be a live person. That much was almost certain. Until now, he had not believed in ghosts, but henceforth he would have to. He would become ridiculed like the old sailors when they shared similar experiences in connection with the sea. His only hope was that he would never have to recount his experiences because pretty soon, he would "die of an accident in the line of his professional duties." But after that, he himself would not give such nighttime serenades. This was a stupid thing to do. These are the habits of Her Grace – a real woman's thing. She had gotten herself shot because she had been flirting with *spahi* captains, and now she would not leave him, a complete stranger, alone. What did she want from him? Did he hurt her in any way?

All of a sudden, so close that he imagined being able to reach her with his hand, the humming ghost appeared and sang loudly, her voice carrying far in the air!

Even with the deceiving perspective created by the moonlight, she could not have been farther away than fifty steps! He ran after her:

"I've got you!"

What in the world?!

He was absolutely sure that he had seen her run right behind the dune. He ran around the dune from the opposite direction. The woman was not there!

"*Si l'on savait...*" sounded from very far.

And this proved that she could not have been a living human being. To move from this close to such a distance in an instant, and then to sing again from fifty steps – it was impossible! On the other hand, the prints left behind by her boots were clearly visible in the sand.

He started to track her footprints.

The indentations generated by her heel and sole were evident in the dust all around. Wait a minute! The sand caves in under the feet of Her Grace the Ghost? This was evidence that she had weight! Volume! And she put one foot in front of the other like any mortal! Not even his grandfather had seen such a ghost. In that case, this had to be some sort of a ruse, and he resented such behavior.

The prints returned towards the oasis, but then…

He froze in astonishment!

Behind a sand dune that was followed by a short plane in the landscape, the footprints abruptly disappeared.

They simply stopped.

This was incredible!

The track ended in the sand between two dunes on an empty plane as if the lady had flown away. The last two prints were clearly visible, but then nothing followed them but smooth dust.

He decided he would no longer be concerned with the matter. Alright. He accepted the fact that ghosts do exist after all. And they could be most gorgeous at that.

He sat down again among the bushes and continued searching the contents of the wallet. He gave up the game with the ghost. Her Grace had won.

He found a letter in the wallet. It was addressed to Monsieur Henry Grison, and urged him to make swift arrangements in "the matter" because Kalimegdan could not wait later than next autumn. *Hmm,* Pigeon thought. *Mr. Kalimegdan will not stick around because I doubt Mr. Grison will be able to make timely arrangements – for it's highly unlikely that Judgment Day and the resurrection associated with it will occur before autumn.*

Nevertheless, Pigeon learned from the letter who the victim was: Henry Grison, *9 Avenue Magenta.*

What else have we got here? he wondered.

He found an ivory plaque. Very interesting! On it was written: "*At the rank of major,*" but there was no name or anything of the like. But there was something near the bottom: "*Personally issued by General (illegible),*" and a number: "*88.*" Above that, in gold letters: "*General Staff. Department D.*"

Mr. Grison must have been some sort of an honorably discharged rheumatic veteran, and this must be a commemorative plaque issued for squadron reunion on the battle's tenth anniversary. Alright; and here is a notification...

What the hell?!

Not far, at the foot of a sand mound, the ghost was sitting with her knees pulled up and arms around them, and she was singing.

Pigeon watched her. He didn't move. To what avail? To start the whole game all over again? He just sat and watched her. He then lit a cigarette. The ghost stood up and spread her arms towards him in an embracing gesture. Harrincourt waved his hand in resignation. He had had enough of this. He resented being haunted. They should leave him alone. Had he hurt anyone? What did they want from him?

Above the farthest waves of sand dunes, a pale chalk-colored stripe separated the horizon and the sky. And the lady sang.

All of a sudden, Pigeon had an idea. He thought that politeness, even towards ghosts, counted as a military virtue. He pulled out his harmonica and, with his eyes closed, he accompanied her singing by flourishing the tune beautifully and emotionally. He opened his eyes because the woman had stopped singing. Hmm, the ghost appeared to be caught off guard. She just stood there and looked at him, astonished.

She then turned around and ran away. "Hello! Your Grace! Mrs. Ghost! Stop for a second, please, and don't be frightened. I won't hurt you!"

But the ghost disappeared behind a mound.

Pigeon honestly regretted that he had scared the ghost. He returned to the camp, ate half a *boulot*,[42] and comfortably fell asleep.

CHAPTER TEN

1

When they resumed marching the next morning, Pigeon was already marched with the column. Troppauer was honestly saddened by Pigeon's being four pairs behind him in the line. When they left Oran, all of them were fresh and in good spirits, but now, more than halfway through the Sahara, they were in a region where the oases were separated by at least three or four days of marching, and the exhausted soldiers wearily pressed on in the dust.

They set up camp for the night in the desert. Sergeant Latouret was already waiting for them with the forward patrol. This trying assignment barely showed on the old soldier. If he had lost some weight, it was only because of melancholy.

The company fell down on the hot, desolate dust like a bundle of rags. Latouret made his picks for the next duty and assembled the following day's patrol.

As he was setting up his tent, Pigeon suddenly caught Latouret's eyes.

"Private!"

"*Oui, mon chef!*"

"You were given the order to travel in the wagon. How did you wind up in the column?"

"Upon my request, the lieutenant permitted me to give my place to an invalid in serious need."

"I think you will become an invalid in quite serious need pretty soon! In the morning, half an hour before line-up, you will report to me for duty in the forward patrol. *Rompez!*"

Pigeon rubbed his hands together with satisfaction when Latouret walked away. The good old angry Latouret would make sure that he died "in the line of his professional duty."

Pigeon then took a walk among the sand dunes, hoping to catch sight of the ghost. He had grown fond of this haunting lady. He sat down and pulled out his harmonica to lure her there, but to no avail. It appeared that he had scared the departed lady away.

"It is a wonderful evening, comrade!" Troppauer said, standing next to Pigeon. The poet's short, chunky body was gray with dust from head to toe. With his arms embracing the desert, he exclaimed, "Oh, Sahara, thou art the queen of barren planes! Blessed is thy dust thou art welcoming the great poet with…"

"You have glorious thoughts," Pigeon said approvingly. "Just proceed, press on… Do you have something to read for me? I haven't had the chance to enjoy a single one of your rhymes in days."

"I have come up with a few beautiful lines, but farewell, for now, Pigeon, I won't read tonight. The desert is calling for me. I feel something stirring inside me tonight! A poem. A thought. See you!"

And then he waddled away with his flat feet. He pondered new rhymes while he kept rearranging his Napoleonesque locks of hair. Soon he disappeared in the dark. Pigeon, on the other hand, pondered the case of the dead man in order to clear his conscience. He would pack and deposit everything in the military warehouse. When he died, the package would be opened, and they would find the address where the money and the valuables should be sent to the heirs of Monsieur Henry Grison. Henry Grison's last address was *9 Avenue Magenta*. That should be a sufficient start for tracking down the heirs.

Bang!

It was a gunshot! He jumped to his feet and looked around.

The alarm bugle was already sounding from the camp.

He ran to his own platoon. A lieutenant, wearing a hair net, rushed out of his tent while the gramophone continued playing inside. *Why do all lieutenants in the Legion have portable gramophones?* flashed through Pigeon's mind.

"Where did the shot come from?" the lieutenant inquired. Nobody had an answer. Patrols left in every direction. They returned in ten minutes.

Holy God!

Troppauer was being carried. The poor poet! Pigeon had a hard time restraining himself from breaking ranks and running up to him.

"Speak up!" the lieutenant said to Troppauer. "What happened?"

Troppauer sat up. His flesh wound was not serious; the bullet only pierced his arm.

"I don't know who shot at me or from where," the thick man said. "I was walking in the desert, daydreaming, because I am a poet – Hümér Troppauer, the lyricist…"

"Man!" the lieutenant shouted at him. "Give me a report!"

"Yes, of course, Sir," Troppauer tried coaxing the lieutenant into calmness while the physician was cleaning his wound. "As I was walking, all of a sudden I heard a bang, a bullet pierced my arm, and I collapsed. I figured that if I had tried to flee, the assassin would have taken another shot at me. This way, he believed that he killed me."

"Get the bugler to signal for line-up," the lieutenant said to a petty officer.

The bugle broke into the air.

"*À terre!*[43]" the lieutenant commanded.

Each soldier lay down his weapon. The officer and the petty officer proceeded from rifle to rifle. Whoever fired the shot had no time to clean the barrel. They examined the barrel and the lock tile on each rifle, one by one.

"This was the one," the sergeant finally exclaimed, pausing at a rifle.

He was holding Pigeon's weapon in his hand.

2

"Private!"

Pigeon stepped out.

"Where were you when the shot was fired?"

"I was taking a walk. But I didn't have the weapon with me."

"Who saw you?"

"Private Troppauer. We had a chat five minutes before the shooting."

"Did you have an argument?"

"On the contrary. The poet is my best friend."

"Follow me! Move!"

The lieutenant led them and Pigeon followed, flanked by two petty officers. They went to the hospital wagon, where Troppauer's arm was being bandaged.

"Private! The round was fired at you from this man's weapon."

Troppauer rose in astonishment.

"That is out of the question."

"How do you dare to use such a tone with me?" the officer scoffed at him. "Did you meet him before the shooting?"

"Yes, Sir! Pigeon asked me to read a few poems to him; he loves my poems because, you know, if I haven't mentioned it yet, I am a poet, and…"

"Shut up! Did this man have a rifle on him when you met?"

Troppauer exclaimed triumphantly:

"Not a single one! He was sitting at the bottom of a dune in the middle of the Sahara, and he had no other weapon but his harmonica."

The lieutenant returned to the scene of the crime. He counted the steps between the dune where Pigeon was sitting to the camp and back. This took at least half an hour at a quick pace. Pigeon was therefore cleared.

"Do you suspect anyone?" the lieutenant asked Troppauer.

"It had to be someone who is jealous of me. An artist is envied by many."

The perpetrator was not identified. Pigeon contemplated whether to report the ghost. It was, after all, weird that a ghost had pursued him, and then someone had gotten wounded with his rifle. What on earth did they want from him? Was it possible that this sad, pretty enigma was the assassin? But what did Troppauer have to do with the story?

He stayed by Troppauer, and he read the poet's own poems to him while the wounded man listened with his eyes closed.

"Excuse me, Pigeon?"

The Count interrupted the reading. His melodious, delicate voice was full of concern and politeness.

"Dear Troppauer," he said to the patient. "Your boots are too tight for me. I limp because of them all the time. Could we switch them back?"

The poet exchanged boots with the Count. Pigeon, curious, inquired after the reason for the unusual situation.

"It happened while still in Oran, the evening before we took off," Troppauer explained. "The Count asked me to exchange boots because I was headed to the city and had to clean my boots anyway, and he wanted to go to bed, but his boots were covered with a thick red gooey stuff, and he didn't want to bother with it. You know how poets are. I switched boots with him, and, in the morning before we knew it, we were already marching. It appears that my boots are too tight for him. Now, please read me that one in which I compare love to a blossoming apple when it falls."

Pigeon read that one, and the poet, with his eyes closed, listened with joy.

CHAPTER ELEVEN

1

The next objective was to reach the Oasis Murzuk,[44] with ten rests and four camps along the way. Sergeant Latouret continued his reconnaissance duty. Everyone knew that the assignment as a forward patrol was unnecessary and served as punishment. Not exactly without joy over his misfortune, the soldiers watched as Latouret took off for the desert half an hour before line-up. However, they were mistaken if they expected the old soldier to become tired or glum. His scarred face showed no emotion. His burned, white bobcat whiskers pointed at the legionnaires as fiercely and rigorously as ever, and he discovered every bit of sloppiness and disorderliness, as always.

Behind Sergeant Latouret, the eight men, Pigeon among them, left in the darkness of night. Pigeon was paired with Ilyich, a Russian student. Ilyich, or as he was called in the Legion, the Kid, was breathing rather rapidly – the first sign of exhaustion. When this happens, the lungs' vessels are already dilated.

"What a damned road," he wheezed. "If I only knew how much further! This part of the Sahara is yet unknown."

"No way," Pigeon calmed him. "Oasis Murzuk is a major center at the crossing of the caravan roads of Morocco and Algeria!"

The Kid shook his head sadly.

"I know more than the average soldier. Oasis Murzuk is the last point of civilization. From there, only a few explorers have reached the equator. This area should always have been important to know about because, if we could reach the Niger from Murzuk, they then could build a railroad to British Guinea. This passage was sought there by Hornemann, Barth, and, first among them, Suetonius Paulinus, but they all perished. There is a large unmapped area in the Niger region that will be claimed by the power who will be first to reach it."

"Tell me, Kid, where do you pick up all this useless stuff about explorers who put their noses where they don't belong? It is utterly futile at your age to waste your breath on so much inconsequential. We will settle in Murzuk, that's all!"

"You are wrong. Murzuk has a garrison staffed by *spahi* and Senegalese soldiers."

"You seem to know it all too well!" Pigeon looked at him with suspicion. Lately he did not like soldiers who possessed unusual information. To hell with this much mystery!

The Kid became uneasy.

"Yes, by coincidence, I made several acquaintances through a lady. I know quite a bit, and, strangely, they shared with me a couple of interesting aspects of Saharan politics."

"Please, I beg you to share these aspects with someone else. Sonny, to be frank with you, I am more interested in your last lover, provided that Her Grace said something humorous and had a favorite tune that I could play for you with my harmonica..."

The Kid looked at him probingly.

"I believe that you are mocking me. Although, if we could talk honestly..."

What is going on with these fellas? Pigeon thought. Since he had come up with this first-class, stupid joke of asking Troppauer to read poems to him, the whole company honored him by sharing their intimate secrets. The Count wanted to tell him the truth, and now this Kid!

"Let's neglect honesty, pal. It is useless to chew on the past of your family. You simply embezzled the money, period."

"No, I didn't!"

"You then lost it in a card game; end of the story."

"It didn't happen that way!"

85

"Alright, alright! You then killed her, that's all."

The Kid suddenly looked up.

"How did you know?"

"Everyone is like that. Lost it in a card game, embezzled it, killed her, or perhaps also married the other one as well, or something like that. Don't bother with it, I tell you!"

From time to time, Latouret glanced back at the two soldiers in conversation, but he made no comment. *You just keep talking! You may even smoke if you wish, but once opportunity comes! When the real opportunity comes! Nom du nom!* he thought.

The sun was sizzling, and the constant yellow, blinding reflection of the desert was unbearable, as if it were, with almost a drone, streaming from the sea of endless, barren waves of sand through their eyes and into their brains. Phew!

"Let's not just plod along, damn it! You are not on the promenade! Let's hear the march of the Legion! Sing it... *un... deux... trois... Allons!*[45]"

The song crackled up exhausted and off key from their dry, almost chapped throats:

"Tiens, voilà du boudin,
voilà du boudin, voilà du boudin...[46]"

At that moment, Koller, the carpenter, fell from the line with a resounding thud. *"Nom de Dieu!"*

One man was left behind with him. They put up a tent, and the two men were to wait there until the company caught up with them.

"Garde à vous! En avant! Marche!"

The patrol continued its journey in the Sahara. They did not sing anymore. The sergeant did not give such a command. *Softies!* Latouret thought. In "his time," when the *crapaudine*, *silo*, and similar punishments were par for the course, when the soldier falling behind was tied to the end of the wagon to make him walk or be dragged, when only the gear was collected from the lads who collapsed and everyone just marched past those lying unconscious – in those days, they sang. And if one could not or did not want to sing, he was tied up with his body stretched and bent into an agonizing ring. But times had changed in the Legion since those days. The newspapers dealt with and scribbled about the Legion so much that one new regulation after the other was issued to make the Legion comfortable for every city slicker.

"I can tell you, Pigeon, if you are interested," panted the Kid, while stumbling on an imaginary rock, "if you are interested. It's a secret, but I'll tell you."

"Don't!" Pigeon quipped. "If it's a secret, I am not interested, and I ask you seriously not to tell me!"

"But, nonetheless, it is better if you know."

"It's better if I don't!"

"Until now, the road leading there has been considered a cunning expedition. There is no road, in fact. From Oasis Murzuk to the Niger, the road is impossible, yet they have established a garrison. The greatest scandal of the twentieth century! Along the way and there at the garrison, people die by the scores! But they need a road to Guinea, and Timbuktu is too far to the west, making it unsuitable. Phew! I won't make it!"

Another soldier dizzied off the line. He, too, was left behind with a more or less fit companion.

"If the good old Latouret – may the Lord rest his soul if His Unchangeable Benevolence would call the Sergeant away from the Legion – did not keep looking at me so suspiciously from the corner of his eye, I would try playing my harmonica for the boys. It would perhaps counter this drudgery. Hmm... I could try. What could happen? There are some that smoke cigarettes, and he lets it pass. The most that could happen is that Latouret would yell at me to stop it. That much I could do for the Sergeant."

The sun's fire burned.

They had been marching for six hours in the middle of the endless sea of yellow dust when Sergeant Latouret suddenly jerked his head up in amazement. He heard some sort of a gentle, quiet, whistling buzz. *What is this?* he thought. What was happening in the unbearable last hour of this deadly march? For a mere sixty minutes separated them from the site of the next rest. What was going on?

He turned around.

"*Sacrebleu!*[47]" The milk-face was squeaking his harmonica, and, what the devil?! He was carrying two rifles on his shoulders! He had taken one over from the youngster marching next to him. This was against regulations, but if the Sergeant had objected, he would have punished that kid who should have stayed at home with his mother rather than coming here to be a soldier. *Well, just carry the other's rifle, my boy! Soon enough you will be grateful if you can even lift your feet. But that this lad can keep blowing the harmonica with this lousy, dusty, choking air! He is a complete idiot, and he will drop dead during the second leg of the march. Just let him drop! Just let him blow!*

And Pigeon kept blowing, by now quite cheerfully. And not a single one dropped out during this hour.

"*Halte! Fixe! À terre!*"

They had a two-hour rest.

2

Only five of them kept marching: the Sergeant; Pigeon; the Kid (whose rifle Pigeon carried); Nadov, the giant from Turkestan who, on the average, spoke less than two words a day; and Minkus, the Austrian physician. They had completed four hours of the second 7-hour leg of their march.

And Pigeon kept playing the harmonica.

He then suddenly stopped. Latouret turned back, expecting to see him at last drop out from the line; instead, he saw Pigeon fish out from his *musette*[48] a cold mutton chop, which wasn't too appetizing even when fresh and warm, and take a big, gratifying bite out of it.

Who had ever seen such a display? The old Sergeant, who had marched in the desert on numerous occasions, was already pretty dizzy. On the contrary, Pigeon was smiling, eating, playing music, and carrying two rifles, and he looked as if he had enrolled here in a weight-gain program.

Nadov, the giant from Turkestan, as if he were a column, fell down with a huge, resounding thud. Minkus bent over him to listen to his heart, but, with a somersault, he ended up sprawled out next to him.

"Private!"

This was directed to the Kid. He was still more or less on his feet, even though his blue lips were quivering and his eyelids were drooping.

"You will set up a tent above the invalids and wait for the company to catch up. Take your rifle back. Patrol! Attention! *A mon commandement, en avant, marche!*[49]"

The patrol, which now consisted of Pigeon all by himself, followed tautly on the heels of the Sergeant.

After a few steps, he hesitantly squeaked his harmonica, and, when he saw that Latouret did not comment, he started playing loudly and beautifully.

It was dusk. The faint shining of early stars already glowed above the desert in the bluish sky, and the patrol's two members kept pressing on. The Sergeant, with his three bobcat whiskers, was in the lead and Pigeon was behind him, playing the harmonica and with his bayonet erect on his rifle.

"Private!"

"*Oui, mon chef!*"

"When did you get acclimated to the tropics?"

"During the past few weeks, *mon chef!*"

"Why are you lying? This is not your first time in the desert."

"With all due respect, Sir, I have never lied. It's unbecoming behavior."

They kept marching. Here and there hyenas encircled them from a respectable distance, sometimes running in front of them and other times lagging behind. Some of them occasionally shrieked menacingly, sounding like the raucous laughter of a hysterical woman.

A weak light appeared on the horizon. They had reached Oasis Murzuk.

CHAPTER TWELVE

1

Oasis Murzuk was the gendarme of the desert. *Spahis*, Saharans, and Senegalese riflemen were stationed there. All these made incursions to keep the Tuaregs, Berbers, and Riffs in check. South of Murzuk began a vast nothingness.

But Murzuk had electric lights, a radio station, a hospital, and roads paved with ceramic bricks. The company from Oran filed in between the colonnades of *spahis*, the band played, and Arab onlookers, with their jaws dropped, admired the exhausted battalion.

Murzuk had a separate presidio for auxiliary squadrons in transit. The arriving company was directed there. The gear and supplies of the dust-covered, exhausted company were replenished, they had a medical check-up, and they got three full days off-duty.

A cordon of *spahis* surrounded the guerilla marauders and led them to a distant site in the oasis, where they were barricaded with barbed wire that was twisted around poles hammered into the soil. Saharan guards were posted at the entrance, which was left free of barbed wire. The irregular troops were thus separated. These people were not very sensitive; they smoked hemp and baked *kesra* behind the barbed wire, taking the situation in stride. At the entrance, a scrawny, gray-bearded Arab sat, wearing a burnoose; his eyes were red and swollen from trachoma. He set up his ember stove and brewed coffee for a few *centimes*.[50]

The legionnaires were surprised to realize that they were being treated as if they were beloved relatives or seriously sick patients. Even the *spahis*, who were otherwise reputed for turning up their noses, gave them tobacco and pastries as gifts and invited them to drink the excellent coffee of the red-eyed Arab who ran his business at the guerilla camp. And, at no cost to himself, every legionnaire could drink as much red wine as he wanted.

"I don't like this overt kindness," Pilotte said to the taciturn Nadov.

"Why?" the Turkestani giant asked in his double bass-toned deep voice.

"It seems they feel pity for us."

A fat Negro sergeant from the Sudanese hunters slapped their backs jovially.

"Where are you headed, boys? Come, I'll buy you a drink of brandy or coffee."

"Tell me, Sergeant," Pilotte said as the red-eyed Arab "Methuselah" placed the coffee in front of them, "what is your post?"

"Department B of the Commissariat. We supply everything from underwear for the soldiers to frieze for the prisoners."

A vivacious voice shouted from behind, interrupting them.

"Ahoy! What have I just heard? Are we marching on in prisoners' uniforms?"

The next moment, Pigeon jumped over the heads of the squatting soldiers, landing among them and sitting down with his legs crossed.

"Didn't you know that from now on you will escort prisoners?" replied the sergeant.

"Give the soldiers as much coffee as they want," said a captain behind them, wearing a blue hussar uniform, presumably the commander of the *spahis*. "You don't have to jump up, boys; just remain seated, eat, drink, and have a good time."

He waved at them with a friendly gesture and went on his way.

"I get the impression," Pigeon said, "that this is not a military camp but some sort of a missionary hospital where the nuns are disguised as captains."

The *spahi* captains were certainly not famous in the Sahara for their jovial manners.

"You will be away for quite some time," a tall, bald, black-bearded *spahi* said. "You will go far as a replacement. To Aut-Taurirt. It is customary in Murzuk to treat those well who replace the people in Aut-Taurirt."

"And what do these folks tell who are replaced and come back?"

Silence.

Now the Kid joined them. He stepped to the edge of the circle, leaning against a pole of the barbed wire fence. He smiled and chewed gum as usual.

"Why aren't you telling us what they say?" Nadov asked anxiously. "If the replacements march through Murzuk, the company being replaced also must come through here on their way back."

Because there was still no answer, Pilotte impatiently broke the silence:

"Speak up, damn it! Don't pamper us as if we were infants, but tell us if trouble awaits us at Aut-Taurirt so that we may be prepared for it. What do they tell you, those who come back from there?"

"That's exactly it...," said the Negro sergeant quietly.

"What?"

"That we have never spoken with anyone who came back from Aut-Taurirt."

They all fell silent.

"And," Minkus asked in a somewhat coarse voice, after wetting his lips and clearing his throat, "have many squadrons passed through here on their way to Aut-Taurirt?"

"Well, the frontier garrison has been in operation for only a year and a half," the tall one said, evading the answer.

"Tell the truth!" shouted Minkus. "Since you have been stationed at the commissariat, how many squadrons have gone through here to Aut-Taurirt?!"

"Hmm... Twelve."

A gloomy mood took over the small group that sat under the shiny palm branches in the sultry night.

"So you are saying," Nadov said with a protracted drawl, "that twelve squadrons have gone to the garrison as replacements but nobody has ever returned from the post?"

Then there was silence again, save for the millions of flies of the oasis buzzing in dense swarms.

"Where is the garrison?" Minkus asked.

"Well, to be honest I don't know the precise location," the *spahi* answered. "Other than the army, very few people have ever wandered into that region. But I understand it is an area that has thick forests."

"But that's splendid!" Pigeon was overflowing with joy. "That means that we will be at the Equator! We can be proud to tell that we have become well-traveled men."

His joke was received with a chill. Nobody was in the mood for laughing. Was it possible that the Legion would send them from Murzuk through the Sahara to the rain forests of the equator? And was it possible that there was a garrison at this god-forsaken, remote site of the globe?

"You mentioned something," Pencroft turned to the sergeant, "about us escorting prisoners?"

"That's correct," the Sudanese nodded. "There is some sort of a prison colony in the area."

The cracks of whips and the bellowing of camels sounded from afar, and unbearable numbers of flies tortured the group during their conversation. A huge, shiny-skinned Arab joined them. A horned viper was coiled around his arm. He was a fortune-teller who also sold amulets, such as the little finger of a fetus stitched into a leather pouch and tiny parchment rolls with Arabic magic spells. The gigantic brown man had a long mustache and large hooked nose.

"Hello, my old friend! Haven't we met before?" Pigeon shouted to him. He had the vague feeling that he had seen this man before, perhaps in Marseille. Or was it in Oran?

"I don't know, Master *Rumi*, if we ever met."

"But I am sure we did, only at the time, you were not peddling from door to door with this toothless snake."

"Toothless?" the Arab asked politely, and he gently pressed the snake's neck, and then held it close to Pigeon's face. "Please, take a look!"

Everybody jumped up from their seats, and the circle suddenly widened.

Both fangs of the horned viper were visible. Its bite meant certain death within minutes, in hellish pain, and there was no antidote.

Pigeon held his grinning face even closer to the snake's mouth, and peered into its throat like old doctors do with their patients.

"Take it away!" a few legionnaires shouted impatiently at the magician. "Take it away, you devil!"

"I only wanted to show that it was not toothless," the long-mustached Arab replied obligingly, "unlike Master *Rumi* said."

"I was wrong in that, mate," Harrincourt admitted with a cheerful nod, "but I stick to my guns that I have seen you before."

"I don't remember. Your Grace must be mistaken."

"Now, now, although to err is human, it might also happen to me. Well then, come and sit with me, my old friend, merchant of curses. Put your favorite lap-snake away somewhere so that the members of the honorable council can sit back down in their places, and then tell my future. Preferably a pleasant one! In that case I will treat you to a coffee," and he called to the gray-haired, red-eyed Arab who just kept on brewing coffee. "Give a cup to the snake-nursing mister. On the double, little boy!"

The "little boy," who was at least eighty years old, took a small copper container from the ember. The magician untwisted the snake from his arm, let it glide into a leather sack, tied the opening of the sack, and then looked at Pigeon's palm:

"You will have a long life," he started.

Pigeon became angry. This was the last thing he wanted to hear.

"Listen, there is no need to falsify the facts. Just tell me the truth! I won't live much longer."

"Master *Rumi* will have a long life. This is absolutely certain. The life line is here, starting below the thumb and crossing the palm. Yours is a long line."

"Look, my friend, it is not that long; rather my hands are dirty, and that's why you can't see it well. But if you look closer...," he tried to talk him into it, almost begging him. But the magician didn't budge:

"This is the truth. You will have a long life. And here, this is interesting, peculiar. You are being pursued by the ghost of a woman!"

What was that? Uh-oh! The ghost! Would you believe it?

"Listen here, old Ali Baba! Do you know anything about this ghost?"

"Yes, I know about her. The ghost of a beautiful but sad woman is following the troops."

Nadov interrupted him, murmuring:

"On my life, if it ain't the truth! I can tell you now that the other day, at one of the oases... I thought that it was because of the wine since I get drunk at every oasis. I saw a woman sitting in the desert beyond the oasis, and she was singing."

"Nadov! You were not drunk! I saw her too," Pigeon nodded, and he turned to the magician. "Listen here, Aladdin! If you know the ghost, the next time you see her, tell her, please, that I send my regards. Tell her that she should not be afraid of me because I don't bite and I find her very attractive. I would like to get acquainted with her."

"What kind of stupidity is this?" Hildebrandt, who thus far had not spoken a word, blurted out nervously. "Listen, Pigeon, it is not wise to mock a ghost in the Sahara."

"It's not stupidity, mate," Pigeon informed him. "A ghost is following the troops, an elegant woman who has a triangle-shaped birthmark on her hand. This is her favorite song."

And he pulled out his harmonica.

Millions of stars glowed over the desert; unusually large red and vibrant silvery stars shone through the motionless tapestry of palm and ficus trees. And Pigeon, with his eyes closed and quivering the harmonica in his palm with feeling, started to play the song softly yet clearly from the corner of his mouth:

"Si l'on savait..."

Two monkeys in transit from the top of a tamarisk to a neighboring poplar stopped and watched them curiously from the branches. In the silvery light of the moon, the dust was clearly visible in the distance as it hovered over the desert like fog.

And Pigeon played "*Si l'on savait.*" All eyes were directed at the distant Sahara as if expecting that the ghost would appear because of the song, as if it were a calling.

Instead, something else, much more unexpected happened.

"Villain!" the Kid shrieked. "Murderous villain!"

As if swimming through the air, he made a long-arched tiger jump and threw himself upon Pencroft.

With both hands, he grabbed and held the American by the throat, the blade of his bayonet flashed, and the Kid probably would have stabbed him, but the greyhound-faced, gaunt man threw a punch promptly, landing a right hook on the Kid's chin. The blow hardly had any swing, but Pencroft must have been incredibly strong because a tiny crack sounded and the Kid dropped to the ground, unconscious.

They all just stood there, astonished. Pencroft panted while he straightened his jacket, and the Kid's entire body trembled, even in unconsciousness. Something had pushed him into a shock-like state.

The bugles signaled taps one fort after the other, and everyone hurried to his own presidio.

2

They marched on.

In Murzuk, the company swelled to the size of a small-scale exodus. First, they received two armored vehicles that were fitted with small-caliber, rapid-fire cannons. Additionally, they received three ammunition-carrying caterpillar vans, and they were joined by a long row of mules with machine guns, flamethrowers, and field reflector lamps, and a huge hospital van with a red-haired paramedic.

In addition, all this was followed by many camels, mules, and carriages packed with miscellaneous cargo and hardware for road construction. Huge trailers carried beams, steel bars, cords, cables, and insulated copper wire.

The two hundred prisoners marched in the middle of the convoy. The indigenous and white prisoners were mixed together. They were tied to each other by their right wrists, in pairs. They were dressed in coarse, light-brown cotton clothes. They were escorted by fifty *goumiers*, Arab gendarmes. These were the most brutal tools of colonial administration: natives dressed in shiny uniforms and outfitted with a haughtiness stemming from the sophistication of a military style learned from drill sergeants.

Even these fifty *goumiers* had to choose between prison and service in Aut-Taurirt after having beaten up a detail of British sailors who were taken into custody because of a brawl, and who were insolent, even at the station; three of them died of their injuries.

Goumiers, unfortunately, had no clue about diplomacy and thus did not have the faintest idea that the British sailor was a precious commodity if he were beaten to death. As long as he lived, he was just as much a poor maritime vagabond as any other sailor, but if he were beaten to death, he became a *file*. A file to which the appropriate response is, "The gendarmes who were found guilty in the investigation were severely punished."

Perhaps they would have found less than fifty *goumiers* guilty if fewer gendarmes had been sufficient in Aut-Taurirt.

And Engineer Lieutenants Burca, Lenormand, and Hilliers had also been found guilty of some misdemeanor and had been transferred to Aut-Taurirt.

Captain Gardone, who drank too much and who, because of a lady, made a scandalous scene at the Opera, was ordered in a telegram sent to his Parisian home to leave for Murzuk immediately, where he was to join the company from Oran. He would assume the duties of Vice Commander under Major *Vicomte*[51] Delahay at the garrison of Aut-Taurirt.

Cursing, he tore up the long telegram. He knew what the glorious phrases meant. He would wind up in a hellish garrison, where he would either kick the bucket or get promoted.

However, he realized the true nature of his assignment only

after arriving in Murzuk when he spoke with a major at the headquarters.

"What? From here… to the Equator?" he asked perplexed, bending over the map.

"Not quite," the major answered. "It's a difficult terrain for sure."

"But what the hell is this Aut-Taurirt? What kind of place is this between the Sahara and the Niger region? I bet no one has ever gone there before!"

"On the contrary. Remember, two years ago, the first reconnaissance mission left Murzuk towards the south, but the patrol was slaughtered in this very region, and the squadron sent for retaliation found no trace of the murderous aborigines. They concluded that *Sokota* Negro native tribesmen were the perpetrators, but they live on the other side of the Niger, beyond the rain forest. Nobody knows how they entered our territory. And then Normand's expedition never returned either. A search party from Timbuktu went after them, and they concluded that all of them were slaughtered. And then Russel's expedition – you must have heard about it since it made the headlines – left for the region, enjoying extraordinary support. He was after some sort of a passage, but he also disappeared."

"Please, forgive me, but this is an unknown, uncharted road."

"Lander, Hornemann, and Caillée charted it sufficiently."

"But not sufficiently enough for armies or garrisons!" Gardone slammed on the table bitterly.

The major shrugged his shoulder.

"For soldiers, there is only one thing impossible: to criticize an order. A year and a half ago they decided that there would be a garrison in the middle of nowhere between the Equator and the Sahara, and ever since, there has been a garrison. This is Aut-Taurirt. A road is needed in lieu of Russel's lost passage. Therefore, there will be a road, and whoever comes back from there when he is relieved from duty will have made a pretty nice career for himself."

"If he comes back," Gardone said turning pale.

"Of course. But if not, even then he will get a beautiful memorial service."

The major made this comment with coldness in his voice, and he stood up. He was a good soldier, and he didn't like Gardone.

This was how the expedition left Murzuk with prisoners and a company full of inexperienced rookies led by a habitual drinker, the fat Gardone, who was accustomed to Parisian comfort.

3

"Tell me, why did you jump on Pencroft?" Minkus, the doctor, asked the Kid. "This must stem from a psychological aberration."

"I don't know. All of a sudden I felt hot, and I don't remember a thing after that."

Behind them, wheels were squeaking. Caterpillar vans struggled ahead with a harsh noise, armored vehicles rattled, and the cracks of drovers' whips sounded as the seemingly endless convoy was trudging ahead in the sizzling desert.

"That happened to me also," Nadov said. "Once I drank so much at the country fair in Smolensk that I slept for two days."

"You have malaria," Pilotte concluded, "It often commences with transient attacks like this one, and then the shivers come."

"Quite possible," the Kid agreed. "It's certain that I was ill."

"Have you ever had anything to do with this Gangster?" Hlavách, the cobbler asked. Pencroft got the most fitting name of "Gangster" from his comrades.

"No! Never!" Ilyich said.

They then stopped the conversation. The air became hotter and hotter. A sirocco-like, southern wind brought upon them sluggishly swirling funnels of sand and unbearable headache. The mules were coughing, braying, and kicking; the whips were cracking, fists were thudding, and drovers were cussing. The captain was riding his horse at the front of the convoy; a mixture of indisposition and anger nauseated him, and every suture of his skull hurt separately. From time to time he pulled out a bottle from his saddlebag and drank.

They camped in the shade of an unusually large sand dune. It was impossible to proceed. The driving rod of one of the vans had broken, and it required a lengthy repair job. The horses and mules were stumbling blindly.

Pigeon realized with joy that he had numerous excellent opportunities here for dying. He already felt the ten thousand dollars in his family's pockets. Somehow death was not a painful thought to him. Those who don't find life painful accept the thought of death more easily.

He thought he would look up Troppauer who still was not on his feet.

"Pigeon," the Kid called to him.

"What's up, boy?"

"I must speak with you."

"I'm at your service, mate."

"I want to entrust you with a great secret."

"Let's leave things alone, please. You have all gone nuts with your secrets! And why did you choose me? I must warn you that I am irresponsible, superficial, flighty, blabbering, gossipy, and untrustworthy."

"Please, just drop the pretense. Come with me away from the rest for a few minutes. I know that the villain is now on duty as a sentinel. We can speak without worries. They will sooner or later put me away. I must tell you everything!"

He was so sad and desperate that Pigeon felt pity for him. To hell with all secrets and mysteries!

"Well, boy, let's talk, but I beg you to quit making such a miserable face all the time."

They sat in the shade of a distant mound.

"I attended university in Paris," Ilyich started. "I was a truly happy man, in spite of often going hungry, but poverty didn't matter; student life was beautiful, I looked ahead with optimism, and... And then I met a woman."

"Trouble always starts like this," Pigeon noted pompously, running sand through his fingers and contemplating how good it would be for him to stay in the desert as hourglass filling.

"This woman promised to aid my career. She had a prominent friend, a certain Henry Grison…"

"Who?!"

"Henry Grison. Why were you startled like that?"

"I met this gentleman."

"Where?"

"In an interesting house. He welcomed me in his pajamas on the floor."

The Kid was looking at him.

"I know who you are!" And then, after a brief pause, he stared into Pigeon's eyes, and said: "*Batalanga.*"

He expected a great impact. However, Pigeon looked at him quite stupidly. He then touched the Kid's forehead:

"You might be right about that; however, it might do you good to get your temperature checked."

The Kid stared at him with a fixated and sarcastic look, he then repeated the word, emphasizing every syllable:

"Ba-ta-lan-ga!"

What do these people want from me? Now, this is the latest one. This Batalanga! Pigeon thought.

"You are a gifted comedian," the Kid said, "but I think you will stop pretending if I tell you that I have been in *Batalanga* before."

"That's all right, my son. You have been there before; I accept the fact. Just tell me one thing: Who is this Grison, and where do his relatives or heirs live?"

"I don't know much about him. I was accepted to join the Russel expedition based on his recommendation…"

Pigeon perked up again.

"Russel! Wait a second! Wasn't this the explorer whose widow married… Yes, Bretail. Wow! But this is fascinating!"

"I knew you would be interested."

"Beyond measure! The late Mrs. Bretail, who was murdered, is following our convoy."

The Kid jumped to his feet with his face turning pale as whitewash.

"Don't say that! I beg you, don't say that! I will go crazy!" And he threw himself on the ground, sobbing desperately.

Harrincourt lifted him gently. He now took seriously what the boy had said, and he was sorry. He didn't know what was hurting the boy; he just saw that the Kid was suffering.

"As far as I know," he said quietly to Ilyich, "Bretail shot the woman, a captain, and himself."

"It's not true," the Kid whispered. "All three of them were murdered!"

A million tiny, burning-hot grains of dust stung their faces, and the air stood above the desert without moving in the sweltering heat.

"Strange," Pigeon mumbled. "And do you know anything more? Like who killed them?"

"I did!"

CHAPTER THIRTEEN

1

For once, Pigeon was shaken to the core. Even his superficial, carefree, cheerful mind grasped the full tragedy of this horrific secret. Never mind *Batalanga!* And the fountain with the Marquis was a joke. The corpse in front of the bathroom was okay; the most important thing was to turn the lights off. The Field Marshal recognized him as a private – who cared? Macquart did not come to the soiree – that didn't matter. But this was different, much more staggering, as the twenty-year-old Kid sat in the middle of the Sahara and cried because he had killed a couple of people. For a superficial man like Pigeon, the most disheartening aspect of this situation was that he was the only one who knew it. And now he had to do something. Make no mistake about it: he had to do something other than play the harmonica or a stupid prank; he had to do something really serious.

"Listen to me, and stop sobbing! I already regret that I did not go on to listen to Troppauer's poems. They are just like your story: exhilarating, depressing, and no one understands a word of them! Here is a cigarette; light up and tell me everything truthfully."

With a few sighs, the boy more or less calmed his irregular breathing. From time to time, he had a hiccup. He was trembling with so much emotion that his chattering teeth reduced his speech to stutter.

"You will now learn everything," he whispered. He then added emphatically: "Major, Sir."

Pigeon jumped up, and threw his cap on the ground in desperation.

"Will you cut the crap, please?"

"Okay, okay! We shall not talk about that. Let's pretend that I don't know a thing."

"In this entire case I am the one who knows nothing! And the more it is explained to me, the less I know."

The Kid smiled with understanding:

"All right then, listen. Let's pretend that you know nothing. You are only a courageous comrade of mine to whom I am telling this horror so that if I die, there would be someone who could throw a noose around the necks of the villains. First of all, you need to know that all those men in the convoy will never return from the place where we are headed. And for all this, the same few villains who killed Russel are responsible."

"What kind of elixir did this Mr. Russel discover?"

"A two thousand-year-old passage. *Suetonius Paulinus*,[52] who visited the Niger region as early as the first century, in one of his records mentioned the 'Road of the Crocodiles' that led through the plains to the empire of the 'Black Giants' without any obstacle. Since the stretch of the Niger that Suetonius described is inhabited by dwarf pygmies, Russel hypothesized that Suetonius had been referring to the *Sokota* Negroes as giants who are giant in size, albeit only in comparison with the pygmies. Thus, the record that had been dismissed by serious scientists because of the reference to giants, in a sense, became as credible as the journey of Herodotus. Now, let's compare all this with Herodotus."

"My friend, let's not compare. Or, let's do it at some other place, and not in the Sahara. I had trouble with those ancient authors even at the Naval Academy."

The pastel moon was glowing through a gray vale of dust. The subdued rays were shining down on endless sand dunes. A startled mule gave out a desperate bray, and hyenas kept replying from afar.

"You must listen to this," the Kid said. "Lots of people have died and will die because of this."

"Forgive me, but it is nonsense that here in the desert people will die because of various classical writers. The weather is hot, and the climate is unhealthy. However, neither Vergil nor Shakespeare is responsible for it."

"I know that you are being sarcastic. Nevertheless, I am asking you to be patient. According to Herodotus, the Nile and the Niger are connected. Rather obscurely, he explained this connection with crocodiles. Russel assumed that the 'Road of the Crocodiles' led through Senegambia, and Herodotus, who followed the same path as Suetonius, mistook the Gambia for the Nile. If somebody were to find this passage that connects the Sahara with the Niger region, the discovery would be one of the most useful contributions to modern colonial expansion. The problem of the Sahara Railway would be solved. The line could connect the Mediterranean Sea with the ports of Western Africa. Moreover, the discovery would secure *Batalanga*, the uncharted lands of Senegambia, the land of the *Sokota* tribe, for France. The *Sokota* aborigines know the passage that has been sought by so many since Suetonius and Herodotus. Russel firmly believed that his hypothesis about the site of the secret passage was infallible. But Russel disappeared and never returned. Only Dr. Bretail arrived in Morocco – seriously ill - – and also this Henry Grison."

"This Grison, was he there with Russel?"

The Kid cracked up in a hoarse, annoying laugh:

"Was he there? He was the man who shot Russel dead!"

2

Thus, the man whose wallet was now in his pocket, who was stabbed to death with his bayonet in Dr. Bretail's house, that very man, Henry Grison, killed Russel!

"How do you know all this?"

"The woman, who I suspect was either the lover or the agent of Grison, introduced me to him. To gain Russel's trust and confidence, Henry Grison pretended to be a wealthy lion hunter and traveler of Africa. As a practical man, he organized Russel's expedition, and he got me involved."

"And who was this man?"

"Now I know: he was an infamous political soldier of fortune. For a hefty payment, he would instigate riots in Arabia as a Muslim prophet, or he would stage a strike at the Iraqi oil wells as an ordinary worker. In Russel's expedition, a hunter by the name of Laporter and I were the youngest.

"We camped in the desert, near the jungle, at the site where the garrison of Aut-Taurirt was later founded. The native pygmies who lived in the forest helped us with the work around the camp. Russel left for his last trip from there. Dr. Bretail alone escorted him. Perhaps he asked no one else because he suspected that dubious characters were among the members of the expedition. Laporter, Lorsakoff the Russian, Grison, an Englishman named Byrel, and I had endured the trip up to that point; the rest of the expedition dropped out because of illness or other reasons.

"In the evening, our four pygmy helpers, among them a chief named Illomor, held a little fiesta and hosted their white masters.

"They impressed me as guileless men; they offered us *kivi*, a drink made of the shoots of a special palm. It is a colorless, odorless wine. According to ancient tradition, virgin maidens must chew the shoots and spit them in a pot that is passed from hand to hand. You will find similar drinks fermented with saliva in most primitive cultures. The other members of the expedition were teasing me because, for a novice tropical explorer, this was a most trying moment. Because refusing the clay pitcher from the chief's hands was a deadly insult. They built a big fire and buzzed with their primitive instruments, and we all drank. When I drank the second cup, I was no longer disgusted. It was an etching drink, reminiscent of whiskey, but it kind of sparkled in the mouth. Before long, the natives were yelling wildly and were dancing and jumping around the fire in a weird ecstasy.

"Peculiarly, without knowing why, I suddenly felt that I had to join their jumping. My head became hot; the fire, the forest, and the wild aborigines swirled around me; and then I felt my arms and my legs twitching, and finally it seemed that I was jumping among them around the fire, but I was no longer aware of myself.

"In the morning, I woke up to find myself tied up, lying on the ground, with Laporter sitting by me.

"'Just remain calm,' he said in a placid, encouraging tone, the way you would speak to the seriously ill.

"I had a terrible headache.

"'Why... am I... tied up?'

"Laporter remained silent.

"'Why don't you answer?!' I shouted impatiently.

"'Look, Ilyich, you were not doing well yesterday, and, well, we forgot that in certain people *kivi* provokes a murderous rage. It happens pretty rarely, but certainly it has happened before.'

"I rose a little.

"It was horrible!

"The chief was squatting with his legs crossed, and Grison was next to him. Two pygmies and Byrel were stretched out in front of them. Dead! I had shot them dead!

"Can you imagine how I felt? In the rage of the narcotic drink I had started shooting and had killed two natives and a European. My emptied revolver lay next to me."

The Kid stopped and stared ahead, panting. Two impertinent hyenas sneaked up on the two soldiers and sat in front of them within a few steps, as if they had joined them to listen to the story. Pigeon threw sandstone at them, and the two beasts took off for the desert with hoarse yelping.

"That was the moment when everything started downhill for me," the Kid continued. "Laporter later untied my hands. I had a terrible headache. It was about noon. The chief just sat there without moving or saying a word. They called him Illomor. It still rings in my ears, for it is such a strange name: Illomor. Grison spoke with him and told him to bury the dead. Illomor did not respond. He just sat there, poking his toes and staring at the ground. Lorsakoff said it was a bad sign. If the chief did not speak, it meant that he had made a vow. After a solemn vow, the natives often remain silent for weeks, and one would never know what kind of vow had been made. Perhaps he would hide in solitude in the jungle for a couple of months, but it was also possible that he would have all of us slaughtered before we could continue our journey.

"They took photographs of the dead. They then made a written record of the evidence, declaring that I had killed Byrel and the natives while intoxicated with *kivi*. Grison and Laporter signed it. Lorsakoff placed the paper in front of me. He said that if I refused to sign the document, it would be held against me in court as an aggravating circumstance. I didn't intend to deny it, anyway. What would I have accomplished against four witnesses?

"So I signed it.

"After that, Lorsakoff recommended that we follow the trail of the professor. Perhaps Russel and Dr. Bretail were in trouble and in need of our help. We buried the dead and then hit the road.

"Following their trail, we entered the thick of the rain forest. Later, Laporter and I got some rest while Lorsakoff and Grison went ahead. They returned about an hour later and said that we should continue searching in a different direction because they could not find the tracks of Russel and Dr. Bretail. By then we were deep into the mysterious land of *Batalanga*.

"We found Russel's corpse in the afternoon. He had been shot dead. Laporter, Grison, and Lorsakoff rushed to the body, seemingly in despair.

"'Murder!' the Russian mumbled.

"'What about Bretail?' I asked.

"'Either he was killed also, or...'

"'Or?'

"Nobody replied. They took a photograph of the corpse.

"We started marching back in silence. The whole story was depressing and mysterious. On our way through the desert, Grison said to me:

"'You have committed a heinous crime, Ilyich. If you won't be locked up for it in prison, you will spend the rest of your life in a mental asylum. I don't want to see your life ruined. Lorsakoff and Laporter will keep quiet, too. Let the record of evidence be our secret. In return, you will work for me. I need the help of trustworthy associates. And I trust you. However, should you ever lose my trust, the record of evidence and the photographs in my pocket will become public. I can sentence you to life in a mental asylum, in a prison, or as a fugitive on the run.'

"'What do you want from me?'

"'I don't know yet. I am in the business of international intelligence. If you follow my orders, you will have no reason to complain.'

"From that moment on, I was a puppet in Grison's hands. I was a weakling, and he had evidence of my serious crime. And anyway, how could I have stood up against such a strong, commanding, powerful man?

"We returned to Morocco and finally arrived in Oran. In the meantime, bit by bit, I learned a lot. For example, that Grison had killed Russel. However, Grison could not find the map on him. It had been taken by Bretail who took a detour because the two explorers had suspected that enemies had infiltrated the expedition. Russel had found the passage at dawn on that fateful day. But he had been ill, and for that reason he had urged Bretail to start the trip home alone, taking a different path to avoid meeting us. Bretail was waiting for Russel in Oran. Instead, Lorsakoff, Laporter, and Grison arrived. They blackmailed Bretail the same way they blackmailed me: photographs and records of evidence about the dead Russel. Bretail could have come under terrible suspicion that he had murdered the professor. Even if he were exonerated by the jury, no one could have cleared him of suspicion. He was also blackmailed with certain letters. Russel's wife and Bretail had loved each other for a long time. The lady had written a couple of letters to him, allegedly compromising ones, and Lorsakoff had gotten his hands on those letters. Mrs. Russel and Bretail were in a terrible situation. They had to comply. Bretail admitted that the map was in his possession. He said that he was willing to share its price but would give it to no one but the buyer. He wanted to negotiate the price personally. Lorsakoff agreed to the terms but only if he could follow Bretail's each and every step. Disguised as butlers, Laporter and I were keeping an eye on the secretary in the house. If he were to leave home, either Lorsakoff or Grison would be on his heels.

"Bretail kept delaying, procrastinating, the matter. He first said that he would work out the detailed, precise map from the sketchy draft. He then had a prolonged negotiation with the buyer whom Grison had brought along. Bretail later married Madame Russel. Nobody had ever seen the map. No one even had a clue where he might have hidden it. After all, a sketchy draft put together in the jungle in haste is not some sort of large, elaborate blueprint. It might have been nothing more than a small scrap of paper. He might have kept it in his pocket or he could have hidden it in a matchbox. At that point, the blackmailers were practically glued to him. And they became more and more furious. But Bretail just laughed in their faces when they threatened to report him to the police. After all, the blackmailers had become accomplices. If they succeeded in framing Bretail for Russel's murder, they could not explain why they had kept quiet about the crime for so long.

"The situation was that they mutually kept their hands on each other's throats. But whoever squeezed the other's throat would have strangled himself as well. Laporter searched the house for the map at night on several occasions but didn't have the foggiest idea where it could have been. Bretail continued delaying the deal with various excuses. In the meantime, Captain Corot started frequenting the house, usually when Bretail was away from home. It appeared that the lady and the captain understood each other very well.

"There was a sirocco on that fateful day. A warm wind blew that ached to the bone, and my carotid artery was thumping in my left ear with a double-pulse. A skull-cracking pressure was hovering over the city. I went to my room to lie down. On such occasions, I would lie in bed for hours and only brandy helped. As usual, I drank half a bottle in one gulp and stretched out on the bed to take a nap. All of a sudden heat rushed into my head; my arms and then my legs started to twitch, but I could neither cry out nor get on my feet. *What is happening to me?* I thought.

"And, as if it were a scene playing out in a nightmare, the closet door opened, and Illomor, the dwarf pygmy chief stepped through it, half-naked and with his nose pierced with a stick.

"I wanted to shout and yell because my arms and legs kept

moving to the rhythm of native drums and whistles, but I just lay there, helplessly convulsing; and the chief quietly said:

"'This was my vow.'

"He placed a handgun on my table, and, in the native tongue of the bush-people, briefly, with a single twitch of his mouth as if spitting, he said:

"'*Nogad!*'

"Kill!

"I remember seeing him leave with the long steps of the dwarf Negroes, shaking his spear over his head.

"Then fires flared up, flutes played, the tam-tam of drums reverberated, and I heard Negro songs springing from hoarse throats. That's all I remember."

The Kid stared into oblivion with ashen face; his voice was hoarse from the long talk and the choking memories of horror.

"When I woke up, I was lying in my bed, tied up, and Laporter was wiping my face with a damp cloth. You can guess what happened."

"No, no," Pigeon said horrified. "Don't tell me. I can imagine."

They fell silent.

Dawn started to glimmer over the desert, and the tiny sparkles of dust began to flash here and there in the whitish daybreak.

The Kid whispered with a stiff, larval face:

"All three of them, I did it, in the rage of *kivi*. Laporter certainly could have prevented it."

The bugler sounded reveille. They had to jog back to the camp on the double.

"I have not mentioned," Ilyich panted while running, "the most important part! Laporter forced me to join the Legion. They were able to arrange that I be assigned to this particular company."

"You can tell the rest later."

"No. No! I must tell you now. Laporter wanted me to enlist. A road is under construction from Aut-Tarurirt – in lieu of Russel's lost passage through the land of *Batalanga* – through the jungle of the Equator. It's an impossible endeavor, but it will be accomplished. Men are dying there by the hundreds! There are many in the company whose goal is to sabotage the road construction. That's why Laporter and Grison forced me to…"

He was out of breath because of running; he was gasping, yet he still tried to continue.

"Laporter is serving in the Legion also, under the name of…"

His voice was completely gone; he could only run with his lungs wheezing. He just wanted to say the name, and…

A gunshot thundered!

Ilyich made a somersault in his run, and then stretched out in the dust, rolling onto his back and spreading his arms. He then moved no more; only his blood burst forth from the corner of his mouth.

CHAPTER FOURTEEN

1

"*À terre!*"

The scene was familiar.

Each soldier laid his weapon on the ground, and the lieutenant, together with the captain, examined the rifles one by one. Pigeon stepped out of the ranks and snapped to attention.

The captain looked at him head to toe.

"Where is your rifle?"

"I can't find it, *mon commandant!*"

The lieutenant recognized the soldier with surprise:

"That chunky man was also wounded with your weapon. Where were you at the time of the shooting?"

The assassin again failed to frame Pigeon. Five soldiers attested to having seen Pigeon running next to the victim.

A petty officer approached, holding a rifle in his hand.

"I found it next to a dune fifty paces from the wounded man."

"Is this your rifle?" the lieutenant asked Pigeon.

"*Oui, mon adjudant!*[53]"

"Most peculiar. You always have an alibi, and in the meantime your rifle keeps killing."

Nothing was uncovered, yet, in spite of the soldiers' testimony, Pigeon was shrouded by inexplicable suspicion, the malicious mist of distrust.

The convoy continued its journey. The bullet had hit Ilyich's left shoulder and also injured his lung. The regimental surgeon and the red-haired paramedic took him under their care.

They were marching in an area of the Sahara where no man had gone in years. They proceeded, writhing with strife. Their feet often sunk above the ankles into the sizzling sand that burned and excoriated their skin, and the daily portion of a liter and a half of stale water did not relieve their misery. Man and beast alike were utterly irritable and anxious. Even Pigeon lost his temper. His harmonica got a lot of lousy dust in it and was now out of tune by half a note. Later it was completely clogged. Pigeon's current mood also resembled a clogged harmonica. He was fond of the frightened, pale youngster. Poor fellow! How sad it is when someone as young as the Kid becomes a killer because of alcohol abuse. But the boy would eventually get out of here, and then Pigeon would encourage him to frequent cafés where live music is played. That is the best antidote against the qualms of conscience. Yes! He would give this advice, as this nice kiddo turned to him with his sorrow. And he would also suggest the Kid not wander in Africa all the time because it would not serve him well. Rather, he should look for some sort of job, say, a railway employee or newspaper reporter, and the modest life would restore him in due course.

To hell with this harmonica!

"Private!" a corporal asked, gasping in the twisting sandstorm as he walked along the platoon. "Are you a rhinoceros?! Or made of tin?! Hoouh! Men are collapsing by the scores, and you are tinkering around with a harmonica? Hoouh... khm... khm... My lungs are about to rupture!"

The southern current stirred up dense funnels of dust.

Pigeon looked at the corporal with polite curiosity:

"Has anyone fallen ill?"

"Man! Four suffered heat stroke just this afternoon!"

"That could be due to the sun."

The men marched coughing, with their knees giving way; funnels of sand twirled in the blazing 120-degree heat and turned the column into a wailing inferno while Pigeon attempted to loosen a screw on his harmonica with a nail file.

The everlasting wandering of dust became more and more tormenting as they got closer to the Equator. They marched in the zone of the *passat*.[54] Sand flew continuously as if the hot soil were smoking, and a shrunken sun glowed like ember through the vales of dust.

"Tighten up! Tighten up!" the corporal roared because the column kept breaking up every minute.

"Would you happen to have a small screwdriver by chance?" Pigeon asked the corporal nicely.

"*Nom de Dieu!*" The petty officer stumbled along in the dust, cussing and coughing. A soldier fell from the column, and many reached for their heads and wailed. The armored vehicle with the small caliber cannons broke down. Three dizzy mechanics bent over the undulating gasoline fumes emitted by the engine and worked on the colossal machine. Someone touched a half-faint mechanic. It was Pigeon who stood behind him:

"Please, would you be so kind, when you are done with this work, to patch up my harmonica as well?"

Pigeon's life was spared only because he ducked quickly, and the hammer whooshed by, missing his head by a few inches.

2

In the evening, when it had cooled down, they forced marching on. The dust funnels that danced with no interruption spread out in white radiance.

The Count, who thus far had endured the trip quite well, was unnerved by the cold. Hlavách, the cobbler, marched next to him. He soon noticed that his aristocratic comrade's teeth were chattering.

"I never imagined that people could be cold in the Sahara," Hlavách said.

"I can tough out anything but cold," the Count replied, shivering. For the first time, his genteel looks showed signs of crumbling under the burden of service. His graying hair around his vaulted forehead, his classical face and remarkable manly figure withered away in shivering.

"My dear colleague Hlavách, I would not mind giving you fifteen franks if you could obtain a shirt that I could wear underneath this one. I have no more undershirts, and if I were wearing two shirts, I would be less cold. It's not exactly appropriate for a gentleman to wear double undergarment. However, at times, here in the Legion, one needs to dispense with etiquette."

"Would you really sacrifice that much money?" Hlavách asked.

"You have my word on it. Would you perhaps have a shirt to spare?"

"No, I don't, but I can steal one," the cobbler contemplated. "What kind would you like?"

"I would not condone such action, but this case is so extraordinary that I am ready to make an exception. If I may choose among the shirts of the company, then I would like to have Harrincourt's. I presume it makes no difference to you whose shirt you would steal, or does it? Harrincourt must have the finest undershirt."

"All right. Harrincourt's shirt it is. But then I will ask for twenty franks."

"Why twenty?"

"What kind of a question is this? A fine shirt costs more everywhere. I can get you Nadov's shirt for less."

The Count could not counter this reasoning.

After eight days of marching, they reached the last oasis on the map, Agadir. They barely knew about the existence of the place. Half of the company was ill. Hellish noise of howling and rattling filled the small oasis that spread out in the humdrum, yellow plain of the disconsolate Sahara, buried with dust and covered by unimaginable clouds of flies.

The animals neighed and brayed because swarms of flies hung to them like clusters of grapes. Any defense against the flies proved futile.

The prisoners and the huge Arab gendarmes were positioned between the guerillas and the legionnaires. It would have been ill advised to let the irregular troops mix with the army. Even with this precaution, a riot broke out because the legionnaires still went to the old coffee-brewer who traveled with the guerillas when they wanted a cup of the hot drink. They could also buy brandy from the old man in secret, although that was supposed to be the monopoly of the canteen. However, the canteen did not have *kmirha*. This hard liquor was fermented from various blossoms and had a horribly penetrating smell of pomade and bitter almond. The coffee-brewer was always surrounded by a small crescent of legionnaires sitting on the ground their legs crossed, discussing current events. They all cheerfully welcomed Pigeon as he approached. As Pigeon always said, he and the old Arab would open a "musical café" in the Sahara.

But today he did not come gamboling as usual. He trudged gloomily. And, after sitting down, he did not pull out his instrument either.

"The situation saddens me," he said somberly.

"Me too," replied Nadov waving his hand in a discouraged gesture. They were indeed hopelessly stationed there, ill and in rags, in a frighteningly deadly spot of the world, cut off from civilization.

Pigeon jerked his head up.

"Was your shirt stolen, too? It's hard to believe what kinds of surprises await one in the Sahara. Somebody stole my shirt. I had only two – especially fine ones. The other one, too, had blue and yellow stripes with white dots like this one that I'm wearing. Genuine faux silk." He was very sad.

"Would you like coffee or *kmirha*, Master *Rumi*, Sir?" the old Arab screeched with his ear-piercing, hoarse, and wheezy voice. "Strong-smelling, delicious *kmirha*? Or delicious coffee?"

"Give me coffee, little boy," Pigeon said mournfully.

"And *kmirha* to me," Rikayev, the Danish barber, stepped up, soaked with sweat. "But hurry up! Phew! The heat!" He unbuttoned his jacket like the others. "The flies! They are killing me!" They swarmed by the thousands, flying into open mouths and eyes, and the coffee-brewer waved his rag in vain. They just kept buzzing in dense clusters. Pigeon got his coffee and sadly stirred it.

The coffee-brewer stepped into his *duar* and returned with a large pitcher in which he kept his reserve brandy. But then he slipped, and oh, horror! He spilled the whole pitcher full of brandy down Pigeon's neck. The stingy smelling drink gushed down, soaking him from head to toe.

"Idiot!" Pigeon cried out in dismay and jumped to his feet. "This terrible odor will kill me for days."

"Forgive me, Master *Rumi*, Sir," The parrot-voiced old man screeched his lamentation and started to wipe Pigeon with his rag. "Oh, how cursedly clumsy I am!"

The soldiers guffawed. At least there was some cheerful event to stir up the stale sultry heat of the oasis.

It was just then that Hümér Troppauer's battle cry sounded:

"Soldiers, come here!"

The poet was fighting with fifty *goumiers*.

CHAPTER FIFTEEN

1

Benid Tongut, the cruelest of all the Arab *goumiers*, surveyed the prisoners who rested in the dust like scattered rags. The prisoners' circumstances were even more horrible than those of the soldiers. Up to this point, they had already buried at least a dozen of them in the desert. They had set their numbers before departure knowing that a third of them would never make it.

The prisoners were grinning, slovenly, disheveled death masks exuding an air of cynicism. Some had the wildly flashing eyes of aborigines; others had tired, sad, intellectual faces. Apathetically aware of irrefutable death, all of them suffered the *goumiers'* snapping whip with resentful, lethargic grimaces.

Barbizon, a stocky bronze-skinned bandit from Corsica, was the most authoritative figure among the prisoners. During the rest, he sang some sort of Italian folksong about love and sunset, and when he finished, a bristly faced, chunky man with the jaws of a gorilla and the eyes of a cow stepped up to him:

"Allow me to reward your royal singing with half a slab of chewing tobacco. I am a poet."

"Thank you. My name is Barbizon. I was a bandit in Corsica."

"I am delighted to hear that," the chunky poet said, "for many people have mentioned that I take after Napoleon." And he pulled his long, thin locks of graying black hair to his forehead.

"Indeed there is a resemblance. Especially your voice. Please, right behind me an embezzler is convulsing; I think he has a heat stroke, and my water ration is already gone. Would you give him some from yours?"

"Help yourself to it." The benevolent Troppauer offered his canteen. Barbizon turned to the embezzler and quickly gave him a drink, but all of a sudden a blow of a whip made him drop the canteen, and the water poured onto the sand.

"Dirty bandit! If I turn my back on you for just a second, you start messing around right away... you... you..." and the infuriated Benid Tongut lashed him two more times.

Before he could strike for the third time, somebody grabbed his arm. It was Troppauer. In a placid, lyrical tone he said:

"Mr. Gendarme, the Bible says, 'Do not let the sun go down on your anger.'"

"What? Go to hell! And release my hand!" He jerked his wrist away, but Troppauer grabbed the lapel of his jacket:

"'Love thy neighbor as thyself.' Please, be a little godly, Mr. Gendarme. After all, you are only human, too."

The gendarme, cussing, tossed the poet by the chest.

Later, when Benid Tongut regained consciousness, he found himself being held by two of his comrades above a pitcher, and they were wiping his nose. The water in the pot was red, and he could never be convinced of his mates' story that the poet had merely given him a single slap on the face.

The slap stirred up the otherwise monotonous camp life. First, when Pigeon saw his poet friend among the pummeling fists of *goumiers*, he threw the empty three-gallon *kmirha* pitcher at them as a first aid – a diversion until he could reach Troppauer. This promptly created some relief because two were knocked to the ground and the rest scattered.

A general fistfight commenced. A gendarme whose clothes caught fire threw himself to the ground screaming; another pulled out his pistol, but someone smashed his face with a leather belt, making him unrecognizable.

Sergeant Latouret with a reinforced guard on his heels arrived at the scene on the double, charging with bayonets.

"*Fixe! En joue!*[55]"

The fight was over in the blink of an eye.

These matters were not taken lightly in the desert. The surgeon came with the red-haired paramedic in tow. They took the wounded away. The rest just stood there.

The inspection was completed quickly. So was the sentencing. Barbizon was tied up. Troppauer and Pigeon had to march with half of their water ration for a week. The rest of the soldiers and *goumiers* who had participated in the fight were assigned double duty in the following twenty-four hours.

"Are you out of your mind?" Pigeon scolded Troppauer while the two of them pulled broom duty, the camp equivalent of confinement to barracks. "Why were you beating up the gendarmes? Come to the company to read your poems; you have already disciplined those guys."

"I didn't want to read poems to him. But he was hurting a respectable bandit, and you know how passionate I am! I quoted the Bible to this beast! What else can a poet do in a situation like that?"

"But why did you have to hit him in the mouth so hard that he landed headfirst at the other end of the oasis?"

Troppauer was fumbling with his fingers embarrassedly.

"Dear me! I am a poet. What else could I have done?"

2

"Are you sure that we will ever reach Aut-Taurirt?" Captain Gardone asked Lieutenant Finley in the tent before maneuver.

"The equipment is adequate. The company was supplied with everything needed. Unfortunately, the personnel are poor."

Gardone was miserable. His face showed the unhealthy, yellowish mixture of anemic pallor and suntan. His breathing was labored, and rivulets of sweat poured down him in spite of having traveled on horseback all the way.

"And," Lieutenant Finley continued, "I'm afraid that there are quite a few suspicious characters among them on special assignment. Some of the Great Powers would be eager to thwart this crazy road construction through the jungle to British Guinea. Suspicious, mysterious things are happening. For instance, those two gunshots. The only thought that gives me peace of mind is that there are most likely a couple of officers around here from the French Secret Service."

Gardone's heavy eyelids were closing.

"What?! Officers?! No way! Where?"

"Who knows? Perhaps they are among the guerillas, but they could just as well be among the legionnaires or the transported prisoners."

"These belong in horror stories! A French officer would never enlist as a private and would never let himself be beaten as a prisoner by *goumiers!* It's impossible."

The Lieutenant smiled.

"Impossible? The case of Captain Poisson proves otherwise. He had been the commander at Ain-Sefra until last year. Major Yves served there for a year to learn the true reason for the mutiny. Poisson was sent into retirement after Yves turned in his report. Two lieutenants, who were well seasoned at going on hunts and who delegated their duties to a sergeant, were dispatched to Sudan."

"I couldn't do such a job!"

He sighed deeply and covered his face with a wet cloth.

The lively bustling made it obvious that these were the last few hours before breaking camp. Everybody was preparing for a march of uncertain duration. Those whose water ration was cut in half grabbed the last opportunity to have a good drink. Pigeon was among them. He had already regained his cheerful mood. His mood was not even affected by the fact that he was nauseated by his own smell due to the *kmirha* poured down his neck.

He suddenly got a glimpse of the brown-colored, gray-mustached Arab who told fortunes in Murzuk. Incredible! How on earth did he get here?

"Hey! Old magician! Did you travel by bus?!"

"I am with the free fighters, Master *Rumi*, Sir," the magician said. "I came with you legionnaires all the way."

"That's pretty clever of you; at least we will not get bored. But where did you leave your little curly friend?"

"Would you believe that it was stolen? Have you heard of such a thing?"

"Why not? In the Wild West, horses are stolen; in the Sahara, it's vipers. It's a rather nice pet."

"I am worried," the magician shook his head. "Many evil deeds have been committed with snakes. Whoever owns a horned viper can kill anyone. It's enough to steal his shirt."

Pigeon's jaw dropped:

"What? What was that again? His shirt?! What did you just say?"

"When an Arab wants to kill someone, he stuffs the person's worn shirt in the sack where the viper is kept. He doesn't feed the snake, and keeps poking at the sack; in short, he torments the animal. And then at night, near the owner of the shirt, he releases the snake. Out of a hundred men, the viper will bite the one whose shirt was in its sack."

"What? Not bad at all!"

"This has been a traditional way of murder for centuries; everybody around here is aware of it, and someone said that it is also in practice in the faraway land of India. Salem!"

The Arab took a deep bow and disappeared in the bustling crowd.

Oops!

"Of course!" Pigeon finally remembered where he had seen the magician before. That bow… He got it.

It was the butler!

He had first seen the man on the *Avenue Magenta* in front of Dr. Bretail's villa together with the woman's ghost. The lady had rung the bell at the backdoor of the villa, and the butler had let her in. This was the man. But then he must have painted himself brown! This was a white man! "Hello! Stop this instant, you stinking movie actor! Where the hell are you? Excuse me, have you seen a snake charmer who is painted brown and is in fact a butler?"

"Idiot!"

Hello! Where could he have disappeared? I must catch him, Pigeon thought. This fellow knew something about the ghost who recently often appeared to Pigeon, albeit only in his dreams; but then she behaved very pleasantly.

But he searched for him to no avail. It was as if the earth had swallowed the fake Arab. Nobody knew about him; no one had seen him anywhere.

Pigeon decided that whatever the Arab said about the shirt was hogwash. A snake is no bloodhound. He imagined Sherlock Holmes going on an investigation, leading a viper on a leash to sniff out the trail of the perpetrator. *They try to make gullible people believe these old wives' tales. They are just like the sailors who talk about death ships and sea serpents to the rookies.* He felt lucky that he was not easily duped. Somebody had stolen his undershirt because he was head over heels about its beautiful pattern.

After taps everyone lay down for a sleep because they knew that they would leave at daybreak. Around midnight, a horrible cry stirred up the camp. Four of them slept in a tent, Pigeon among them. A private named Kramartz frantically ran out of the tent screaming. He had been bitten by a horned viper, and it struck its fangs so deep in the soldier's upper arm that it could not withdraw. It fell off him only outside the tent, and eight gun-stocks simultaneously struck down the reptile.

The unfortunate Kramartz died within a few minutes. There was no antidote against the venom of a horned viper.

Pigeon stood there in shock. When the general commotion subsided, he sat under a distant palm tree. The others went back to sleep. They had to march the next morning.

Pigeon, on the other hand, was really shaken. He didn't quite understand the matter because, after all, if his shirt was stolen, why had the viper bitten Kramartz? Or was the snake's sense of smell broken? Even a snake can have sniffles! How simple everything would have become if the snake had bitten him! He would no longer need to worry about finding a way to kick the bucket.

Was it possible that Kramartz died because of him? But if the viper was angered with his shirt, how did the snake get Kramartz? And who could have stolen the shirt? It could only have been the ghost! That woman! The woman with the triangle-shaped birthmark. The ghostess of the desert. *Just wait until I lay my eyes on you!* Pigeon thought.

Somebody touched his shoulder:

"Good evening!"

The ghost, wearing her horse-riding outfit, stood next to Pigeon.

CHAPTER SIXTEEN

1

A lone parrot was shrieking nearby.

Otherwise it was dead quiet. The ghost stood there facing Pigeon.

"Well?" the woman asked coldly.

Pigeon was smiling ear to ear.

"It's good of you to show up. I was just thinking that weird things have been happening around the camp and that, when I saw you haunting the next time, I was going to ask you whether you knew something more concrete."

The woman exclaimed tensely:

"Tell me, please. Don't you feel anything when you are standing face to face with a woman who has been murdered?! A woman for whose death you are also responsible!"

"I vehemently take offense at this accusation."

"Look, I have been watching you for quite some time," the woman said with her voice trembling. "I admit that you have remarkable nerves, you are a convincing actor, and what you are doing exceeds your fame, but I still believe that you have a heart. I saw you helping the weak."

"My lady! Recently, I have grown accustomed to listening to urgent stories I neither understand nor have anything to do with. I have become resigned to people not believing the truth about me and believing things about me that are untrue. However, on this occasion, you could perhaps tell me something more revealing."

"It's useless to put on a show for me. I know who you are."

"Would you tell me that, please? It would be nice if I also knew."

"You are Major Yves."

Pigeon cried out bitterly:

"All this 'Major' business is sending me to my grave! And then I will come back to haunt as your Ladyship does!"

The woman eyed him, feeling less conviction.

"Well, then, who do you confess to be?"

"My name is Harrincourt. Jules Manfred Harrincourt, dishonorably discharged naval cadet and philharmonic musician. Having told you my name, may I ask whom am I mourning in your person?"

The woman couldn't suppress a smile. But then she pursed her lip in contempt:

"You want me to believe this fairy tale? Don't you dare try that!"

"Please, I will tell you everything honestly. I hope I can trust a ghost; after all, in the great beyond, hopefully there is no gossiping. Please, listen up."

And Pigeon told everything. He began with the Academy, continued with the Superintendent, and, apart from a couple of digressions when he elaborated on some of his female acquaintances, he laid out his story more or less coherently.

The woman was looking at him with suspicion all the while. The story was somewhat supported by the young man's perpetual, childish smiling. In the end, the woman said in an uncertain tone:

"Well, you can easily prove that you are not Major Yves. If this is all true, a shabby watch certainly would have no value to you."

"Unfortunately I gave it to Macquart."

"What?!" The woman turned pale and looked at him, trembling. "But I was told that Macquart would not show up."

"It doesn't matter. Nevertheless he was there. And he took the gold watch."

"Who is talking about a gold watch? I meant a wristwatch with a crocodile head!"

"Oh, I've got that one! I would be happy to give it to you, although it's not mine. Here you go. What the devil?!

Unfortunately the watch seems to have been stolen," Pigeon said.

The watch was missing from his wrist.

2

The woman burst into laughter.

"And I almost believed your charade!"

"But I swear!"

"Don't you swear! And I have been such a fool to have doubts about your identity. I didn't want to believe that it was nothing but a show. I was misled by your act."

"Please, believe me!"

"Enough! You will have the watch delivered where they are expecting it, and I am responsible for this because I saved you."

"Saved me from what, please?"

"Man! If the Arab coffee brewer had not poured *kmirha* brandy on you, you would be dead now. How stupid I was to save your life!"

The *kmirha!* The snake was unable to find the owner of the shirt because he was surrounded by the awful smell of *kmirha*. Not wanting to leave without its job done, the viper had bitten poor Kramartz. So the Arab coffee brewer saved Pigeon's life.

Or rather, this woman had. She shouldn't have done it. However, it was at least an indication of fondness on behalf of the departed lady.

"Please, believe me," the man begged. "I am not happy that you saved my life because this counts as a blow of fate to me. However, I am delighted that you have been concerned about me, and that you have developed an interest in me. Because, you see, I have been thinking about you beyond measure."

Pigeon took her hand in his. It was a warm feminine hand, the kind that is rare among the dead. But she jerked her wrist away abruptly and angrily.

"Don't you dare touch me!"

The woman pushed him away and was on the run again. Pigeon was on her heels. *You won't disappear now as you did in the desert!* he thought. But wait! She could not go beyond the turn because a mimosa hedge blocked her way.

The woman was running and she had just reached the hedge; Pigeon had followed her with giant leaps and had almost reached her when, from behind the trees, someone hit him on the head and he collapsed to the ground, unconscious.

CHAPTER SEVENTEEN

1

When Pigeon regained consciousness, his head was buzzing. He felt no pain, only the illusion of carrying a barrel on the back of his neck from which ten thousand trapped bees were trying to escape.

It was dawn.

He felt his head around the nape. It was slightly swollen and was tender to the touch.

Dang it! he thought. He had been knocked out soundly.

He returned to the camp.

So the ghost saved his life via the coffee brewer. Of course! The coffee brewer had heard that his shirt had been stolen and knew that the snake had disappeared and probably had surmised a connection. For that reason, he at once poured the stinky brandy all over Pigeon. What kinds of schemes were possible in this desert! One was playing with his life! And if he could at least lose it. God forbid that he failed at trying!

So the ghost found him appealing. It was too bad that she had not believed him. He really would have been glad to give her that tasteless baroque junk. A watch minted after a crocodile's head! And with a pop-up lid at that! These days, this kind was worn on a brass chain threaded through a vest only by retired fire-hose operators. However, it had been stolen. Only the devil knew who needed that stuff.

"Trarah! Trarah!"

Line-up!

Yikes! I should quickly get to the others to have an alibi, Pigeon thought. This was the usual time when his rifle was used for assassinations.

However, as an exception, nothing like that happened this time. Everyone was running to his platoon, people were lining up, engines were humming, cars were rattling; cussing, popping, and commands filled the air; the company was ready to roll.

Troppauer fell in line. In the oasis he had recuperated from his wounds and had fully recovered by the time of departure. He called ahead to Pigeon:

"Where the hell have you been wandering? I have been looking for you all over the place! That Ilyich fellow sent a message. He wants to speak with you. He is in the hospital wagon in pretty bad shape."

"I am sorry I wasn't around. Poor fellow! As soon as I can, I will go to the rear to see him."

A long whistle and a sharp voice sounded from afar…

"Company! March!"

In the afternoon, during an hour-long rest, Pigeon went to the red-cross wagon at the rear.

"Hello, boy; what's up?" he shouted to the patient.

Ilyich lay there, his skin had turned yellowish, his face had thinned into a skeleton, and his eyes were ablaze. When he saw Pigeon, he moved his head in an agitated manner, as if he were impatiently waiting for him.

"You mustn't talk," Harrincourt gestured to him. "We'll write letters. Here is a pencil and paper. Write, just like Troppauer. But make sure I understand it."

The patient nodded, took the notepad in his hands, and wrote:

"Ilyich Rodion, with his own hand. I killed Bretail, his wife, and Captain Corot. Only two of us were in the house, Laporter and myself. Before we notified the police, he forced me to help him search the room. A small piece of paper fell from the hand of the dead Captain. I hated Laporter. I disposed of the note at once. It had said, '*We are being watched. If you want to know what time it is, set the hands of the watch in the sun, and watch the second hand closely. Your watch will be accurate at midnight. Dr. Bretail.'*

I knew I was eliminating an important clue. Laporter instructed me what to tell the police."

Pigeon read the note.

"My friend, I don't understand much of this rubbish. However, I would be happy to kick this Laporter's butt. It's too bad that he is not here in the Legion."

The patient looked at him with astonishment. After Pigeon pocketed the paper, the Kid picked up another one and anxiously scribbled:

"Laporter is serving with us under the alias of…"

"Garde à vous!"

Pigeon jumped up. The regimental surgeon stood there.

"What is this, a casino? Get out of here at once!"

Pigeon scurried away.

What kind of craziness was the Kid scribbling? But if Laporter is indeed here, I will give him a hard lesson in boxing, Pigeon thought.

"Excuse me…" As he stepped down from the carriage, he bumped into the Count. Would you look at that? Was he eavesdropping there? Could he be Laporter?

"Tell me," Pigeon scoffed at the Count, "do you live under an assumed name here among the soldiers?! Do you?!"

"But, please!"

"Cut the pleasantries. Watch out! And don't prowl around the wagon because if you ever hurt this kid again, that will be the last of you! What's your real name? It's Laporter, isn't it?"

"No, it isn't!"

"You are lucky that it isn't," and Pigeon left him.

The Count shot a dark glance after him. The paramedic came up from the side.

"What a rude buck," the redhead said.

"So, in your opinion, there is no hope?" the Count asked the paramedic.

"The doc said that if the wagon were to shake him a little more, he would die because he would have internal bleeding."

"And there is no hope whatsoever for his recovery?"

"Absolutely none." The redhead waved his hand and pulled out a large slice of bread. He took a big bite. "A blood vessel has ruptured and to clamp it, we would need surgery. But it can't be done here."

"Thank you," he gave a coin to the paramedic and walked away, deep in his thought.

In the meantime Pigeon was setting up his tent when a petty officer approached the platoon:

"Two men have come down with typhus among the guerillas," he announced loudly. "Everyone needs to clean his clothes thoroughly to make sure that neither worms nor lice are in them because mainly these will spread the disease. You must wash your undergarments. The paramedic will give you carbolic solution."

Darn! Pigeon thought. *And this is the time when I don't have a spare undershirt. Someone brazenly stole it. No matter. I will wash the one I am wearing during our rest. Out with the soap!* He opened his sack in which he kept his belongings.

He had hardly reached in it when he dropped it on the ground in surprise and all of his stuff scattered. His shirt was there.

His beautiful colored shirt, although somewhat wrinkled, was in the bag.

Yahoo! This was indeed a pleasure. Well, well, these were really honorable assassins. Since the viper had no further need for it, they had returned the beautiful shirt.

He unfolded the shirt joyfully. And that led to the second big surprise:

Something fell out of the shirt, landing with a clack.

The wristwatch!

The beautiful crocodile-head wristwatch that the ghost had been asking for so eagerly, the one that had been stolen, was right there. It was wrapped in the returned shirt.

2

They broke camp and resumed marching past midnight. They now had to be pretty close to Aut-Taurirt.

The usual order broke up in the column. It was impossible to discipline the men under the conditions this section of the journey presented them with. Captain Gardone sat on his horse like a melted wax figurine, and only the brandy kept him going. He was unable to fulfill his duties. Lieutenant Finley had to take on the commander's role.

Having marched in dust and heat for weeks, the company was undertaking a punishing task, and every single soldier used up the last drop of his strength.

At night, the soldiers lay scattered in the camp without any formation; they did not erect a barricade around it; whoever wanted to set up his tent did so; whoever didn't want to just dropped on the ground and fell into a comatose sleep immediately.

Meanwhile, up front, by the light of a carbide lamp, Sergeant Latouret spread a map on a table. The officers sat around it. Finley was looking at the route thus far, marked on the map in red.

"It is possible that here, right after Agadir, when we went around that *hamada*,[56] we might have steered away from due southeast by a few degrees."

"It is unlikely, *mon adjudant*," Latouret said, "because we would already have arrived in Bilmao."

Not far from them, the red-haired paramedic was holding up a lamp, and the regimental surgeon was attempting to revive Captain Gardone with caffeine injections.

"We will keep our current southeasterly direction," Finley concluded the discussion. "Give signals with blue flares every half an hour. They might see our signal from the garrison."

In this vast uninhabited land, like a needle in a haystack, there was a tiny garrison somewhere; if they didn't find it soon, it meant their end.

It was daybreak. In the sunlight, spreading to the farthest edge of the horizon, they were surrounded by the infinite, maddeningly uniform, sizzling yellow waves of dunes.

"But, how much farther do we have to go?" Gardone panted, as he was hardly able to hold himself in the saddle. Finley was sucking his teeth.

"I think we have lost our way."

This the Captain understood. He almost fainted off his horse because of the terror that ran through his veins.

They had lost their way in the Sahara!

"*Eh bien!*[57] Sergeant!" a cracked voice shouted harshly at Latouret. "Why should we continue? Just order us to fall out. *Rompez!* Damn it! At least let us bite the dust peacefully, and let us lie or sit down."

"I will put an extra machine gun on you to carry. Stupid *bleu!*[58] We'll arrive by nightfall."

"You know very well that we are lost! Just tell the honest truth! Even you don't believe what you are saying!"

The Sergeant strolled on, cursing. They had a long rest in the midday heat. In the evening, the soldiers did not want to continue. Lieutenants Finley and Bruce, together with the petty officers and the small fraction of the troop that still obeyed orders, formed a crescent, and pointed machine guns at the company. Finley ordered the armored vehicle to drive into the crowd of resisting soldiers while he himself, with pistol in hand, ran among them, shouting at each and every one of the legionnaires.

It was hell. Even the officers felt that this was no mutiny but the exhaustion of nerves.

The disintegrating caravan got to its feet once again. But after, it would do so no more. That much was certain. If it were to stop, this company would never get going again, regardless of threats with machine guns or cannons.

Despair took hold among them over and over again, though it was only dusk, and in the distance nothing was in sight but the Sahara.

And then, somewhere in the column, something started buzzing quietly.

It was a harmonica!

Its sound filtered through ever more cheerfully, ever more playfully, and the imbecile Chalky, who had marched since Oran almost without saying a word but with the perpetual smile and proverbial stamina of a mental patient, unexpectedly burst into a yell.

The yell prompted laughter among a few. The imbecile, enjoying the moment of popularity, started to sing inarticulately to the tune of the harmonica:

"*Le sac, ma foi, toujours au dos!*[59]"

It was a foolish military song which said, "The pack, I swear, is always on our backs; we are always on the move and never have time for embrace."

At first, they cackled, but then a driver at the wheel of a van started singing. Who could resist a harmonica? By the time the waves of dunes swallowed the swollen crimson and violet sun, the entire company was singing crazily, with the last energy of those who are about to die:

"*Le sac, ma foi, toujours au dos!*"

This Moses' Staff of a harmonica made melody burst up from the rigid rock of exhausted souls.

Later, Pigeon tuned his orchestra with a nail cleaner because the Sahara was beginning to take a toll on the delicate instrument.

Finley knew what the harmonica playing meant under the circumstances. Perhaps it meant their lives. He approached Pigeon, patting his shoulder.

"You played the harmonica well."

"Maybe, although I am out of practice. I would be better at playing the *Sérieuse*." And he immediately commenced with playing the Legion's love song:

"*L'amour m'a rendu fou...*[60]"

And they pressed on.

Around midnight, as a reply to one of God knows how many signals of rocket flares, a long blue serpent of light crawled in the distance to the middle of the sky vault. And then another one...

The company burst into thunderous, exuberant cries of joy. The rejoicing soldiers hugged each other and threw their hats in the air. They shot in the air repeatedly with flare guns, and a blue serpent arrived from afar as a reply to each of the signals.

Aut-Taurirt was signaling!

3

They were still far from the fort. They didn't miss the direction anywhere. The journey was just impossibly long.

When Lieutenant Finley reached Pigeon in the column again, the soldier stepped out of line and stood in front of the officer at attention:

"Well?" Finley asked. "You are a good soldier. You may have a request."

"One of my friends is seriously ill and, *mon adjudant*, I would like to visit him in the hospital wagon. The poor guy is all by himself."

"How do you know?"

"I have seen the surgeon and the paramedic up front with the Captain for some time now. No one else may step up on the hospital carriage. Since noon, nobody has given water to the poor fellow or has changed his bandage."

"Go on! Sergeant! This private is permitted to care for his friend on the carriage. Enter it in the daily order."

This prevented the regimental surgeon, who outranked Finley, from pushing Harrincourt off the carriage.

Pigeon walked happily toward the wagon. For one thing, he liked Ilyich and, by then, the case had captured his imagination. For instance, there was the woman. She was clearly sneaking about the same case for which the Kid was shot at. Moreover, Troppauer was shot at, too. What did the resolute poet have to do with this case?

It was obvious that the key to murders, a military secret, and the mystery of numerous treacherous men was a single person: Ilyich. Pigeon decided that he would be negligent no more. He stepped on the wheel hub and climbed in under the canvas of the carriage.

He flinched at the sight and stood frozen.
Ilyich, the Kid, lay in bed – dead.
He had been murdered.

CHAPTER EIGHTEEN

1

He had been dead for hours.

He had been murdered in a most peculiar manner. They found six or eight red spots on his body. They couldn't tell what might have caused the spots. They looked like the marks of pinching or scratching. Only the surface of the skin showed marks, as if it had been pinched between a finger and a thumb at a few places. At a few other places of the body, blood was oozing through pores of the skin in extremely tiny droplets.

"I have heard about such symptoms, but this case must be different," the surgeon said. "The main veins of the victims of South American coral snakebites are clogged, and the blood, after accumulating in the arteries, is pressed through the pores. But there is no sign of snakebite on this man, and we are not in South America. One thing is sure: he was murdered."

Pigeon again had a perfect alibi. When he had stepped under the canvas, Ilyich had been dead for a long time.

The officers were sizing Pigeon up with dark glances. They were acutely aware that the company might have hidden some unusual people. They had been forewarned from above before departure to be on the watch for suspicious individuals.

"He must be shackled," Gardone said when Finley reported the event to him. "We'll interrogate him and send him to court martial in Timbuktu under strong escort."

"With what kind of report? That his rifle was used for shooting someone when he wasn't there? That an ill man was murdered whom he was about to visit?"

"There is no need to play the advocate. This is the military! When he blows up the road under construction or the ammunition depot, it will be too late to send him anywhere!"

"If you don't mind, Captain, Sir, I would like to talk you out of it. We should first ask his sergeant. The court martial can do something with him only if you give them the opportunity to press charges."

"Just stop being a wiseacre," replied Gardone whose conceit had returned with the proximity of the fort, and he felt ashamed to have shown weakness under the threat of inescapable death. "Nevertheless, I will interrogate the sergeant, and then I will issue my orders as special higher military interests currently dictate."

Latouret came.

He said that Harrincourt had attended military school for petty officers, but his privileged assignment had been withdrawn because of deserting the Legion. He had endured marching as if he had already been in Africa, but he had denied that fact. There was nothing objectionable about his military conduct except for the occasional petty officer's complaint for being addressed as "old-timer."

"You see!" Gardone said triumphantly. "The man enlisted as a rookie, although according to the *chef*,[61] it is obvious that he has been in Africa before! This proves that my suspicion is well founded. Sergeant Latouret! Keep an eye on this individual. Assign harsh duties to him. You will face no recourse should this suspicious character be unable to cope with the strain. *Rompez!*"

Finley remained silent, and Latouret left.

"I am sure you would have taken a different course of action," the Captain said haughtily. "Remember, my friend, that in the military, one must sometimes exercise merciless precaution. Here, any suspicious characters will one by one receive assignments that make them croak. This is the kind of action that they expected from me when they entrusted me with this special mission."

Since Finley still had not said a word, Gardone continued in a more official tone:

"Lieutenant, see to it that this gang shapes up and does not march through the gate of the fort like a Gypsy caravan. I must tell you that while I was indisposed, order, so to speak, broke down entirely. Unfortunately I can't be personally present everywhere."

Finley clicked his heels together and left.

The Sergeant reported to him in front of the tent:

"As per regulation, we are to leave the four suspected typhus cases behind so that the garrison can later arrange their quarantine."

"Under what conditions do you want to leave them behind?"

"With a tent, supplied with medication and food, under the care of Private Harrincourt."

Finley looked the Sergeant up and down and said with disdain:

"It is in line with the regulation. *Rompez!*"

2

Finley would not have been so angry if he had known how happy Pigeon was about the cruel duty. Yippee! One could catch typhus here! It would certainly count as a death occurring in the course of his professional duties.

In the distance, the others were already marching towards Aut-Taurirt. It was daybreak, and Pigeon was sitting in front of the tent. The four ill soldiers were inside.

He felt a terrible weight in his heart. He had grown fond of Ilyich. *Oh Lord, oh Lord! Poor Kid! What an ugly, bad life he had, and how monstrously and nefariously had this nice, frightened boy been murdered,* Pigeon thought. He decided that he would not leave this case unsolved. He had read enough detective stories to know what to do. It was quite simple:

First of all, deduction was necessary. Deduction with ironclad logic.

Let's see. Only Laporter could have murdered the boy. But who could Laporter be? That must be deduced with ironclad logic!

But he couldn't.

Well, that would have been too much to ask, even from a detective. Perhaps the woman was involved in the case. *But who is this woman? It doesn't matter. The woman killed no one. That is simple and clear, and, if needed, I will prove it with systematic, ironclad logic. Its' very simple! Why did this woman not kill the Kid? Answer: because she did not kill him, period. Then who killed him? Laporter did. And who is Laporter? The Count has the type of face that belongs to a butler in an aristocratic household, and he was the one prowling around the wagon. Hmm... Ironclad logic dictates that public enemy number one is therefore the Count.*

Pigeon suddenly had an idea. Yes! He got it! He had been mistaken for a major on several occasions. A certain Major Yves. What was the conclusion from that? There had to be among them a major in disguise. That sounded stupid. Why should a major march in the uniform of a private when he could ride a horse if he put on his own uniform? Yes, but this was a major with the Secret Service. *He must be after Laporter!*

That had to be it!

The Major must have observed the others mistaking Pigeon for him, and he quietly let them be mistaken. Thus, everybody was bothering Pigeon while the Major watched them from a distance.

But who could the Major be?

Let's first take a look at the watch. Let's see if perhaps some sort of document is hidden in it, Pigeon thought.

He opened the lid of the watch. Nothing! It was an ordinary, run-of-the-mill, old-fashioned watch. He then opened the back of the watch but saw nothing but clockwork. Once a heavy object must have fallen on the clock-face because it was cracked in eight or ten places. Pigeon eventually concluded that nothing was hidden in it.

And yet, this watch must have been extremely important. He was sure of it by now.

In summary: I must find out which soldier is Laporter, who the Major is, and who this woman is, she, who is so beautiful, especially when she is worked up.

Laporter must have stolen the shirt and the watch.

Then, the Major was the one who had stolen these items back. Of that he was certain. He had to find out who had stolen his shirt back for him.

At that very moment, someone in the tent moaned:

"Return... the shirt... to Harrincourt..."

CHAPTER NINETEEN

1

Pigeon immediately rushed into the tent. Four patients lay there, tossing and turning with fever. Their cheeks were all ablaze.

One of them had to be the Major.

The one who knew about the shirt.

Let's see. Here on the right, this is the honorable Dr. Minkus. Well, this one couldn't be the Major. He is a slow-witted, ever-sleepy boozer. He could not be entangled in espionage. This one next to him is a Berber. That left two patients: Hlavách, the cobbler, and Rikayev, the Danish barber.

Pigeon waited.

Not much later Hlavách blurted out:

"Harrincourt's… shirt…"

Thus, Hlavách was Major Yves!

Bravo, Pigeon! Now you have gotten closer to solving the riddle! he thought. *The little Hlavách, who poses as a cobbler, is in fact a major in the French Army. Who would have thought that I have just the right nose for sniffing things out?*

He gave drink to the ailing men. He touched them with his bare hands. They left carbolic solution for him but he didn't use it. This way he would certainly catch typhus. He put on one of the patient's jackets. He used the other's cup for drinking. With that, he must have swallowed at least twenty million germs. Now he would just wait until he started to feel dizzy and his head started to ache. That would be the sign of typhus.

He sat in front of the tent and kept waiting. He sat there for a couple of hours.

Finally, a convoy approached. Paramedic soldiers came with a canvas-covered van. Lieutenant Finley's first business upon arrival was to make the arrangement.

They first loaded the patients, then the tent and the soldiers' belongings.

Pigeon sat up front with the driver. He was hoping to have acquired typhus. He observed himself for any symptoms. He sighed with resignation.

He was bothered only by a single aching feeling:

He was very hungry.

2

Pigeon did not go up to his room. He walked out of the Fort. Exiting was unrestricted here because leaving the Fort's immediate vicinity was impossible.

He walked over to the guerillas. The woman and the snake charmer could only be there. They could not have been hiding among the legionnaires on the way here. He surveyed the Arab camp. He looked at every single man and entered every single tent. He could find them nowhere. The woman could not have traveled through the air in a single horse-riding outfit! And where could the magician have disappeared from the desert? He also could not have taken off in a hot-air balloon. *Dang!*

He was sure of one thing. They could not have been hiding anywhere, and they were neither among the guerillas nor among the soldiers. A bearded Arab called out to the wandering legionnaire:

"What are you looking for, Sir?"

"The snake charmer."

"The one who told the *Rumi*'s fortune in Murzuk?"

"That's the one."

"He didn't come with us. He stayed behind in Murzuk."

"Your fairy godfather together with his entire family – they stayed behind in Murzuk! I spoke with the magician on the way!"

"That's out of the question, Sir."

Hmm, this was like a real madhouse. But wait! The old coffee brewer, the one who poured the *kmirha* over Pigeon to fool the viper, still had to be there! He was part of the bunch also!

"Tell me, my dear friend, do you know the coffee brewer who travels with you and sets up his business at every stop?"

"Abu el Kebir?"

"Yes, Abu el Kebir! That gaunt, red-eyed devil! Where is he?"

"The poor man! He died last night. But Master Rumi, how can you use such profanity?"

Pigeon turned his back on him. He had had enough of this. This exceeded the capabilities even of a master sleuth. That was the end of it. There was nowhere to go from here. Some people disappeared; others died, like this Abu el Kebir had. Everybody died except him, to whom it would have been so urgent and important.

Later, it turned out that he had worried needlessly. Aut-Taurirt offered exceptionally favorable opportunities to all who wished to die in a hurry, no matter the reason.

The garrison was built in the barren desert a few hundred yards from the jungle running along the Niger, where the temperature rose to one hundred and twenty degrees in the early hours of morning. Staying there was maddening even to those otherwise acclimated to a tropical climate. Those who had the misfortune of being in this particular spot received their fair share of tortures unknown to them in the desert: the pungent odor billowing from the rotting mangrove swamps of the nearby forest, the moldy breath of the jungle, the torturous headaches, the bone-grinding rheumatic fever, and the vapors of disease and miasma. The Saharan heat had but one healthy aspect – its dryness – and even that was missing here. The dense vapors of the jungle hovered over the sizzling fort with a soggy, foul-smelling presence.

Pigeon returned to the fort. The courtyard was practically

empty. He went up to the crew's quarters. The men, half-dead with exhaustion, were asleep. Marching obviously had taken its toll on them. But where were the soldiers who had already been stationed at the Fort?

The corporal on duty was drafting a table on his desk, drawing the lines with a pen and ruler.

"Tell me, please, is it true that other than the company that just arrived, there is no other soldier here?" Pigeon asked.

"And what am I? A chaperone for young maidens? Idiot!"

"And how many are here beyond your petty officership?"

"If I do not count the one who will die by tomorrow, then me, the Major, two petty officers, and nine privates, and me. Taken together that's fourteen."

"You listed yourself twice. Are you taking double shifts?"

The calm corporal, who had a deep voice and spoke with a deliberately even pace, looked up and gently said only this:

"Shut your mouth!"

He then carefully aligned his ruler, drew a line, and said syllable by syllable as he wrote:

"Three laun-dered ap-rons. Period."

Pigeon reclined on his bed. Was it true then that, ever since Murzuk, they had taken for a usual legionnaires' frightening rumor that nobody ever returned from Aut-Taurirt? Several companies had been sent here, and altogether nine privates survived, and none of the lieutenants.

Gardone was contemplating these depressing statistics, too, as he stood in front of the Major. Major Delahay was a classy, thin-boned man with a fragile physique. He was a soldier distinguished by polished manners, closer to his sixties than to his fifties. His opinion was highly regarded in delicate matters. His amiable tiny face sometimes assumed a sly expression of malice. He had served as commander at this horrible place for almost a year, and he had not gotten sick until the last few weeks. His ever-cheerful face was now weary, his skin had acquired an unhealthy yellow tint, and he was powerlessly sitting in an armchair in the tobacco-smelling command office. Gardone stood in front of him.

"And couldn't this situation be helped with a better healthcare facility?" he asked.

A momentary, sly grimace flashed over Delahay's weary face:

"Sure it could be. Even I myself gave it some thought before. We will request a little Alpine air from headquarters." To avoid offending Gardone with his joke, he immediately added: "My friend, we must accept that the globe has a few spots where the environment is not suitable for human survival. Soldiers must do their duty in such areas, and one must not get bogged down with miniscule details. That's also the case here."

He was weak, and, in any case, unaccustomed to talking much. His voice faded, and he bent his head back with his eyes closed. Gardone paced nervously.

"I am surprised that men die here obediently by the hundreds and there has never been a mutiny."

"Mutiny is impossible. In the backyard of the Fort, there is a vault with an incredibly complicated combination lock – eight letters and eight numbers. The central water faucet is in the vault. Twice a day, I open it for one hour at a time. Other than me, only one officer knows the combination. Should my adjutant and I suddenly die, then, within twenty-four hours, the entire garrison and all prisoners would die of thirst. For you see, the pipe leading to the forest branches off from there also."

"And where is the adjutant?" Gardone asked somewhat perplexed. Delahay immediately saw that he was dealing with a coward.

"I am the last officer in the Fort," he replied. "My adjutant died the day before yesterday."

"Then tell me the code quickly!" Gardone exclaimed, terrified of the thought that the sick old man could die at any moment and would take the secret of the water faucet vault to his grave.

"Because we have two officers now, and because my condition warrants that I appoint a vice commander, I will share it with you and Finley at the same time."

Gardone swallowed deeply. *Where the hell is that damned Finley?* he thought. *This aged, ill man could die any moment.*

"Perhaps it would be better if you would tell it to me right now, Major, Sir."

"Why? I will stay alive long enough. Yet, here one must not shrink from death. It prowls around you in a thousand different forms every day."

To the Captain's great relief, Finley arrived.

"Finley, please, the Major wants to tell us something about the combination lock."

"Yes, yes," Delahay said, and he poked for a cigar from his pocket case with his slender, tiny fingers. He cut its tip with care and lit up. He then turned to Finley.

"Finley... Finley... You are not French, are you?"

"My father was English, but I was born in France."

There was an unusual resilience in this suntanned, rugged-faced, stern-eyed officer. His nostrils often flared with suppressed emotion.

"Finley, please," Gardone said, "the Major will share with us the combination of a lock that is necessary for accessing the water faucet in a..."

"Yes, yes," the Major waved with his hand. "As to the circumstances around here, well, the scum of the colonial army is being sent to Aut-Taurirt. In addition, there are the prisoners. We don't even know their numbers because it would be ill advised to go among them. They somehow put up with the engineers."

"Would it be possible to restore order?" Gardone asked.

"We herd the prisoners into the forest, but we can't go after them." At this point Gardone trembled because the Major sighed a long sigh, rubbed his chest with his palm, and, with a grimace of disgust, extinguished his cigar. "They can't leave the jungle because they don't have an hour's worth of reserve water or food. They must build the road; otherwise they receive nothing to eat or drink. However, going among them to investigate, to punish, is impossible. I am tired and weak. You two must take charge. And you may always do whatever you want, whatever you consider appropriate. Time and human life don't matter. Whoever comes here – either prisoner, private, or captain – he has slammed the door behind himself," the Major said. He then wrote something on a piece of paper. "You must memorize this at once. This must not be written anywhere. The secret of the combination is our only power over the garrison. If it is leaked, if they learn it, they will slaughter us."

Finley took only a brief glance at the sheet. Gardone paced back and forth for quite some time to learn it. However, the following day he could open the faucet only with Finley's help.

CHAPTER TWENTY

1

Line-up was at five in the morning.

Latouret assigned the patrol, designated the men to their posts, and assembled the *corvée*.[62]

The *corvée* had the worst duty: to guard the prisoners at the beginning of the paved road leading to the forest.

The *corvée* consisted of fifty men in full combat gear. Three platoons took turns every eight hours. They took position at the beginning of the paved road between the desert and the forest and kept an eye on the prisoners; their order was to shoot in case of even the slightest disorder. They supervised the eight delegates of prisoners who took over food, water, and other supplies. If more than eight prisoners approached the *corvée*, their order was to open fire.

With the diminished number of personnel, every petty officer and private (less than twenty men) was assigned to the *corvée*. The real sentry, however, was the supply of water and food, of which the prisoners must not have accumulated reserves. For the prisoners did whatever they wanted to in the forest, farther away from the patrol.

When a legionnaire was punished by being sent among the prisoners, it was equivalent to a death sentence because as soon as he was out of sight of the *corvée*, the prisoners beat him to death. The soldiers were keenly aware of this, and if someone was, for instance, sentenced for a week of *travaux forcés*,[63] his identification tag was retained. When the time of punishment was up, they entered in the garrison's registry the name of private number this or that who, due to his death, was removed from the staff of the company.

The apathetic *corvée* was sitting in full gear in the yard when the voice of Battista, an Italian corporal, reverberated:

"*Debout! En route! En avant, marche!*[64]"

The fifty men marched.

One of the lieutenants, Hilliers, walked over to the prisoners. He was an engineering officer brought here for the road construction. Delahay forewarned him to be nice to the prisoners and to try to be on good terms with them. For the prisoners didn't kill engineers because they were needed for the construction. However, even he could be protected by nothing but the prisoners' goodwill.

The *corvée* delivered the breakfast. Eight dour prisoners pushed the breakfast cart. There was no salutation, just hostile glances.

The patrol suffered beyond measure in the heat of the sun. Millions of mosquitoes swarmed from the jungle, and armies of flies buzzed around scraps of food. It was unbearable. Everybody was bleeding from mosquito bites.

Quinine was handed out to the legionnaires. Pigeon secretly spat his pill out. This way he would certainly get malaria. He was glad to put up with the mosquito bites. It was impossible that none of them were spreading malaria.

The stench was horrible. A plague-like smell emanated from the direction of the prisoners. Like skeletons wrapped in rags, the prisoners loitered about or pounded with their hammers in the distance. Some started to work near to the *corvée*. Amazing! From the sleeves of their shirts, white sticks were poking out in lieu of arms, and their angular cheekbones protruded as if they were about to pierce what little skin was left to cover them.

Chalky stood next to Pigeon. He was jaundiced and imbecilic, but he was calm. The soldiers envied him because his paralytic, moribund nervous system was to a great extent impervious to pain.

"Swallow your quinine!" Corporal Kobienski shouted at the imbecile.

"Thanks, but I don't have a headache."

Kobienski punched Chalky's face with his fist. Pigeon's fists tightened in anger.

"Take it, or I will crush your head!"

"Now I have a headache after all," the grinning imbecile said with his nose bleeding. Pigeon stepped out of line and snapped to attention.

"I report to you, Sir, that this comrade is retarded."

"What?! You dare reporting?! You, you dare to step out of the *corvée*?" The Corporal had raised his fist, but Pigeon's hand slid down a little on the strap of his rifle, as if he were about to throw his weapon in gear. Kobienski was a good judge of character, and he knew that if he struck down, the rifle would fly off Pigeon's shoulder, and its bayonet would stab him.

"I have already swallowed the quinine," Chalky reported, grinning. But Kobienski yelled:

"Gamberich! Pelli! Hammer and Bouillon! *A moi!*[65]" These were four men of the old guard. They came over immediately with a petty officer. "Disarm this private and tie him up!"

Pigeon calmly put up with it. He was thrown in the dust. His *képi*[66] fell off, and no one put it back. He was lying in the sizzling sun with his head uncovered.

"Men, carry him to the Fort! One hour in tie-up," Kobienski said sternly. "Report to the sergeant that the private left the *corvée*."

2

The crew watched the familiar scene from the windows with disgust. In the middle of the yard, in the sun, disrobed to the waist, Pigeon was tied to a pole. His hands were tied together behind his back and he was pulled up by his wrists so that his toes barely touched the ground. They then tightened the rope.

He lost consciousness in fifteen minutes. He was then untied, and they poured water over him. He lost consciousness four times within an hour, and they repeated the process four times. He was then carried to his room and tossed onto the bed. Latouret watched the punishment with a stern expression on his face. *Now the impertinent one may lie half-dead. If he does not regain consciousness until the evening, he may go to the infirmary for a day*, he thought.

He could not believe his eyes when he entered the canteen fifteen minutes later and found Pigeon there, sitting with a bottle of wine and cheerfully playing his harmonica.

"Private!" Latouret roared.

Pigeon jumped up. The Sergeant continued quietly:

"Listen here, Private. Based on Corporal Kobienski's report, I recommended you for two days of *pelote*, but the Captain topped it with another three days with a double-load and two hours double-quick."

No such punishment existed. Nobody could have survived it. Originally the *pelote* consisted of bread and water once a day and one hour running at noon with forty-five pounds of rocks in the knapsack. Gardone, however, who wanted to destroy Pigeon for being a suspicious character, ordered ninety pounds of rocks and five days with two hours of running. Latouret expected to see the private's cheerful face to wince. But he was mistaken. To his amazement, the private's eyes flared up with joy, and he was smiling ear to ear.

"What are you chortling about?! Man! This will make you kick the bucket!"

"I report to you, Sir, that I am grateful for the punishment."

He was pushed into a *cellule*,[67] nothing more than a dirty, damp pit. There was no bench in there. He would now indeed kick the bucket and be rid of this foggy tale of mystery. After all, as a dead man, what would he have to do with convoluted stories of fraud? He had come here so that his relatives would collect the ten thousand-dollar policy. This would happen as soon as he suffered a stroke or pulmonary embolism in the sun, and that would be the end of it. Thanks to the Captain, his problems were solved. Nevertheless, he discarded the dose of quinine that the warden had brought for him – although acquiring malaria was no longer necessary. The *pelote* would suffice. Still, it was better to be safe than sorry. He didn't want to take quinine.

It was a hundred and twenty degrees at noon, when Corporal Battista shouted:

"*Pas de gymnastique! En avant, marche!*"

He began to run in the sun. It was relatively easy. The troops watched from the windows, horrified that he ran a full forty-five minutes before collapsing. And within ten minutes, he started running again. My God: He ran a good half an hour! He then ran fifteen-minute intervals three more times. In the meantime, Latouret sat somewhere in the warehouse, somberly smoking a pipe.

Whatever he was thinking, no one knew.

Two lads carried Pigeon to the solitary *cellule* as if he were a bundle of rags and threw the soaking-wet, unconscious man on the dirty ground.

The next day, Latouret observed as Pigeon was brought forth. Now the boy was crushed! His face was sunken, his eyes were exhausted, and he reported in a hoarse voice.

"Hey! You braggart!" Latouret called to Pigeon. "If you are religious, you may request suspension of punishment for a day; it's Ascension Day tomorrow."

"Thank you, *mon chef!* I do not request any suspension of punishment; I will pray in my cell."

"Well then, *pas de gymnastique!* You! You! A man like you should drop dead!" he muttered angrily and rushed down to the warehouse to smoke his pipe. *This one will never break, this... this...* he thought.

After two days, Pigeon lost consciousness every five minutes, and he felt that his heart, vasculature, and lungs were totally exhausted. By the next day, the fuss would be over. From that point on, his sister, Anette,[68] and his mother could live securely.

It was a hot, stinky night. He lay faint on the dirty slate floor of the pit. A rat chewed on something nearby.

"Farewell, beautiful little mystery! How did it go? An officer turns the lights off around a dead man, Lambertier waits for me at the fountain, and although Macquart did not come, it doesn't matter."

If he could only see the woman once more! This woman – she was different; she was beautiful! He wished he could hear her singing just once more. As he had this thought, the prison's door opened, and Pigeon happily concluded that, behold, he had gone mad, and his end was imminent, for he saw the Arab coffee-brewer entering through the door.

He saw Abu el Kebir, who had died days ago.

CHAPTER TWENTY-ONE

1

He lay on the floor all wet, soaked in his sweat, and just watched. He could hardly speak. The coffee-brewer went over to his *pelote* knapsack. The moon was shining through the window. The Arab's trachoma-stricken eyes and long gray beard were clearly visible. Would you look at that! He took the rocks from the knapsack and packed them in a bundle.

Hey! What's going on? Pigeon thought, seeing the coffee-brewer replacing the rocks in the *pelote* with pieces of wood.

Pigeon gathered all his strength and pushed himself up.

"Get away from there, you snotty fellow!"

Abu el Kebir raised his finger to his lips. He then took the bundle with the rocks on his back and sneaked out.

Pigeon could not move. *This… this is impossible! Never mind. I will tell the warden to get my rocks back.*

He fell asleep.

When they shook him awake next morning, he scrambled to his feet with his head buzzing. Well, he knew that he would meet his end this day. He still remembered his stupid dream about Abu el Kebir, the dead coffee-brewer with the rocks. The warden picked up the knapsack and put it on Pigeon's back.

What's this? Pigeon thought. *This has hardly any weight!* Ninety pounds of rocks, and it felt like nothing, even though the knapsack was bulging as usual.

This is impossible, he thought. They had to let him to die. He angrily turned towards the warden and…

Battista's eyes flashed menacingly while he secured the straps of the knapsack and, between his teeth, he sneered at Pigeon:

"Keep quiet you pig, or else!"

Well…

That was completely different. One could not argue too much in such a situation, and if the warden was involved in the late Abu el Kebir's dirty business, Pigeon had to keep quiet or else Battista would be punished to *travaux forcés.*

He stepped to the yard with the enormously bulging knapsack that was light as a feather. Fine kettle of fish, one might say! Such a thing in the Legion! Corruption, flimflam, and fraud! Phew! He should have thought twice before joining the Legion to die. Apparently, all these men were working for the insurance company. Goodness gracious! He just realized that all were watching him with their jaws dropped because he was running like a gazelle. *Uh-oh! Battista may get in deep trouble because of this,* he thought and collapsed.

He lay there without any certitude, his eyes closed. Later he ran again. Ten minutes after he had been returned to the prison, Battista showed up with a large bowl of food and wine. Pigeon wanted to say something about his mandatory starvation on bread and water, but Battista's eyes flashed again:

"If you open your mouth, I will cut you down, you, you… Pig!"

When Pigeon had completed his sentence, Latouret ordered him to report. My Lord!

This man gained weight!

"*Rompez! Rompez,* you villain, or … I will trample you down!!!"

"If only I knew why they are so rude," Pigeon thought on his way to the crew's quarters to get his harmonica. What had he done to be cursed at and threatened?

He blew the dust from his harmonica, discarded his dose of quinine, and went to the canteen.

2

The men sat around in silence. This was the bleakest, quietest canteen in the colonies. The *corvée*, the monotony, and the maddening heat turned the soldiers into lethargic zombies. Innumerable flies buzzed in the room.

"Hello, gentlemen! Is this a canteen, or a funeral parlor?" Pigeon's lively yell splashed the hot, depressing air away. The men stirred. And then the harmonica sounded the tune:

"Le sac, ma foi, toujours au dos…"

A few of them sang along. Even the imbecile Chalky grinned and moved his hand as a conductor. He exclaimed from time to time, making everyone laugh. But even this day did not pass without a tragedy.

The dazed men were stewing in the humid, pestilent steam of the canteen that was heavy with pipe-smoke.

They heard the sound of the bugle that announced the departure of the *corvée*. And the door opened.

Troppauer rushed in. He was in a panic, frightened.

"Boys! My rifle! It's gone!"

They fell silent in astonishment. This certainly and inescapably meant *travaux forcés*. The chunky poet looked around helplessly with his sad, vacant eyes.

Pencroft tossed a one-frank coin on the tin-covered bench of the bar and left quietly. Hildebrandt remained seated.

"What kind of stupid joke is this?" Pigeon yelled at the poet. "What do you mean by your rifle being gone? A *Lebel* repeating rifle is not a fairy-tale sprite to simply disappear in thin air!"

"I put it on the rack. I must now go on duty with the *corvée*, and I can't find it! It disappeared!"

A rifle's stock thumped at the door. It was the patrol.

"Private! You failed to report to the *corvée*. You will report for a hearing in working clothes in five minutes."

P. Howard (Jenő Rejtő)

Even Pigeon's harmonica was muted. His best friend, the large-headed, chunky poet, was to take off for *travaux forcés* in the afternoon.

He was sentenced to two weeks, but, after all, time made no difference. He would be killed the first day. Latouret allowed him to talk with Pigeon for the last time.

Pigeon couldn't speak. He swallowed as if something were choking his throat, and he squeezed his friend's hand for a long time. Troppauer smiled and he licked his wide, clownish mouth. He was so ugly and so endearing. He self-consciously stroked the blue-gray stubble on his ape jaw, shifting his weight from one of his waddling feet to the other, and he finally gave a bundle of writings to Pigeon.

"My opuses" he said loftily. "One hundred and ten selected works of Troppauer. Save it. You owe this to posterity."

"*Debout!*" the corporal shouted, and Troppauer left with the *corvée*. At the paved road that started at the edge of the rain forest, he proceeded alone.

He disappeared from their eyes after just a few minutes. They all knew well that it was forever.

Troppauer waddled quietly along the road toward the thick of the jungle. Lieutenant Hilliers was just then supervising as the cold bitumen was poured and spread over the cleared dirt.

"Private number 1865 is reporting for two weeks of *travaux forcés*, Sir!"

The Lieutenant entered the information in his notebook and waved.

"Go to the bungalow!"

And he went.

The large trees hid him from the officer. Hilliers sighed. He knew all too well that the soldier would disappear. It was horrible. And nothing could be done about it. The road was needed at any cost.

From afar, Troppauer saw the scornful and menacing group of prisoners hanging about the tent-house. Something wrung his chest.

A giant figure at the edge of the group menacingly shook his fist from the distance. He was a Tarzan-like, half-naked man, with a bony, angular, horse-shaped head and a Santa Claus beard reaching down to his waist-belt. He was swinging a club in his hand.

"Boys! There will soon be one less soldier once more," the Tarzan exclaimed. "But bury this one farther away because the last one drew a crowd of hyenas here."

And he approached Troppauer to be the first to hit him. Troppauer thought for a moment that he would run away. But where to? He was surrounded by the thick, impenetrable jungle. He proceeded straight ahead.

"You dog! Filthy bloodhound!" the Santa Claus-bearded wild man shouted, and he raised the club. But someone grabbed his arm and threw him aside as if he were a small piece of luggage.

"Nobody will harm this man!"

The skeletons dressed in burlap and halfway covered in mold approached with a menacing shriek.

Barbizon, the Corsican bandit, stood in front of Troppauer spreading his arms in protection.

"This was the soldier that gave his water so that I could give you a drink, Grumont. This one was the one who beat that *goumier* because of us. I will kill anyone who dares to touch him. I swear by the Madonna!"

The Corsican's threat in itself would not have proven effective. The shaggy haired Santa Claus-Tarzan shrunk back only when he heard that the soldier had given a drink to a prisoner. These zombie-like, nerve wrack characters were, in their hysterical state of mind, swaying between committing a heinous deed and being overcome by sentimentality. Finally they slapped Troppauer's shoulders and grinned at him.

The stocky man straightened his back and said with his widest smile:

"Then, if you will allow me, I will read you one of my poems," and he drew out a dirty sheet. "*Roses of dawn over the Sahara.* Written by Hümér Troppauer."

The prisoners stood there, mortified.

3

Pigeon got himself bitten by mosquitoes until he bled and continued to discard his quinine. He took not a single gram. On the other hand, Rikayev acquired quinine-deafness because of overdone protection against malaria. Pigeon just let the mosquitoes bite because he knew that if he was taken to the hospital with malaria, it was as good as if he had already kicked the bucket.

However, in the evening it was yet again not fever but impatient hunger that tormented him in the canteen. And when dinner was eventually served, Rikayev fell from his chair all of a sudden, threw himself half a yard in chills, and his clenched teeth gnashed as if two rough pebbles were rubbed against each other.

The doctor just looked at the Dane:

"Malaria," he stated with a wave of his hand. And Rikayev was carried away.

I cross my heart and hope to die; fate is pulling my leg, Pigeon thought bitterly.

Yet I must die! I must die! he kept repeating, and he swallowed big chunks of his meal. *Poor Troppauer!* Pigeon put Troppauer's poems in the same waxed canvas sack in which he kept Grison's wallet and the ivory plaque with the number 88 on it.

Hlavách dragged himself into the canteen. He had just recovered from his attack of fever that was first believed to be typhus. He sat by Pigeon's table modestly, with a somewhat guilty conscience. Hlavách was indeed a cobbler. Two years earlier, he had set his shop on fire and was locked up for insurance fraud. After being released, he joined the Legion and was unaware that due to his thievery, the overly imaginative Pigeon surmised him to be an undercover major.

Pigeon slammed his heels together under the table and winked. He had just realized that he had not seen Hlavách since learning that he was Major Yves. Of course, the alleged cobbler did not have any idea about it because he had been running a fever. Pigeon winked again at the cobbler who looked at him aghast, and then leaned close to him and whispered in his ear:

"I know everything."

Hlavách turned as pale as corpse. Here comes the shirt affair!

"I don't understand," he stammered.

Pigeon winked again and added emphatically and quietly:

"The shirt! You made a slip of the tongue while you were unconscious with fever."

Hlavách's lips trembled, and he clutched at his chair.

"I beg of you! I… I… If they learn…"

"You can trust me. I am a good guy and an excellent sleuth. You'd better believe it!"

"Please," Hlavách stammered, "Spoliansky told me to! Really, I am not responsible."

"Okay, okay! The most important thing is that you may count on me if it comes down to it. I almost became a French naval officer. They may have taken my sword tassel but not my patriotism. *Vive la France!* Hush!" and he put his finger to his lips. "I can keep quiet. But I tell you: You can count on me! Good bye, Major, Sir!"

And he waltzed away. Hlavách sat numbly and kept wiping his sweat. He felt he would be in really deep trouble if this man indeed had gone crazy.

CHAPTER TWENTY-TWO

1

Like many others', Captain Gardone's face also assumed the yellowish brown, bile-like tone that was a peculiar waxy Creole mixture of brown and pale: the opposing colors of intense sunshine and acute onset anemia. His head buzzed all day long, and only brandy made this fatal duty bearable.

Pigeon became the object of his obsession in his idling, helpless anger, and irritability. He had made up his mind while still in the desert that he would destroy "this suspicious individual." And they kept reporting that Pigeon had survived one deadly punishment after another. Gardone was furious that, in spite of the many petty officers unleashed on Pigeon, he was still alive here where death was not in short supply. The Captain found relief for all his despair in the hate that he attributed to some sort of suspicion.

As the Captain lamented over his unsuccessful attempts to put the private out of the way, Pigeon was walking toward him. And he dared to whistle! Gardone snapped at him:

"Private! Where is your waist belt?!"

Pigeon stood in front of him in the Fort's sizzling yard.

"I am not on duty, *mon commandant*," Pigeon replied.

"Where is your waist belt?!"

"After the *paquetage*, I always let it dry so that the wax will not get smudged."

"You are to report to the corporal that you crossed the yard without wearing your waist belt. *Rompez!*"

Kobienski had already had his share of inconvenience because this legionnaire was still in the way. He understood the Captain quite well; that Pigeon was still alive really was not the consequence of the petty officer's goodwill.

Kobienski listened to Pigeon's report with a face distorted by anger, and then this distortion converted into a beastly grin.

"This time I will teach you a lesson for good. Dirty *bleu!* Twenty-four hours *en crapaudine!*"

Sergeant Latouret went to see the Captain: this punishment was forbidden even for two and a half hours. Twenty-four hours in this climate ultimately meant torturous death. He was unwilling to take that responsibility. The Captain, however, profusely berated him:

"We are not at the Army Service Corps. We are dealing with unusual situations, and there are many things that go against regulations. But it won't work any other way."

Latouret went to get the prisoner. Pigeon was already waiting for him, dressed in work clothes and, *nom du nom*, he was grinning!

"Harrincourt! You are getting twenty-four hours *en crapaudine*. I must tell you that it wasn't my doing. And if... What are you grinning about? You idiot! You will die ten times in twenty-four hours!"

Oh Lord God, at last, make it happen just once. Just once! Pigeon was praying in his thoughts, and he was unequivocally glad.

He was taken to the guardhouse. The *goumiers* shared the house with the guard next to the gate. When they arrived, the petty officer was beating up Spoliansky, the Count, with the buckle end of a waist belt.

"You pig! You dared falling asleep on duty?! You dirt bag, you! The lieutenant will punish me because of you, you wretched... You dare to fall asleep?!"

Some men of weaker physique often would fall asleep, as if fainting, after meals in the tropics. Nothing could be done about it; this type of drowsiness is uncontrollable. Spoliansky fell on the ground with his face bleeding.

"Tie this Spoliansky guy next to the other scoundrel for two hours."

The *en crapaudine* is a medieval punishment. The ankles and wrists are tied up, then, with the man lying on his stomach, the hands and feet are pulled to each other on the back until they touch. The man is then pushed into a covered pit.

Pigeon felt his head fill with blood, and his heart beat wildly as he lay in the pit.

The unfortunate Spoliansky was tied up next to him. The temperature was over 120 degrees in the sun, which was not uncommon in the Sahara. The pit was covered with a canvas. It would become terribly hot in the pit within half an hour.

Hmm... Pigeon noted that his head was no longer congested with blood, and his heartbeat became pretty regular. This way, it would eventually take several hours for him to die.

"Harrincourt," Spoliansky moaned. "I won't survive two hours!"

"Come on! One can play poker for two hours like this. Not to mention playing harmonica."

"But I have an aortic aneurysm!"

"If you are *that* aristocratic, you should not have come to the Sahara. Try to avoid movement because it helps to slow down your circulation, and the rope will not strangulate it that much."

"Then, why do you keep moving?"

"Because I would like to die."

The heat was growing thicker under the canvas, and the carbon dioxide the two men exhaled was trapped and made the blazing pressure even deadlier. The canvas exuded scorching heat as if it were the wall of a stoked furnace, and it did not allow the radiating heat to escape.

"Harrincourt," the Count panted, "listen to me! I don't want to take to the grave what I know. I must tell you who I am."

"Officer of the guards, and you lost it in card games. Or a marquis, and you killed her. It makes so little difference."

"I was a state official in Poland."

"A ministerial counselor?"

"No, an executioner."

"What???"

The "Count" an executioner? With those looks? Why not? Poor

Troppauer looked like an executioner, yet he was a poet. This one, on the other hand, looked more like a poet, yet he had been an executioner. Fine kettle of fish with all these incognitos.

"Yes, I was an executioner. I inherited the trade; my father was one also."

"Don't get hung up on it too much."

Spoliansky heaved a great sigh. He turned to the other side, which made him feel somewhat relieved.

"Listen to me, Harrincourt – although I am not worthy of your attention because I wanted to steal your shirt."

"You, too? Did the entire company want to put on my underwear?" he stopped amidst panting. "Doggone!"

"A soldier undertook the job of getting it for me. He delivered the goods, and then this Pencroft fellow pounced upon me. He told me that if I did not give the shirt to him, he would report me! You know how it is – it's horrible! The thief gets lynched. I was at his mercy. Phew!" It's getting hard to talk. "He took the shirt. What a fool I was! I told him my secret, my invention. For I was dismissed from my job because I invented something."

"It wasn't a smart move. A state official should dedicate himself entirely to his profession."

"Well, that was the very problem. I approached the executioner's profession as a religious man. I wanted to execute without pain. I invented a method, but it was not accepted. In spite of the fact that hanging is horrible, you can believe me."

"If you say so."

"I had thought that if I proved it to them, they then would approve it, and I used it on a convict before he was lead to the gallows. But it malfunctioned, and I was fired. Since then, I have refined the invention and have lived only to give it to humanity. The guilty man should not suffer when he dies. I joined the Legion so that if there were a hopelessly wounded or ill man, I could try it."

Suddenly, Pigeon understood:

"Tell me! You whispered with the paramedic when Ilyich lay wounded."

"Yes. We made an agreement – that if the surgeon were to give up all hope, he would allow me to try."

"So it was you who killed him?!"

"No! Because when I wanted to apply my invention... It's a long, bent wire mattress with clips that can be adjusted. If you place the wire mattress over the body, you can position each clip over a main artery. The rod is bent in such a way that if you press a clasp at its upper end, the clips close, and all vessels are clamped down in a blink of an eye. The heart, brain function, and the respiratory center all stop instantly. Because if the radial artery and... ouch!"

"Tell me about the murder," Pigeon panted.

"The paramedic said that Ilyich's condition had made a turn for the better, and there was hope. So, I didn't do it. But then this villain took it from me – the blood vessel clamp, and he killed him with it!"

"Pencroft?!"

"Yes!" He threw himself high and fell back breathing with a rattle. He added with a mournful sigh: "But he has another name, too."

"Laporter!"

"Y...Yes! Ouch!"

2

Thus Pencroft and Laporter were the same person? He should have figured it out. How stupid he was! After all, when he had played *"Si l'on savait"* in Murzuk, the Kid had shouted *"murderer"* and jumped at Pencroft's throat.

Pigeon was still conscious as Spoliansky was untied and as water was poured over him.

Is he dead? he wondered.

He was covered back up. He felt that his mouth was foaming. How much time could have had passed? Everything went dark. The blood hammered in his brain with a buzz, and he lost consciousness. It was over. *Thank God; now it's finally over.* This was the last thought of his consciousness as it bid farewell.

As he regained consciousness, he found himself in a hospital bed, and the doctor was standing over him with concern. So was the Captain. The red-haired paramedic held a lamp high. Sergeant Latouret was in the background. *What's this? Did I survive the twenty-four hours?* Pigeon wondered.

They poured brandy into his mouth. It made him feel warm, and his blood started to circulate. *To hell with my indestructible body*, he thought.

The regimental surgeon listened to his heart.

"This man is made of iron. The heartbeat is already rhythmic."

"Sergeant," the Captain said, "when the patient feels better, escort him to the commander's office. Get well, my friend."

What? What did he mean by saying "my friend"? And "get well"?! How long had this man been on such good terms with him? What had happened? Did these men conspire with the insurance company to prevent him from dying? What kind of monkey business was this yet again?

However, he did not yet have enough strength to say any of this.

This is what had happened earlier: Pigeon had lost consciousness at four o'clock in the afternoon. The patrol, led by the Captain, came for him at half past four. The regimental surgeon and the paramedic, carrying a stretcher, accompanied them. Had they come just half an hour later, he would have been dead.

And what had happened?

Finley went to see Delahay and reported to the ill, bedridden Major that a lad, whose conduct had been exemplary on the way, was tied up *en crapaudine* for twenty-four hours.

"What?!" the Major had exclaimed. "Petty officer! Tell the Captain that I asked for him!"

Gardone had almost drawn his sword on Finley, but the Major had given a perfect cover for the officer.

"I asked Finley to report to me about punishments," Delahay had said. "He could not have hidden the case from me."

"Well then, in my opinion, this private is a spy. I was forewarned from above when I got my new assignment to watch out for suspicious characters, and, since I cannot prove the private's guilt that is nevertheless beyond a doubt, he must perish! Human life and service regulations are irrelevant when important military interests are at stake!"

"If it is as you say," the Major replied, "you should have searched his belongings long ago. Finley! Tell the bugler to signal for line-up, and, while the men are standing down in the yard, examine that lad's knapsack."

"I'm coming too," the Captain said.

Upon opening the waxed canvas sack, Troppauer's poems had surfaced first. They then had found the identification plaque of Secret Service Major Number 88, General Staff, Department D.

Gardone had turned as pale as death.

He put back everything in the sack, and he took it and its contents to the commander's office.

"Please, do you believe?"

"I think," Finley replied, "that there is only one officer at the rank of major in Department D of the General Staff: Yves. I believe the man whom you have tied up is Major Yves!"

"But, but who? Who had him tied up *en crapaudine*? Hey, Sergeant! Patrol! Get the doctor and a stretcher!" In the meantime he handed the sack over to Finley. "Please, lock it up in the safe."

Finley locked up everything in the safe and handed the key over to Gardone who immediately took off for Pigeon.

And so it was that Harrincourt, fit as a fiddle and for that reason sadly, stood in front of the Captain.

"Private! Here some brutish men have treated you nefariously. I have punished those individuals. Latouret has been assigned to full-time duty with the *corvée*, and I have sentenced two petty officers to *cellule*." He added somewhat more quietly, "When I was transferred here, I was warned that I might have to aid some confidential envoys. They entrusted me with the task because I have a knack for strategy. Just let me know what you wish, and I will make it happen."

Pigeon did not understand the story at all; nevertheless, without hesitation he blurted out:

"A friend of mine, Troppauer, was sentenced to *travaux forcés*."

The Captain turned pale again. Good grief, that would be a man of the secret service, too. He would get himself into a scandal like the captain from Ain Sefra did! Phew! How awkward!

"Why didn't you trust me, Ma... Private? That man must be dead by now. This was brought about by Latouret and, foremost, Finley's cruelty." He lifted the handset. "Patrol commander? The *corvée* is to inform the prisoners that we will not open the water faucet until they return the soldier who was sentenced to *travaux forcés*. At least we must learn something certain about his fate." He hung up and went to the safe. "We secured some of your belongings here. You can have them back, if you wish. I didn't want anyone to gain access to them."

Gardone stepped back in astonishment. The compartment of the safe where Pigeon's sack had lain a short while ago was now empty!

CHAPTER TWENTY-THREE

1

"I am sorry, but your bag has disappeared," the Captain turned to Pigeon. "However, if you need anything, you can count on me."

"Captain, Sir, I would primarily like to know if Troppauer..."

"Oh, yes, the other soldier!" The phone rang and the Captain answered it. "Is that so? Very good! A patrol should leave from the *corvée* at once and bring him to the Fort." He hung up and looked at Pigeon. "Interesting! That Troppauer fellow is alive. If you wish, you may leave to meet him on his way."

"Hooray!" Pigeon exclaimed, forgetting about everything, and he ran.

Troppauer returned somewhat thinner and ragged but all smiles. They hugged each other for a long time. The poet reported for duty to the Sergeant perfectly unharmed. They then went up to the crew's quarters so that Troppauer could change into his uniform.

"How did you manage to stay alive?" Pigeon asked.

"It's simple. They did not bludgeon me to death," the poet explained cheerfully. "The moral of the story is that it is sometimes useful to slap a *goumier*. Ever since, my palms itch every time I see that beautiful Benid Tongut down there. That Corsican bandit to whom I had given water back in Agadir gave me a warm recommendation to the execution squad. He intervened with a half-naked gentleman not to kill me. But to change the subject,

Pigeon… There is a delicate matter I need to discuss with you. Those prisoners behaved oddly."

"They didn't listen when you read your poems to them?"

"No. On that account I had relatively few fights. However, they want to stage a mutiny."

"Are you sure?"

"I don't know anything definite. A native pygmy visited them, the likes of those who live in the jungle. Some sort of *Sokota* tribe will come over. They only have to wait until the water level of the Niger falls. The prisoners will then riot. Many of the soldiers stationed at the Fort know about it. Kobienski is a part of it, and also this guy who goes by the name Hildebrandt."

"What about the water? Only the officers have access to the water."

"Somebody will come and bring explosives. Once they have ecrasite, they can blow up the pipe vault and get water."

"What should we do? If we report them, we'll get many legionnaires in trouble. On the other hand, I am a French cadet!"

"And I am a poet, and the devoted patriotism of such men is proverbial. Who the hell knows what should be done under the circumstances? We can't betray our comrades."

"I already know what to do. We'll seek advice from the undercover Major whose identity I unveiled. We can trust him."

"Who is it?"

"Hlavách!" Pigeon declared triumphantly.

"I would have never guessed him!" Troppauer marveled. "Hlavách, the cobbler?" He just couldn't come to terms with that.

They went to see Hlavách who was brooding with a bottle of wine in the canteen. Pigeon sat by him.

"There is trouble," he whispered.

Hlavách turned pale.

"I knew that this Spoliansky fellow would betray me!" he said, thinking that the Pole had reported him for the shirt theft.

"It's a different matter. You can trust Troppauer; he is a poet. Some fellows are planning a riot for the day after tomorrow." He called to the waiter in the canteen, an Arab youngster. "Can't you see that are you under foot here? Bring a bottle of wine!"

The brown-skinned young man went to the bar and poured wine into a pitcher.

"I don't understand," Hlavách said. "What do you want?"

"Look, we need your advice. Some sort of mutiny is brewing around here; the soldiers want to take over the Fort."

The Arab boy brought the wine to the table and poured it into glasses.

"Something must be done," Pigeon urged Hlavách. "You must see that, Major, Sir!"

"But please," Hlavách was perplexed.

"Excuse me," Pigeon said revoking the indiscretion. And, at the same time, he scoffed at the Arab youngster, "Get away from here!"

"You must tell us what to do," Troppauer prodded him.

Hlavách wiped his forehead nervously. If he only knew what these men wanted of him! He drank up a glass of wine with a trembling hand.

"First of all, who are the rebels? And, well, how many are those who will not join the mutiny?" he inquired meekly and uneasily.

"Splendid. We'll learn who the rebels are."

"Or rather," Troppauer interposed, "we'll learn whom we can trust. That's already half of the victory."

"Victory! We drink to that," the cobbler said because he grabbed every opportunity to imbibe.

"Nadov and Rikayev will side with us," Troppauer started the list.

"And Spoliansky," Pigeon continued. "A man who lived on state pension has loyalty to the land. Further, Dr. Minkus is also a good guy; then there is Pilotte, that aged veteran."

"To his health!" the cobbler gladly drank to Pilotte.

"I already know what you are thinking." Pigeon turned to Hlavách excitedly, taking his jacket off in the unbearable heat. "You are thinking that we'll assemble the trustworthy people, and, if it comes to it, we'll restore order."

"Something like that," Hlavách commented tentatively.

"All the prisoners and many legionnaires will side with the rebels," Troppauer interposed.

"I think we'll first pretend to side with them," Pigeon said.

"Don't you agree?"

"But of course!" the cobbler replied in pain. "Only, we'll have to watch out. To your health!"

"You can rest assured," Pigeon encouraged him and put his jacket back on. "Come," he said to Troppauer. They bowed to Hlavách and left to see Pilotte.

"He is a smart man, that's for sure," Troppauer said after they were in the courtyard.

"Of course, my friend. You can expect no less from a secret service major! However, I would be happy to punch out both eyes of this Pencroft-Laporter fellow. Only I don't want to incriminate Spoliansky. That's why I'm giving him a break for the time being. What's wrong with you?"

The poet embarrassedly stroked his gorilla jaw.

"I know that it is not easy for you to part with them," he said with his eyes cast down. "But I nevertheless ask you to. My opuses that I trusted in your care?"

Pigeon fell silent. How should he break the terrible news?

"Buddy," he finally said with a heavy heart. "Be brave."

"Holy God!"

"The poems were in a waxed canvas bag, and all of them were stolen." They stood in silence. The poet sighed. Pigeon tried to comfort him. "My wallet was taken together with them, with fifteen thousand francs."

"Ah, what's money? The wretched man was after my poems. I knew it. He already wanted to kill me for them! Oh!"

A tear trickled down from his eye.

They walked side by side without a word. They found Pilotte buck naked in the sleeping quarters. Even the veteran soldier had a hard time tolerating the heat.

"Listen here, old-timer," Pigeon began. "The word is that a few people here want to mess around. I don't know how you feel about it, but even in this godforsaken place, I say that I will not be a traitor to France. What's your take on it?"

Pilotte gave it a thought.

"What do you want? If there is a fight, you can count on me, but I will not be a tattletale to the higher-ups."

"That's not what we had in mind," Pigeon assured him.

"Only to fight," the poet said absently and licked his lip. After that, they sought out Spoliansky who had been released from the hospital earlier that day.

"Look," Pigeon explained, "you are a state official who owes loyalty to his country. It would be shameful to the guild of executioners if there were even one among them who proved unworthy to wear the black tie and top hat."

"Gentlemen," Spoliansky declared in his aristocratic manner, "you can put your trust in me. I am loyal to the state. I hanged a number of rogues but only in the service of the country."

"And you also proved," Pigeon praised him, "that you can be a good soldier when others are on the ropes."

Minkus, Nadov, and Rikayev who had recovered from his attack of fever, all joined them. They swayed these men by telling them that Hlavách was a major in the secret service, and he had said that a punitive squadron was on its way. After that, Hlavách's persona was seen in a different light, and some of the soldiers were happy to buy wine for him. The cobbler did not understand the reason of his newfound popularity, but he accepted it because he found drinking pleasurable.

"Come, let's go now to the canteen," Pigeon said after they had succeeded in recruiting a few men, and he saw how much Troppauer was devastated by the loss of his poems. "I will play a couple of nice songs for you."

But the poet somberly walked with Pigeon and sighed deeply.

"They stole my most beautiful poems. Among them was my epic, '*The squadron will leave for military drill tomorrow*. Written by Hümér Troppauer.' You were very fond of it."

They sat down at a corner table. The proprietor brought wine, and Pigeon reached into his pocket for his harmonica.

He was startled.

Instead of the harmonica, he pulled out Grison's wallet containing the secret service plaque, the fifteen thousand franks, the notebook, and the newspaper clipping!

He stared at them, stupefied.

"What's that?" Troppauer asked.

"This stuff was in the waxed canvas bag. The one that disappeared from the garrison's safe! And now it's in my pocket!"

"My poems! They were there too!" Troppauer exclaimed anxiously. "Search your pocket!"

But Pigeon poked around in his pocket to no avail. The poems were gone.

"They are not here," Pigeon stammered. "They returned everything, even the fifteen thousand francs!"

"I should have known," the poet said bitterly. "The scoundrel knew what he was after. He wouldn't be foolish enough to keep the fifteen thousand francs when he was able to get his hands on all original works by Troppauer."

His lips quivered, and his big gray eyes glistened with tears.

2

Pigeon rose ominously from the table.

Of course! No one else could have put this in his pocket but the Arab lad who earlier had been underfoot near Pigeon's jacket, which he had shed. But where was the boy?

He left Troppauer and rushed out without saying a word. He headed behind the canteen's bar towards the kitchen. He found no one there. He crossed the kitchen. He reached a small garden surrounded by stonewalls where they peeled potatoes, discarded the water after dishwashing, and wiped the dishes.

There he was! The Arab lad stood there and was busy polishing shoes.

Pigeon caught him!

"Speak up, you little devil, or I will break your neck! How did this stuff end up in your hands?"

"I will tell you everything, but please release me, Master!"

However, as his grip loosened, the boy slipped from his hand and ran into the house in the narrow alley next to the kitchen. Pigeon grabbed his wrist. Both of them had their hands squeezed between the entrance and the wall, but the Arab lad tore himself loose and jumped into the room where the canteen's manager lived. Pigeon pressed his shoulder against the door; the lock broke easily, and he was immediately standing on the threshold.

A petty officer's huge revolver was pressed against his stomach, held by the lad's trembling hand.

"If you dare to touch me, I'll shoot you!"

Pigeon looked at the brown-skinned kid's resolutely glinting eyes with surprise. He then looked at his hand. He was numbed with astonishment. Where the doorpost had scraped the skin, it was white, and a triangle-shaped birthmark was visible. The ghost! This was no brown Arab lad but a white woman. He stepped back in shock.

"Forgive me! I didn't know that..."

The Arab followed the soldier's glance, saw the birthmark on the hand, and covered it hastily. There was a moment of silence.

"How stupid I was," she said finally with resignation. "I should have guessed that you would figure it out if I returned everything to your pocket."

"Naturally," Pigeon waved condescendingly. "Didn't you know that in the meantime I have become an excellent sleuth? But now, tell me please, who are you? For I stubbornly don't believe in ghosts."

The woman was thinking for a second.

"I am Magde Russel. My father was the explorer who was despicably murdered, and my mother later became the wife of Dr. Bretail."

"I get it. That's the source of the resemblance and the birthmark."

"Please, for now, I cannot tell you anything. For a long time I thought that you were a traitor. For example, when I asked for the watch in the oasis. You must remember."

"Faintly," he replied in an ill mood, reaching for the back of his head.

"Later, I became convinced through somebody that you were quite a good man, and..."

Pigeon stepped to her with his eyes glowing, and reached for her hands:

"I have been yearning for a conversation like this for a long time. For I must tell you…"

"No, don't tell me anything," the girl interrupted him hastily, and she blushed as red as fire.

"By the way, the watch. If you would like it…"

"No, I don't want it. Just keep it with you, but I beg you," she added with genuine concern, "watch out for yourself, because these guys want to kill you for it."

"But they never deliver!" he exclaimed with exasperation.

The bugle sounded. It was taps.

"When will I see you?" Pigeon asked quickly.

"Perhaps there will be another opportunity. Please, leave that to me. I am not my own master now, but I promise that we'll meet again soon."

She couldn't prevent Pigeon from kissing her hand. Although, apparently she didn't even want to.

CHAPTER TWENTY-FOUR

1

A peculiar restlessness had taken over the soldiers of the garrison. Groups whispered left and right. Kobienski, that merciless man, now fraternized with the grunts, and they shot stealthy glances at Latouret and Battista and grumbled behind their backs.

In the evening, Finley discussed the petty officers' report in the ailing Delahay's room. Whenever the Major's condition improved, the officers sat with him for a cup of tea because, even in his utterly weakened state, Delahay was the heart and soul of the garrison.

"Around this time of year, in the dry season, they are always restless," he said when Finley briefed him about the petty officers' report. "It's possible that in the rage of the *cafard*[69] they will attempt something, but eventually, through the control of the water faucet, you can quell them by keeping them thirsty for half a day in this hellish heat."

"Don't you think," Gardone remarked, "that they might succeed in breaking the vault open?"

"There is no way," Delahay replied and sighed deeply. "It can be blown up only with ecrasite. For that very reason, there are no explosives in the warehouse of the Fort."

Delahay sank back to his pillow:

"Here, success depends on your wisdom to know when to apply merciless discipline and when to look the other way. You need to know that. Now let me sleep."

He slumped back in exhaustion.

In the office, a fat civilian wearing glasses was waiting for the officers.

"I am Dr. Borden. I have come from Timbuktu with a detachment of the Red Cross. The Niger Mission received a permit to conduct medical examinations among the prisoners."

Gardone looked at the paper. It was a permit properly issued to Dr. Borden and his staff for the purpose of collecting blood samples in the Niger region in order to assess the spread of sleeping sickness.

"How many are in your company?" the Captain asked tiredly.

"Three. Our caterpillar truck is parked outside the Fort. Two paramedics came with me. We were here three months ago, and the prisoners welcomed us because we distributed useful things among them."

Gardone signed the permit and made arrangements for the *corvée* to escort the mission's personnel.

Dr. Borden returned to the truck and sat behind the wheel. Two other men were in the truck.

"Everything is all right," he told them.

Macquart and Lorsakoff were his companions.

Four or five huge packages, each labeled with a red cross, were scattered around inside the truck.

Ecrasite was in all of them.

2

In the morning, Spoliansky pulled Pigeon aside:

"It will begin this afternoon when the second *corvée* is to be released. Rumor has it that the prisoners have gotten their hands on weapons and ecrasite. They will blow up the water pipe. They will unite with the *corvée*. Kobienski is joining them."

"The insolent…"

"It's not only him but also almost every soldier. Most of them are capable of anything because they cannot withstand the idling and the choking hot monotony, and they are ready to rush headlong into disaster simply for the sake of doing something. I know this because at one time I studied psychology."

"It's good that you did. Don't you think that we should report this to Finley?" Pigeon mulled.

"I think it's too late for that. The men have been fanaticized. Not much is needed for that in such a place as this. Now the events will keep rolling at an ever-increasing pace, like an avalanche. I read that expression in a novel."

"We'll try everything humanly possible. First of all, we must gather a war council. The events of the afternoon will find us prepared."

With that, Pigeon left to find Hlavách, and he also included Troppauer in the war council.

They were in the last, most depressing cycle of the dry season. The air sat on the men with an almost palpable weight; their bones were strained with tension from within, and the southern breeze made the soldiers of the garrison half-crazed.

At noon, Hilliers reported to the office, and there was a prisoner with him: Barbizon. By order of the Lieutenant, the *corvée* let him through with his large toolbox. Hilliers rushed to Gardone immediately.

"This man is Barbizon. The secret service sent him with the prisoners." He presented Barbizon's document. It said that the bandit was pardoned for a patriotic act and was recruited by the secret service. He was dispatched as an observer among the prisoners headed to Aut-Taurirt.

"Well?" Gardone asked after taking a look at the paper. "Do you have anything to report?"

"Plenty," the bandit replied. "The mutiny will break out today. Clever organizers infiltrated the prisoners under the pretense of working for the Red Cross. They brought ecrasite."

Gardone turned pale.

"The mutiny," Barbizon continued, "cannot be prevented. They organized the riot masterfully. Their plans had been ready back in Oran. Their men are in the majority among the guerillas, *corvée*, *goumiers*, and prisoners. There isn't a reliable group of men to assemble a patrol. The ecrasite is the most dangerous aspect in the story. If they blow up the pipe outside the Fort where it branches off toward the prison camp, we will be without water here. Moreover, a tribal chief from the forest repeatedly visited the prisoners, and he promised them that the *Sokota* tribe would come to their aid from the other side of the Niger. After taking over the Fort, the *Sokotas* would lead them to British Guinea through a secret passage."

The pale Gardone was stroking his chin. All this sounded rather hopeless. Finley shouted out to the hallway:

"Battista!" When the Italian Corporal entered, Finley commanded: "Tell Latouret to have four machine guns and twenty belts of ammunition brought up here."

The Italian hurried away.

"In the evening, on the cue of a previously agreed upon light signal, the prisoners will unite with the *corvée*. They will invade the garrison and will quickly eliminate anyone who would still resist."

"Hilliers," Finley said, "please, go and give an order to close the gate of the Fort, and tell Latouret to have machine guns delivered to the parapet. You and Barbizon will disregard everything happening inside the Fort, but you will be on watch toward the outside; and, should the *corvée* return together with the prisoners, you are to mow them down. This might yet help." Hilliers and Barbizon rushed away. Gardone was useless. The fear of death weighed down on his heart with a chill.

"But," he eventually said with a hoarse voice, "if they have known everything, why didn't you let us know? So that we could have requested help? The *spahis* could be here in a week from Timbuktu."

"I think," Finley replied, "they let this uprising mature on purpose. There are a couple of people here from the secret service who might want to find Russel's passage by tracking the *Sokotas*."

They fell silent. Battista returned with the belts. He threw them down. He appeared calm, yet there was something ominous about the way he was laying out the belts loaded with ammunition.

3

Pigeon held the last meeting of the war council with Major Hlavách and Troppauer. They casually sat at a table and drank wine as if they were just having some innocent fun.

"We can count on sixteen men," Pigeon said. "We were asked to join the mutiny. We gave an evasive answer. What's next?"

"Well," the cobbler answered insecurely, "first of all, we perhaps need to know what they want, and, well, what can sixteen men do against so many? I don't know, to be honest." He really didn't know why the revolt had to be crushed altogether. But who dared to argue with two lunatics?

"This afternoon," Troppauer said, "the *corvée* will return together with the prisoners. They will receive a signal from inside the Fort."

Pencroft entered and stared at them.

"What are you whispering about?" he said provokingly. "Listen here, Harrincourt. It would be wise to understand that all your labor was in vain. I know that you understand me. It's not important that anyone else does. Such a smart man would be a great loss. For your whispering is too late now. Do you get it?"

"I have a feeling, Pencroft," Pigeon replied cheerfully. "The two of us will soon get into a brawl with one another. You are very strong and an excellent boxer. I am always delighted to knock out the teeth of such a man."

Pencroft looked him up and down with a sarcastic smile and left.

"Let me know when you are to about beat him up," Troppauer said. "I would like to deliver a few punches to him myself."

"Just give us one last direction," Pigeon turned to Hlavách. "What should we do when the party commences here?"

"Please, I wouldn't like to give any advice," he replied in obvious pain. *What do these fellows want from me?* he thought. He didn't want to pick a fight with so many mutineers. He finally groaned, "Probably it would be wisest to bring up some rum and alcohol from the cellar. Because, you know, there's plenty of excellent drink in the warehouse."

Pigeon jumped to his feet:

"Ingenious! Splendid!"

Pigeon attracted the attention of the soldiers who were seated even at some distance; he consequently continued somewhat more quietly:

"Thank you. It's a remarkable idea. Yes, the rum!"

If I only knew what he is gleaming about! Hlavách pondered. If there were a riot, everyone would eventually be shot in the head; therefore, it's only logical that they would get drunk at least, before it happened. But why was this ingenious?

"Do you get it?" Pigeon asked Troppauer when they got to the courtyard. "This is a first-class idea. When the party starts, we break into the warehouse. Let the soldiers who are in the Fort get soaked, while we do not drink any rum."

"Perhaps we could risk having a few sips," the Poet interposed "as long as it's…"

"No! We'll remain sober," Pigeon said emphatically. He parted with Troppauer. He had not seen the girl for four days.

At noon, he had found a small piece of paper by his plate: "See you at five." That was all.

It was precisely five o'clock. He hurried behind the canteen. When he reached the room, the door quietly opened. Magde was waiting for him.

Pigeon smiled from ear to ear in happiness. Instead of the Arab youngster, he was received by the ghost in white breeches. The beautiful, sad-faced woman that had sung in the desert.

"We can be together only for a short time," Magde Russel said. "We shouldn't even risk this much."

Pigeon, before anything else, kissed her hand.

"You can relax. Trust me."

"Be careful because a mutiny is in the works."

"I know about it," he replied grinning. "Now I can tell you that Hlavách is not really a cobbler but a French Major. With his help, we shall extinguish the riot."

Magde grabbed the boy's hands and didn't know whether to cry

185

or laugh:

"For God's sake, please don't do such a thing. You are so naïve, reckless, and rash!"

"You are wrong," he replied with a conceited smile. "Those days are over. It would be nice if you could now tell me something about yourself."

"You already know that I am Russel's daughter. My poor father was a tense, tyrannical man. He was warm-hearted and ingenious, but also quirky and explosive. He was the reason why I left home when I was sixteen. We didn't get along. I became an actress like my mother. And then came this tragedy. My father disappeared. Now I know that they murdered him. My mother was framed to make it look as if she had cheated on her second husband, Dr. Bretail. My mother had loved Bretail for a long time and had suffered by my father, but she had always remained honest and pure. Because of this, I decided to find out the truth. First and foremost, I took up this bitter fight for my innocent mother's smeared honor. However, my father's great discovery, the passage, for which he struggled so much, was inseparable from my mother's tragedy. And I had no one to support me in this battle but an old servant, a half-blood Arab, who left my father's house together with me. That was Mahmud, whom you once saw as a butler and later as a native fortune-teller, making his rounds with a viper in Murzuk. I also did a pretty good job myself. I am an actress, and I am experienced in make-up. I observed the men who returned from my father's expedition. I knew that the guilty one was among them. To mix in with the folks of the periphery, where a European woman cannot go unnoticed, I wore a burnoose, painted my skin brown, and, to make it impossible to be recognized, I masqueraded as a man. If you remember that old coffee brewer in Oran, on the *Avenue Magenta*?"

Pigeon almost fell back.

"What? You were the ugly old man? You glued a beard to your chin? Of course! I get it! That's why I saw no one entering the house from which you came out. You sat there wearing a burnoose and a beard! And while I was stitching the sleeve of my trousers, you changed, and you came out as a woman. I followed you and didn't understand. So you were the coffee brewer in Oran!"

"And I was also Abu el Kebir, the trachoma-stricken, red-eyed, skinny geezer with the long gray beard and the screeching voice!"

Pigeon's jaw dropped again.

He then pulled the girl to himself and kissed her.

"Forgive me," the soldier stuttered, "but you saved my life. With a kiss, I can't even remotely express my gratitude."

"For now, don't express your gratitude any further. Mahmud escorted me everywhere as a snake charmer. When he realized that his viper had been stolen and that your shirt had also disappeared, he warned you, even though he thought that you were a traitor; although, by then, I... Well, I already suspected that we had been wrong about you. For that reason, I poured *kmirha* on you." She jumped back. "Not now! This is not the time to express your gratitude. So this was the reason why…"

"And the wristwatch?"

"That wristwatch hides the blueprint that shows the location of the passage, but nobody can solve the secret of the watch."

They fell silent. Pigeon reached for her hand. Magde didn't pull it away.

"Shouldn't we take another look at the watch?" the soldier asked. "Perhaps we can come up with something. Wait! I've just remembered! The poor Kid scribbled a few lines."

The paper on which the wounded Kid had written was still in Pigeon's jacket. He had completely forgotten about it. The woman tore it from his hands and read it excitedly:

"We are being watched. If you want to know what time it is, set the hands of the watch in the sun, and watch the second hand closely. Your watch will be accurate at midnight."

"For God's sake, how can you be so superficial?" the girl whispered with her voice trembling. "This is extremely important! We should have known this long ago."

She took the watch to the window and clicked its lid open. The sun shone on the cracked clock-face. The woman turned the winding knob. Perhaps a secret compartment would be opened.

They tried it for several minutes but to no avail.

"I have an idea," Pigeon exclaimed. "The instructions say: 'Your watch will be precise at midnight.' Set both hands to twelve. That's midnight."

"That might work!"

She turned the hands rapidly. When the two hands covered each other pointing to twelve, she waited. Nothing!

She gave the watch back to Pigeon with a sigh.

"Put it on, and please," she said while Pigeon was strapping the watch on his wrist, "I beg you to watch out and take care of yourself because…"

"Hello! What's going on here?" Pencroft entered. "Would you look at that! Now that's really interesting."

Pigeon turned to the girl in a grim mood:

"Forgive me Magde, but I am obliged to beat this gentleman to a pulp right now – although it is a most inappropriate behavior in the presence of a lady." And because Pencroft had gotten closer to him in the meantime, Pigeon slapped him with such vehemence that he plunged headfirst into the cabinet, broke through the door of the dilapidated piece of furniture, and fell on the floor along with all kinds of odds and ends.

Pencroft jumped up immediately and threw himself at Pigeon. They exchanged four or five boxing punches, and Pigeon realized that this time he had met his match. Pencroft's fist felt as heavy as if Pigeon's head had been stricken with a sledgehammer.

Magde, frightened, retreated to the corner of the room and pushed her fist into her mouth to restrain herself from screaming.

The two men clashed wildly. A punch landed on Pigeon's chin. He tottered back and then rammed Pencroft's stomach with his head, toppled him, and beat his face with both hands. Both men were covered with blood as they tore and lashed at each other. And then a bayonet flashed. Magde cried out with a muffled scream. Pigeon jumped back but to no avail: Pencroft had thrust the knife. Pigeon grabbed Pencroft's wrist. They struggled. If the American freed the hand with the bayonet, it was over. Pigeon punched the gangster's chin from below with his left fist. He tottered back dizzily. The same fist landed another punch, followed by a kick. By then, Pencroft was wobbling and still unable to free his wrist. Pigeon's fist now, like a machine, landed another cool, calculated blow, then another, finding his opponent on the nose, the mouth, and the chin. And Pencroft slumped. Another kick. He ceased moving. Pigeon looked at the girl, panting:

"I believe," he said, "this dispute is settled for the time being. First let's tie up our man and keep him in storage while the critical events unfold. That couldn't hurt."

While he spoke, he tore the rope from a package, tied Penroft's hands and feet very tightly, gagged him, and rolled him under the bed.

"The case is closed. We can go now. I will send Troppauer over because he made reservations for a couple of kicks." He had just realized that the woman was struggling to stay on her feet. He embraced her shoulders. "You are not disturbed by this fuss, are you?"

"Don't think that I'm weak. But so many things have happened, and this climate is terrible even for me, in spite of having been raised in Africa."

"Even so, it's too much for a woman. Well, you would be smart to take my advice and go to bed to rest for the duration of the riot."

"Are you out of your mind?" she said in astonishment because Pigeon spoke of the riot as if it would be an insignificant incident. "It's possible that they will slaughter everyone, and..."

"Nonsense!" Pigeon waved his hand with a smile whilst he rearranged his garment somewhat. "We'll conclude the entire matter in no time. I just don't understand why it is necessary to blow everything out of proportion. We'll derail the mutiny with some sort of joke. These are nice guys here; only, a couple of bad ones filled their heads with this riot. We slap the bad guys, and it's done. And it's also possible that the mutiny will be aborted. And, should we not see each other again..."

"Tell me, why do you want to die at any cost? If you feel that my question is intrusive, you don't have to answer."

Pigeon turned somber. How he had forgotten about that! Even though the ten thousand dollars was needed at home in a hurry, it was now beside the point.

"Mademoiselle Russel, unfortunately this is such a moment when I cannot avoid giving some serious thought to the matter. Until now, I have been cheerful. After all, it was only a matter of my life. But now the situation is serious. I must stand up for my military honor. And that interferes with my plans. In the event of my death, an insurance company would have taken care of my mother and sister. I have to tell you something: If it happened on occasion that I wished to stay alive and frowned at the thought of death, it always happened when your departed, nonetheless charming, spirit haunted me in the desert. For it is my suspicion that I have fallen madly in love with you."

They fell silent. The furnace-like heat sizzled around them, and an Arab scavenger at the nearby camp sang some inarticulate melody in a guttural voice. Throngs of huge humming flies buzzed thickly everywhere. This was a repulsive, deadly side of Africa – a barren, lifeless, aching heat. And yet, as their eyes met for a moment, smiles gleamed on their faces, and Pigeon pulled Magde to himself in an embrace.

"If you discover the secret of the watch," the girl whispered, snuggling up to him tamely, "then you will become rich. You could easily get a million francs. It is invaluable. The Russel map is worth as much as its finder is asking for it. If you knew its secret…"

"The watch is your inheritance. Even if I knew its secret, can you imagine that I would accept the money that is duly yours? Only if," he mumbled embarrassedly, "if we could share it. I mean only if the whole thing would be ours, together. That is, if the money would stay in the family."

Magde leaned her head on Pigeon's shoulder, and he stroked her hair. They stood like that for a while. Both of them knew they were talking about something they didn't have: the secret of the watch was unsolvable. Something creaked under the bed. Pencroft had regained consciousness but couldn't move. They heard someone pouring out a pail of water in the kitchen's garden. They stood there, facing each other.

And suddenly, in the hot afternoon silence, a gunshot thundered.

"It has started! Dress as an Arab youngster, you'll then be safe. I must run along now!"

"But…"

He quickly embraced the girl, kissed her, and ran away.

4

Battista and Latouret carried machine guns up to the office. Battista arrived first and dropped his load on the floor.

"Why don't you have it carried by a lad?" Finley asked.

The corporal calmly looked up.

"There were none I could trust."

And then Latouret arrived. He had found a trustworthy soldier. But this was even more depressing. The only lad who was helping him was the imbecile Chalky. They dared to rely on only one man in the entire garrison: a retarded one. Chalky, grinning, dropped the machine gun and saluted. His eyes were moving about in a crack-brained manner, and, with the two deep grooves by his mouth, his face resembled an infantile clown.

He was the one and only soldier to whom they dared to give orders in Aut-Taurirt. He grinned and panted.

They already had a clear picture of the situation. Finley sympathetically said to the last faithful private:

"Son, there is a bench by the door; sit down and light up."

"I report to you, Sir: light up what?"

"A cigarette."

"I report to you, Sir: what cigarette? Because this private has no cigarette on him."

In spite of the sad circumstances, Finley broke out in laughter and gave Chalky a cigarette.

"Son, take the clerk's bayonet rifle off the wall. You don't need to stand post. You just sit down nice and easy, but, should anyone try to enter without permission, you can shoot him without any qualms. Do you understand?"

"More or less."

He, the only trustworthy private in Aut-Aurirt, the imbecile Chalky, strutted out with a grin.

"Couldn't we," Gardone asked while he lit a cigarette with trembling hands, "attempt to round up the leaders, and prevent them from…"

A gunshot thundered.

"It's too late," Finley said.

CHAPTER TWENTY-FIVE

1

The bugler wanted to sound the alarm, but the bugle was knocked out of his hands.

"Don't bother! Cut it out! We have had enough!"

Adrogopoulos, the Greek wrestler, and Benid Tongut, the gendarme, were Hildebrandt's bellwethers. They gathered the majority of the disgruntled soldiers in order to surround the legionnaires rushing forward.

All the men were embittered, dead tired, and anxious, and most of them were ill. It was already six o'clock in the afternoon, and the last wave of desert heat raged around them.

Hildebrandt stepped onto a bench:

"Folks! We've had enough of the Sahara! We don't want to die in the desert. We'll break out together with the prisoners who were sentenced to perish here just as we were. Many armed fighters of the *Sokota* tribe will soon arrive to our aid and, through a secret passage, will lead all of us to British territory where we'll be free. That's all we want. We must provide security to our *Sokota* rescuers. Therefore, we must take over the Fort so that no one can fire at them from here. We'll harm no one. Even the officers may flee if they wish – either with us or on their own, as they please. But should they resist, we'll kill them all. We are not afraid of a water shortage. By evening, it will be resolved. By evening, we'll have ecrasite to blow up the pump's armor. But if it comes to it, if they do not give us the code to the vault, everyone who does not side with us will die. Until then, we'll maintain order and harm no one." His eyes were restlessly seeking Pencroft, but he didn't see him approaching. *Where could he be?* Hildebrandt thought, and then continued his speech: "I will go up to the office. I will speak with the officers. It might take a long time. Wait with discipline and patience. We want neither blood nor chaos; we just want to leave this hell."

"Well said!" the men roared in unison.

"The *goumiers* will accompany us, too. Only three of them refused to join," Hildebrandt continued.

Benid Tongut, the huge Arab sergeant, stood among the rioters. The legionnaires were patting his shoulders. Barbizon, longing to squeeze the *goumier*'s neck, rubbed his hands together on the parapet.

"Until I return, maintain order. If I am not back in an hour, they finished me off up there. In that case, have mercy on no one," Hildebrandt concluded his speech and then headed towards the main building with determined steps. The soldiers clamored.

And where was Pigeon? Where were Latouret, Battista, and the others?

When the gunshot resounded, Latouret and Battista had been on the staircase leading to the office. The Sergeant had pulled out his revolver. Battista had followed suit. At that very moment, somebody had grabbed his hand from behind and had wrestled away his pistol. The same had happened to Battista. Pigeon, Troppauer, Spoliansky, and Nadov had disarmed them.

"Tie them up!" Pigeon said. "Go on, Spoliansky!"

The Pole pulled out a rope and turned to the Sergeant who was cursing helplessly:

"If you will allow me," he said politely, and he tied the Sergeant tightly with obvious practiced efficiency. He then turned to Battista as if he were asking him to dance: "May I have the honor?" But before he could learn whether or not the Italian would consent, he was already done with tying him up. He then led them to a lavatory.

"At ease, good old Latouret," Pigeon encouraged him,

"everything will turn out fine. I am a good boy, and I will think of you, and you two must be stashed away only temporarily."

"You know, Harrincourt," the Sergeant said with contempt, "until now I thought that you were only undisciplined and conceited. I even felt pity for you when you were tied up *en crapaudine*. But now I see that you are a common traitor, a wretched coward, and I regret ever having said a single kind word to you."

"Just keep muttering, old man. I know that you like me nonetheless. Don't you worry about a thing. Pigeon is a good boy. He likes the old papa soldier. Let's go lads."

After that they went to the barracks. The "Harrincourt Detail" – Minkus, Pilotte, Hlavách, Rikayev, and another eight trustworthy men – gathered there, led by Pilotte.

"Boys! We are all under the leadership of Major Hlavách. We'll all go downstairs and pretend to join the rioters. We'll break the door to the warehouse, and everyone can drink rum or whatever drink is available."

"That's the ticket!" Hlavách exclaimed enthusiastically.

"Forward!" Pigeon commanded, but he kept the pushing Hlavách back. "You'll stay behind. You must not risk your life. That's the privates' duty."

"But I would like to be there when the rum is brought up," Hlavách mumbled in disappointment.

"I respect that you want to lead us heroically, but we are responsible for your life, Major, Sir. Let's go boys!" He pushed Hlavách back and locked the door on him. At first, the cobbler just stared in desperation, but then he became angry. *What kind of treatment is this?!* he lamented. *The whole rum idea was mine, and I am the only one left out of it! Darn!*

However, he could do nothing about it.

Meanwhile, Pigeon said on the staircase:

"Boys! Any of you who drinks from the rum throws away his military honor, and I give you my word that I will shoot him on the spot."

"You don't have to be so stingy," Troppauer the poet grumbled. "A small glassful wouldn't hurt." But Pigeon looked at him in such a way that he quickly fell silent.

They arrived running among the soldiers who crowded the court:

"Hello!" Pigeon exclaimed. "Freedom is here at last! We are going home! And until they open the water faucet, let's not remain thirsty. Boys, there is rum in the warehouse. After so much misery, we deserve a couple of drinks."

"Well said!" exclaimed Troppauer.

"Well said!" the alcoholics roared.

They pried open the door of the warehouse in a minute.

They tapped the large barrels with bayonets or axes, whatever was at hand. Within moments, rum was flowing everywhere; guffaws and shouts filled the air.

"Hey! This is whiskey!" one of them mumbled, and they thronged like a herd. Soon a harmonica started to play.

The backlash of long-lasting monotony was terrifying. The men shrieked and sang, and some gulped so much rum at once that they collapsed, falling next to the bottle dropped from their hands as if they had had a stroke.

"What's going on here?!" Adrogopoulos shouted at the top of the staircase leading down to the warehouse. *This man is dangerous. He has been whispering with Pencroft and that other fellow for weeks*, the thought flashed through Pigeon's mind.

"Folks!" the Greek yelled desperately, "you must not get drunk. Everything is over if…"

Pigeon stood in front of him wobbling as if he were drunk:

"Why are you butting in? Come and have a drink, too! Why should you be the one around here giving orders? Who do you think you are? What? Here you go, drink!"

The Greek angrily pushed the glass aside, prompting Pigeon to burst out in a roar:

"You hit me! I will kill you for that, you pig!" And while the Greek was perplexed by surprise, for he had not hit Pigeon, he was kicked with such force that he fell back and, as if riding a sleigh, slid down the stairs into the cellar. He jumped up immediately, but a zooming fist punched him in the nose so that everything went dark for a couple of seconds. Pigeon knew that the Greek could ruin his plans. He had to finish him.

The legionnaires thought that it was just the usual brawl. They guffawed and gathered around them, shouting.

Adrogopoulos suddenly grabbed his opponent. Pigeon worriedly realized that he was fighting against someone stronger. Adrogopoulos's arms were as hard as marble. Right away, Pigeon received a punch in the jaw from below that made him dizzy, but he blindly threw a hook that luckily hit the target. The Greek staggered for a moment. He backed to a stack of barrels and prepared to jump. His bearded face twisted into a malicious grin, and…

From the top of the stacked barrels, somehow, perhaps because the large body leaned against them, a hogshead fell on his head and flattened his skull into a pie.

The soldiers stood in astonishment for a few seconds.

Meanwhile Troppauer squatted behind the large barrels because if the others figured out that he had tilted the heavy barrel on Adrogopoulos's head, it would have meant big trouble.

"At least you have learned," Pigeon mimicked the slurred tone of a drunk, "not to give orders to legionnaires. Dirt bag! We've had enough of the likes of him."

Somebody yelled that he had found cognac. The others thronged around him, shouting inarticulately, and the corpse of the Greek at the foot of the barrels was soon forgotten.

Pigeon's harmonica started on the legionnaires' favorite song:
"*Le sac, ma foi, toujours au dos…!*"

They sang and they drank. Some of them, in the absence of a better cup, ladled the rum with their caps. Half of it was wasted. In the background, a smaller dispute was settled with a bayonet. A few lay on the ground unconscious. Hoarse shrieking filled the cellar, and the harmonica kept on playing.

It was by then getting dark. Pigeon played relentlessly. A bunch of *goumiers* got into a fight with a couple of soldiers. Gunshots thundered. The revelry already had four or five victims. Nobody was concerned with Hildebrandt and the *corvée*. Spoliansky, Troppauer, Minkus, Pilotte, and the others didn't dare to drink. For Pigeon sat on the stairs, playing his harmonica with a petty officer's large revolver was in his lap.

It was half past six, and the squadron was already soused. They had consumed incredible amounts of rum.

Meanwhile, Battista and Latouret lay tied up next to one another. They had a pretty clear idea about their fate and heard the frantic bellowing. All of a sudden, in an orderly double row, a couple of soldiers came with their bayonets on their rifles. Troppauer and Pilotte were up front, each with a stovepipe-like flamethrower. Pigeon led the detail. He cut the ropes of both petty officers. Latouret jumped up.

"You wretched scumbags! Dirty traitors!"

"If you are finished, old man" Pigeon said quietly, "just let me know because we've got a lot to do. Or wouldn't you rather take over leading the patrol and arrest the rioters than continue insulting us?"

While he said all this, he handed over a revolver to each petty officer.

"What's going on?" Battista asked dumbfounded.

"Had we not tied you two up earlier, you would have come to the courtyard with a pompous attitude, and the rioters would have killed you both. And we are in need of two good petty officers, even if one or the other is getting a little bit long in the tooth." Pigeon turned to Latouret. "We have disarmed the rioters, but they are unaware of it. They pried the door to the depot open, drank up all the rum, and are barely on their feet. Sergeant! Lead the patrol to apprehend them; but now let's go. *En avant*, Gramps! *Marche!*" he commanded in his peculiar military jargon.

"If this is true, Harrincourt, then I don't regret that I sometimes felt pity for you when they were skinning you." His eyes glinted, his few cat-like, gray whiskers fiercely projected ahead, and he stood in front of the tiny platoon: "*A mon commandemant! En route! Marche!*"

Only a handful of soldiers were still somewhat on their feet when heavy steps approached from the outside. The patrol stopped at the doorway. Two flamethrowers were pointed at them, enough to burn everyone in the cellar to death within seconds.

"*En joue!*" Latouret crackled, and bayonets were pointed at the rioters. A couple of drunken men were astonished to notice that their weapons were gone.

They padlocked the doors of the cellar within ten minutes, and the rioters lay on the floor bound tightly. With their weapons ready to fire, they intruded upon the *goumiers'* quarters so suddenly that the *goumiers* didn't stand a chance of resisting them. They tied them up quickly. They untied the three captives who hadn't joined the mutinous gendarmes. Weapons were given to these three. Benid Tongut escaped through the back window in time. He climbed the parapet of the Fort at a deserted segment. He had a rope with him. He planned to climb down on the other side and to wait for the arrival of the *Sokotas* who were supposed to arrive in the desert either the next day or the day after.

However, he didn't expect that a man had been watching him for hours from the parapet – someone who had unsettled business with the Arab gendarme. Long shadows were cast over the stones under the oblique angle of the sunset when Benid Tongut reached the embrasures. Someone stepped to him from the shade and grabbed his throat. The sergeant saw Barbizon's mercilessly stern features up close.

"Just a minute, comrade," the Corsican whispered.

The only thing Benid Tongut felt was an excruciating pain cutting in the back of his neck and something cracking. He then flew over the ridge of the parapet, plunging fifty feet.

2

When Finley looked down from the window and saw the soldiers gathering, he turned around:

"It has begun."

Gardone was wiping his sweating face, yellowed with terror.

"What do you think?" he asked the Lieutenant.

"We are going to die," he replied unfazed. "If they have ecrasite, we cannot hold them in check because they will blow up the pipeline. After that, if the *Sokotas* indeed arrive and if the rioters have not killed us yet, we can shoot ourselves in the head because, naturally, I would not even consider giving myself up to the natives."

"But please, we'd be prisoners of war."

"Don't even think about it! They would slaughter us immediately."

"That is not certain. On the contrary, how would it serve their interest?"

Finley felt disgust. Even if a person is a coward, he should control himself when he sees that he must die and that there is no escape. And this man was wearing the uniform of French officers!

They heard the idiot's voice from outside:

"Would you please stop; otherwise this private must shoot! That is the order!"

"Go to hell," somebody said, and it appeared that he pushed the imbecile aside because the door opened and Hildebrandt entered.

"Private!" Finley snapped at him, "Who allowed you to enter without knocking and permission?"

"Wait," the Captain interrupted. "I am in command here. Why are you here?" he turned to Hildebrandt.

"Captain, Sir! The crew sent me to negotiate with the officers. We refuse to follow orders. We want to go home, and we will go home. Nobody can stop us from doing so. The prisoners, the *goumiers*, and the guerillas all side with us. The officers did not harm us, and we don't want to harm them. We won't do harm to the Fort either. You will tell us the combination, we will get our water supply for the trip, France will retain this garrison, and the officers will stay alive. If you do not cooperate, we'll take over the Fort. If needed, we'll blow up the Fort. We have enough ecrasite, and that makes the officers' resistance futile. One way or the other, we'll get our hands on the water. But if you don't cooperate, we'll blow up the water pipe, demolish the Fort, and kill all who join you. This is the decision of the rebelling garrison."

"Get out of my sight!" Finley exclaimed. "We won't negotiate with mutineers, and you can all…"

"Silence!" the Captain said forcefully. He no longer felt the danger of imminent death, and that made him pompous again. "What is the role of a certain *Sokota* Negro tribe in this matter?"

"The *Sokotas* are on their way to Aut-Taurirt. They sent message with a jungle tribe's chief that if we took over the fort and they would no longer need to fear the French army, they would then lead us on a secret path to British Guinea. We won't harm the *Sokotas*, and we'll protect you also, unless you force us to take different action."

"Step out," Gardone replied to Hildebrandt, "and wait in the hallway."

Hildebrandt knew he had won. He turned around in snappy military fashion and stepped out of the room. After he left, Chalky poked his head through the door:

"Officer, Sir! Should the private be shot?"

"Get out of my sight!"

Chalky grinned and disappeared. Gardone said to Finley with superiority:

"My dear Finley, I believe that this case calls for diplomatic skills. Playing the hero is not a solution. The Garrison and the road are the top priorities, as spelled out in our orders. Let the mutineers go wherever they want to. I won't take responsibility for the destruction of the Fort."

Gardone puffed himself up and haughtily looked down on his deputy.

"Captain, Sir! You don't want to open the faucet vault for them, do you? Or to disclose the combination?"

"But I do! These are not bad guys, only embittered. A little diplomacy, you know! Let them go, and this way, at least the Fort will remain standing. If they blow up the pipe, they will kill the entire garrison! We can't give up this important military strategic site."

"I don't share your opinion, Captain, Sir" Finley replied angrily with his nostrils flaring.

"Is that so? Well, that's not important, anyway. I was sent here because they knew that this was a delicate mission. Lieutenant! I order you to lead the delegate of the mutineers to the faucet, and tell him the combination of the vault."

The officer replied without hesitation:

"I refuse to carry out the order!"

"Your sword!"

Finley unbuckled his sword with a curt twitch and placed it on the desk.

"You will go to your quarters and stay there until further notice. I will disclose the code to the vault myself and will take responsibility for opening the faucet. Private!"

Every word was easily heard through the thin door, so Hildebrandt joyously rushed into the room, and Gardone wanted to say something, but he recoiled in terror.

As he faced the private, a bayonet suddenly poked through Hildebrandt's chest. The soldier stared ahead with his eyes wide open and his jaw dropped, and then he tumbled. Behind him, holding his rifle, stood Chalky, blood dripping from the bayonet of his firearm.

"I am Major Yves," he said quietly, and looked straight into Gardone's eyes. "Captain! Turn your sword over to Finley. You are under arrest for treason."

CHAPTER TWENTY-SIX

1

In the meantime, the detail, now led by Lieutenant Hilliers, continued purging. The guerillas that camped next to the Fort could also have posed danger. Barbizon knew from the prisoners who the ringleaders were among these irregular troops.

From the parapet of the Fort, machine guns were suddenly pointed at the guerillas. A few of them jumped on their camels but they were fired upon, and all who attempted to escape fell. The rest sat down and waited to learn their fates. An Arab gendarme was sent to them with the message to lay down their weapons within ten minutes else they would all be shot.

They capitulated within the ten minutes. They were then surrounded by a patrol with their weapons ready to shoot. Hilliers read thirty names from a slip. These were the ringleaders. They were led away. Under martial law, they were all shot in the head "immediately and on site" as mutineers.

The rest of the Arabs were told that they would get their weapons back. It was possible that it would come to battle that night. If they did not fight well enough, they would be mowed down with machine guns that would be positioned behind them within range.

After this, Latouret assigned duties in the courtyard of the Fort and finally dismissed the line with these words:

"Boys! Everyone now deserves a glass of good wine. You,

Harrincourt, come with me for debriefing."

"Let's go, old-timer," he replied with his usual laxity, and Latouret's moustache trembled; he made some leopard-like grumbling but otherwise said nothing.

2

The sun sank under the desert horizon, and Kobienski, the leader of the *corvée*, was waiting for the signal: the light of a reflector on the Fort's parapet.

But the small white castle stood out silently in the desert dusk, as if abandoned by all living creatures.

Some sort of ominous feeling weighed down on the men. The prisoners gathered at the beginning of the paved road in preparation for joining forces with the men in the *corvée* upon the signal of the reflector beam. The alleged Dr. Borden and the other two strangers, Lorsakoff and Macquart, led the prisoners. They distributed some weapons, not many altogether, but as many as they could smuggle with them in their truck. The ecrasite lay beside them in two crates.

Hyenas laughed with unpleasant voices, and the first faintly glowing stars lit up over the yellow mounds of the Sahara.

"What the devil is going on?" muttered Kobienski, looking at the silent Fort that appeared forbiddingly deserted.

"There must be something wrong," a soldier said.

"But what?"

They fell silent.

"We'll know soon enough," Lorsakoff said from among the prisoners, "when they come to relieve the *corvée*."

Nobody replied. A nightmarish, foreboding feeling weighed down on the small group of soldiers as they were waiting in the desert on the evening of that fateful day.

The time for changing of the guards came and went. And nothing happened. Dark night fell over the Sahara. The prisoners and soldiers saw each other only as shapeless patches of shadow.

At last the gate of the Fort opened. By glimmering lights inside the fort, they could see well, even from a distance, that a soldier was coming.

A single one!

And the gate closed behind him immediately. The shadow slowly and unflappably approached them on the long road while clouds of dust covered him from time to time. Now, he was separated from the *corvée* only by a few steps.

They finally recognized him.

"It's Troppauer!" a soldier exclaimed.

It was indeed the poet. Now it became certain that something had happened.

"Boys!" he said upon reaching the guard. "They sent me because I am on good terms with the prisoners as well. There's trouble. The majority of the soldiers have changed their minds at the last minute. They have locked up the ringleaders of the rebellion; the others have decided against this foolishness in favor of protecting the Fort."

Dead silence followed. The sultry, oppressing night weighed down on the rioters even more menacingly.

Reflectors lit up on the parapet of the Fort. But there was no signal. The beams of eight to ten searchlights scanned the desert, crossing each other's paths.

"Hogwash!" Lorsakoff exclaimed. "The soldiers won't fire at us!"

"The boys' message is," Troppauer remarked, "that anyone who returns unarmed will be allowed to enter. Otherwise, they will shoot. They have closed down the water pipe, and they will not open it until everyone has given himself up."

The astounded soldiers remained silent during the pause that followed. Somewhere from the forest, they heard the raucous voice of a bird as it kept repeating: "Kee-raa-gaa... Kee-raa-gaa..." Wind whisked through the Sahara, and dust rustled in the air.

"The Major sends this message: if the *corvée* returns to the Fort and the prisoners return to their work, he will disregard whatever you had planned. Only the leaders will be punished." And he added with a sigh, "Kobienski, they will probably hang you. However, such is life: sometimes you are down, and then you are up. And after all, up there, nothing hurts anymore."

"Don't listen to this traitor!" Kobienski shrieked. "He tells nothing but lies!"

"And we have ecrasite!" Lorsakoff exclaimed. "If needed, we can blow up the entire Fort."

The determined encouragement was met with little enthusiasm. Only Troppauer replied in a similarly loud voice:

"We won't be fools to die because of you! Why should we seek trouble when we can get out of this mess unharmed? You shouldn't have come here in the first place!"

"You dirty pig!" Kobienski sneered, and he stepped in front of Troppauer. "I will teach you to bother only with your idiotic poems, and..."

In response to this insult, Troppauer, of course, slapped Kobienski who subsequently remained spread out on the ground very quietly for quite some time.

Lorsakoff pulled out his revolver, but a prisoner knocked it out of his hand. Macquart was grabbed by two soldiers.

"We won't be fools to die because of you!" the Santa Claus-bearded prisoner yelled. "Troppauer is right."

"Let them eat what they cooked," another skeleton said, and he raised his parched arm, shaking his fist toward Dr. Borden.

In ten minutes, the *corvée* returned to the Fort unarmed and carried Kobienski, Lorsakoff, Macquart, and Dr. Borden, all of them tied up.

The prisoners sat in their bungalows quietly waiting to learn their fates.

CHAPTER TWENTY-SEVEN

1

They gathered in Delahay's room. The Major was feeling a little better. He rested on his elbow in bed and smoked a cigar. He had had an attack in the afternoon and had thus just learned of the turn of events. Chalky – Major Yves to be precise –, Finley, and Lieutenant Hilliers sat around him.

"Our honor has been saved," the Major said. "However, the Fort is still in danger as long as an attack by the *Sokotas* is imminent."

"If we knew their route, it would be child's play to make them retreat or to surround them," Finley remarked.

"However, we don't know it," Yves said. "And we have little hope of finding it out. All the same, the watch in that Harrincourt lad's possession is the clue to everything."

He didn't notice the astonishment in the eyes of those listening to him. Chalky had undergone an astounding transformation. His slenderness now projected energy. He was a gaunt, sun-tanned man with an air about him reminiscent of an English gentleman, and his eyes gleamed with clarity and intelligence.

"When did you reveal yourself to Finley?" Delahay asked.

"When that kind lad, who had been constantly mistaken for me, was sentenced to *en crapaudine*. I had to save him. I told Finley to report this to you, bypassing Gardone. First I had to prove who I was. Later, Finley obtained the waxed canvas bag from the safe, and it was smuggled back to the lad by another friend of mine. The bag contained Grison's wallet, my identification plaque with my service number, and a bundle of writings. Poems. I wanted to read them because it might have turned out that even my friend Troppauer had been putting on an act and had in fact been a spy. Thank God the poems put my mind at ease about that possibility."

Latouret entered, together with Pigeon.

"Come here, my friend," Delahay said. "You have done a great service to your country, and you'll receive an extraordinary reward!"

"Major, Sir! It is not worth mentioning, let alone rewarding. For his country every man has to stand up. And after all, the credit for the entire success should go to Major Yves. Oh, my God!"

"What's wrong? What happened?" the officers inquired in surprise.

"Major, Sir! I respectfully request your permission to leave for a few minutes. I locked up an officer somewhere in the early afternoon, and it is possible that he might wish to eat or drink something."

The surprised Major waved him in approval. Chalky reemerged.

"This lad is under the impression that a cobbler named Hlavách is me, and he has thoroughly tormented the poor devil."

This was precisely the case. Hlavách was sitting in the room, hungry and thirsty. He was about to climb downstairs through the window, but when Pigeon opened the door, the cobbler, afraid of further complications, bolted out in terror and headed straight to the canteen.

It was time for the changing of the guards downstairs. Upstairs, they could hear Battista's commanding and the knocking of stocks as rifles flew off shoulders and landed on the pavement.

It was midnight.

2

Pigeon didn't immediately return to the Major, and he appeared to abandon all military discipline. There was no saving grace for his carefree action, perhaps with the exception that he was in love, the emotion that has deleteriously influenced even the most serious men.

He rushed towards the canteen, but he wasn't even half way there when, from the darkness of the courtyard, the Arab youngster – Magde – suddenly appeared.

He embraced the girl and hugged her tightly.

"You see," he whispered. "I told you that the entire fuss would not take long."

"I've been worried about you," the girl replied. "But now it's over, thank God!"

"It is not over by any means. First of all, we don't even know what will happen to the prisoners. And then those native scoundrels are supposedly planning some sort of attack."

Up on the parapet, the sentinel's footsteps clicked monotonously.

"You are right," the girl replied with resignation. "The passage my father sought is the natives' secret."

"Yes, the passage," Pigeon nodded his head. "It would be a blessing for the region if we were to find it at last. Could the secret really be locked in this watch?"

They both looked at the ugly, silver crocodile head.

"It's absolutely certain. It's enough to drive you mad, but that's the case. The map of the passage is hiding in this watch. Dr. Bretail wanted to give this to Captain Corot on the evening they were killed."

Pigeon looked at the scratched lid of the watch with despondency. And then, with an instinctive move, he pressed on the winding knob. The lid popped open, and…

As they glanced at the clock-face, both of them exclaimed in surprise.

The map was there!

This was unprecedented! A rushing man stumbled on the threshold of the Major's room, crash-landed on the floor, jumped up and, disregarding all his superiors, kept on shouting:

"The lights! Turn down the lights! We found it! Here it is! Just a moment!" he panted, out of breath because of the stairs. It was Pigeon. Chalky turned the lights off.

And, in a greenish-yellow light, emitting its radiation onto the silver crocodile head, a miniature map of Russel's passage glowed in a few tiny lines!

In the darkness, nothing was heard but the gasping of astonished people.

3

How simple it was! The explorer had drawn the map either with a radium- or phosphorus-based radiating material on the clock-face of the watch. The faint, thin-as-hair lines blended in unnoticeably with the cracks of the clock-face and were virtually invisible, but they glowed at night if the clock-face had been previously exposed to sunlight as the phosphorescent material emitted the absorbed energy. The cartographer Russel, a man who had traveled in delicate diplomatic matters, had charted the first draft of his map on this cracked clock face with an invisible, or – more precisely – a transparent material that absorbed radiation. He had then fixed the draft with glue. If he were attacked or strip-searched or if someone were to disassemble the watch a thousand times they would not find a thing because the map became visible only in the dark after having been exposed to strong sunshine.

Now all of them looked at the watch with their eyes wide open, as if they were watching an apparition from the beyond.

On the clock-face, a very tiny dashed line indicated the road to the Niger from a site labeled with the letter "C." This could only have stood for camp – the site where Russel had set camp for the last time. And that was the site where the Fort of Aut-Taurirt was built. It said at the bottom: 1 mm = 2 km. The road was shown by a line about 2 cm long; thus they were about forty kilometers from the passage. The stripe that indicated the road crossed a dotted line that was labeled with "N." This could only have meant the River Niger. Below it, under the second hand, the script said: from 03.10 to 06.25. This was also clear and simple. From the 10th of March until the 25th of June, the water level in the Niger allowed use of the passage, whereas during the other months the passage was probably submerged.

"Had we known this earlier," Major Yves said in the astounded silence, "we could have spared the lives of many people."

Someone turned the light on.

"Look, it's the imbecile Chalky!" Pigeon exclaimed.

"No, my friend," "Chalky" said with a smile. "I am that certain Major Yves because of whom you have had so many unpleasant encounters. Do close your mouth, my son, because the way you look does not reflect well on you."

For Pigeon had opened his mouth as wide open as it was altogether possible. He bent his neck forward, strained his eyes, and shifted his sight between the surprisingly easy-mannered "Chalky" and the laughing officers, jerking his head left and right in astonishment.

"Wow!" he said finally.

"I repeat what my friend Major Delahay said: You have done a great service to your country. You are the most reckless and the best soldier in the world. And as for Chalky, the hapless imbecile, I shake your hand with gratitude on his behalf."

He shook Pigeon's hand firmly. Pigeon was still shifting his blinking eyes from one officer to the next, and he kept repeating in his embarrassment and surprise:

"Fine kettle of fish; I say, it's a fine kettle of fish."

"And, on top of everything, our friend Pigeon happens to be a lucky fellow," Finley interjected. "Fate has led him to the secret of the watch that was sought after by so many experts."

"It's good that you mention it!" Delahay said, pushing himself up in bed with his elbow. The worn, little old man apparently had regained his strength. "Let's not rest on the laurels of victory while the *Sokota*'s attack can find us unprepared."

"That's no longer that dangerous," Yves said with a wave of his hand. "First, it's only the 8th of March, and it is unlikely that the road to *Batalanga* would become fit for passage in less than four or five days. Russel's map indicated the tenth. Then, having the map allows us to occupy the opening of the passage with the irregular troops. The passage probably leads under the bed of the Niger, where its bedrock is strong enough, so as not to cave in."

"Bed!" Pigeon yelled wildly again and slapped his forehead. "I've forgotten about leaving a villain named Laporter under a bed somewhere."

"Laporter!" Chalky jumped up. "Where is he?! I could have sworn that he had slipped out of my hands. Come with me, my son!" Pigeon and the Major rushed to the corridor behind the canteen and opened the door of the room where the gangster had been left tied up.

When they untied him, Pencroft's limbs fell from the ropes like rags scattered from a dismantled bundle. He was half-dead by then.

Pigeon shook his head:

"Loneliness has taken a severe toll on him!"

CHAPTER TWENTY-EIGHT

1

By dawn, the Fort had grown quiet. Everybody had slept soundly after the hard day.

Some of the soldiers wound up in the infirmary with severe alcohol poisoning. The others lined up after reveille with headaches and sore limbs. Finley informed them in a few short sentences that instead of heavy-handed punishment, they would consider the entire event a simple bar brawl, and every tenth person involved would be sentenced to four days of *pelote*. Should a similar event occur in the future, the participants would be court-martialed.

The men quietly listened. The sun was rising, and the heat intensified almost by the second.

They then assembled the *corvée*. It consisted of a trustworthy crew: Pigeon, Spoliansky, and the others were assigned to the platoon. Finley led them accompanied by Latouret.

For nearly a day, the prisoners had repeatedly tried to open the faucet. But, it had all been in vain and they had been completely deprived of water. The night had passed by bearably, but in the sizzling heat of the morning, thirst made them grow very weak, and more than two hundred human skeletons sat around dizzy and exhausted in the stifling jungle. Blue vessels pulsated under the yellow skin of moribund, scrawny skulls; swollen, large, red eyelids drooped as if dying, and from between the bloodless lolling lips, white tongues protruded hesitantly.

They saw the *corvée* coming. They watched as the officer ordered the *corvée* to present arms and as the weapons were aimed at them. No one moved. Would he give the order to fire? Possibly.

A patrol then separated from the *corvée* and approached them with the lead of an officer. A few prisoners lumbered to rise. They didn't even think about attacking the handful of soldiers.

The collapse of the mutiny had taken their last drop of vitality away.

"Men!" Finley said curtly. "I sent word to you yesterday that if you return to your camp, we'll punish no one. I am a man of my word. We'll open the water faucet, you'll get food, but from now on a small platoon will come among you in every suspicious case. And whoever behaves without discipline will be shot in the head. We'll convert Aut-Taurirt into a normal garrison. We'll start constructing barracks tomorrow; you will get a hospital and a doctor, and we'll put everything in order. The water faucet will be open in thirty minutes. I will leave one soldier here. A single one. And you will drink in the order he commands you to. If any harm comes to this soldier, I will have you decimated. *Rompez!*"

The patrol continued toward the thick of the jungle. The prisoners loafed about, tottering without saying a word; some of them had already fainted. And then Rikov, the soldier assigned to man the faucet, said:

"The water is on its way. Attention! Line up single file and bring your cups."

The prisoners lined up, drank in an orderly manner, and the solo post remained unharmed among them.

2

And the patrol continued its trip along an elephant walk in the jungle toward the pygmy village. The dwarf chief personally rushed ahead to meet them; he thought that the mutineers were coming. He was utterly disappointed upon seeing the officers leading the soldiers.

"Master! I am glad to see you," he faltered.

"And yet, this will be a sad day for you, Chief," Finley replied, "for I will have you hanged, and we'll destroy your village."

"You must not do that, Master *Rumi!* I have been a longtime friend to the white soldiers."

"Loaded rifles are pointed at you and your people from every direction, Chief!" The "people" were made up of a dozen natives in four log cabins. "You will now all go into one of the cabins and stay there until we reach a decision about you. Eight of my men will watch over you."

The natives obeyed without a word. Eight soldiers stayed behind and watched them. They piled up the pygmies' crockery and weapons and burned them. They burned up the other cabins and chopped down the ten coconut palms that constituted the tribe's livelihood.

And they took the chief with them in shackles.

"What is your name?" Finley asked the trembling dwarf pygmy on the way.

"Illomor, Master," the chief replied.

3

Major Yves continued the interrogations in the garrison's office at a feverish pace. After a brief radio communication, they were informed that a contingent of *spahis* was dispatched from Timbuktu as reinforcement to the garrison and that all participants in the incident would be transported to Oran by airplane.

Pencroft confessed nothing. Illomor, the chief, revealed a lot more, and Pigeon recounted everything that jumped to mind.

"Think, my son," Yves encouraged him, "every detail is important."

"But I really have told everything. At most, I might have forgotten a few punches, since I got into numerous fights related to this affair. By the way, I stood on post in the laundry, and I was attacked. This was most probably that scoundrel Laporter. But somebody fired at him from the dark, although I couldn't even guess who it was."

"It was me," the Major said with a smile. "I was taking a nap, and you were concerned about my stuff; nevertheless I heard quite well what you said. I figured that others would hear it, too. So I snuck into the laundry first and saw Hildebrandt, for it was he and not Pencroft, lie down on the floor. I intervened just in time to help you out. The only trouble was that my boots were covered by red, rust-proofing minium paint; however, I cleverly swapped my boots with Spoliansky's."

"The boots! And he swapped them with Troppauer, and then started to limp!"

"That's why they wanted to assassinate poor Troppauer. They believed that you were Major Yves and that Troppauer was your partner. And now, we must have an important cross-examination."
He stepped to the door leading to the adjacent room, and escorted Magde Russel from there. She wore a neat travel dress and watched Pigeon's surprise with a smile.

"Wow! The two of you are acquainted?!"

"We have become accomplices only recently," the girl laughed. "I have gotten acquainted with the Major only here in the garrison. He had been keeping an eye on me for quite some time and finally honored me with his trust."

"Mademoiselle Russel has become my first-class aide. She was the first person I asked to help me. For I trusted no one. This happened to some degree for your sake, Harrincourt. At the time, I didn't want to reveal my incognito to Finley, and I had to find a way to help prevent you from kicking the bucket because of the ninety-pound *pelote*. We used the Mademoiselle's disguise, the late Abu el Kebir, the coffee brewer, who bribed Battista, and thus could help you. You should be grateful to her for this!"

"Oh, rest assured that I will express my gratitude many times over," Pigeon said with enthusiasm, and the girl blushed.

4

They were invited to tea and spent the farewell evening in the convalescing Delahay's room. As an exception, two privates were among them without whom the assembly would have been incomplete. Naturally, Pigeon was one of them, and the other was Hümér Troppauer.

The poet stumbled on the rug and blushed every other minute, wrenching his hands.

And needless to say, Magde Russel also was in attendance, wearing the white horse-riders' outfit that Pigeon was so fond of.

At Delahay's request, Major Yves told the entire story from beginning to end.

"I had known Grison for a long time," Yves started, peering into his tea, as if a strip of film were rolling there on which he viewed the events unfolding. "He was a dubious character but a skilled intelligence agent. Our line of work sometimes necessitates giving preference to skills over decency. I was supposed to testify in court in the case of the mutiny in Ain-Sefra. I knew that many of my enemies would like to learn about my physical appearance. Nobody knows the men of the secret service, not even the chiefs of the General Staff. Only the head of Department D, General Aubert, contacts them personally. On occasion, I used to have other people act in my place and assume my identity in certain cases. That is how I had Grison take my place in court. I wanted to mislead all those who were after me. Grison memorized my testimony in advance and appeared in a major's uniform as Yves. He was never interrogated in the presence of the defendants, and they were never cross-examined. The charge of mutiny was obvious. Grison, of course, rented an apartment under the name of Major Yves and conspicuously frequented Department D of the General Staff, thereby perfectly misleading all who watched him.

"At the same time, under the names of Grison and Dupont, for he used both names, he was also involved in the Russel affair. However, I didn't know about that. Macquart is a representative of the railroad company that has a vested interest in preventing the completion of the Sahara railroad. Macquart presented himself as a wealthy gentleman in Oran. He, Lorsakoff, and Grison wanted to acquire the map of the passage. Grison shot Russel for the same reason, but they didn't find the map on him.

"Then, Grison even double-crossed his two accomplices. He told them that Major Yves, meaning me, would work for them if they paid him well. If they wanted to have confirmation of this, they were told to call the Major by phone. These two had no clue that Grison was coincidentally acting in my place at the time and, naturally, had an apartment under my name. Thus, they fell for the story. Grison answered the phone and cleverly made them believe that the Major was willing to communicate with them through Grison. He put himself forward as my emissary. Why did he do that? He wanted to get two shares of the vast reward upon finding the map in Russel's villa. One share as Grison and one in my name as Yves. This plan almost worked because at the time I wasn't even in Africa. I was away in Constantinople on a different assignment. That's where General Aubert reached me, ordering my return because I was to have an important mission in the company headed to Aut-Taurirt. I traveled to Marseilles and joined the Legion. Foreign intelligence keeps an eye on rookies who enlist in Oran because they suspect that the Secret Service smuggles one or two of its men among them. I sailed to Oran with the company assigned to duty in Aut-Taurirt. I did not report at the Service in Oran. I had no clue about Grison's dealings.

"I learned about them by coincidence. Once, I saw him in the street together with Macquart and became suspicious. I contacted Aubert, who calmed me down. He said that he considered Grison a useful man, and he gave the assignment to Grison in the Russel case. In the meantime, Grison told Mademoiselle Russel that Major Yves wanted to investigate the case and, through him, requested her permission for spending a day in the villa. He got the consent. Grison arrived at a conclusion that was obvious yet ingenious: The draft must be hidden in something that was with Russel and wound up with Dr. Bretail. And it had to be on Bretail on the day of the murder since he planned to give it to Captain Corot. Grison thus figured that the map could not have been in the villa because the district attorney's office took the victims' possessions into custody for the duration of the investigation. He made inquiries at the district attorney's office and learned that the possessions would be delivered to the heirs at the address of the deceased. He also learned the day of the delivery. He asked for permission for Yves to move into the villa on that very day with the excuse that the Major wanted again to examine everything thoroughly. However, by then I had already followed Grison's trail. I ordered one of my men to watch him. This is how I learned that he had gone to the district attorney's office. Then, when he expected me the least, I stepped in front of him in the street.

"The astonished expression on his face pretty clearly revealed that he had been acting in my name with dishonest intent. He told me that he was about to search Bretail's villa, and, when I said that I would join him, he regained his composure and invited me enthusiastically. By coincidence, in the afternoon of that particular day, a petty officer played a dirty practical joke on me and locked me in the cellar of the fort and left me there until the evening. I could not get away and didn't reach the villa until eleven in the evening. I immediately called the man whom I had ordered to watch Grison and learned from him that the late Bretail's belongings had been delivered from the attorney general's office sometime in the afternoon. Furthermore, most peculiarly, Grison, as Major Yves, informed the Service that he had killed an intruder in the villa. The intruder was a spy. Grison requested someone to pick him up and to take him to the soiree at Cochran's, the city's military commander, and the same person should make arrangements to have the body disappear. The men of the Secret Service are often forced to use their weapons when there is no time for presenting evidence in court for a conviction. They are accountable to no one but the General. Such was the case when I stabbed Hildebrandt to death, and I would have also killed Gardone without hesitation if I had no alternative to prevent him from disclosing the combination of the lock. But whom had Grison killed under the disguise of Major Yves?

"I arrived at the villa at eleven. I climbed into the garden and went around the house. I wanted to get in unnoticed. I heard gunshots; I then saw a legionnaire who approached the villa, running. The patrol was on his heels, chasing the soldier. He jumped into the garden of Bretail's villa. I recognized my comrade in arms, Harrincourt. Later he used the noisy arrival of a police car to throw his bayonet through the window – for the siren overpowered the noise of shattering. He climbed through the broken window and proceeded. I followed him and climbed in. In the room, I noticed the legionnaire's bayonet on the floor. He had used it for shattering the glass but had recklessly left it behind. I didn't want to leave any clue that might have led to the Legion. I picked it up, pushed it in my belt next to my own bayonet, and then hurried forward. The night was disturbed by loud commands, orders, and shouting in the street. I tiptoed to the room where the lights were on. I was curious to learn whom Grison had killed. I peeped through the keyhole and, to my surprise, I saw no corpse in the room. I understood the picture immediately. He had an appointment with me. I was the corpse to get rid of. He simply wanted to shoot me and to have my body disappear with the aid of the Secret Service, quickly and with absolute certainty. After all, only General Aubert knew me personally, and he would not have come to the scene. He only would have read Grison's report about the event.

"After that, I entered the room as if I had just arrived for the appointment. He looked at me in surprise. He then started to speak about something, and under the tablecloth he cautiously grabbed a revolver and was about to shoot – but I knew what he was up to. I pulled out my bayonet in haste and finished him off. There was no time for hesitation. I noticed only afterwards that instead of my own bayonet, I had used Harrincourt's, which I had pushed in my belt earlier. And then I heard footsteps approaching. If I had exited the room, whoever was headed that way would have seen me. I turned off the light and hid in the wardrobe closet. Our friend, Harrincourt – God only knows what he might have lost in the villa – had returned instead of fleeing. I thought that upon seeing Grison's stabbed corpse he would bolt in terror, but since then we have learned that Harrincourt rarely runs away."

"Fleeing does not run in my family," Pigeon said as if he needed an excuse.

Yves continued:

"The officer sent by the Secret Service to get rid of the body found Grison dead. However, he knew neither of us. He only knew that Major Yves was waiting for him next to a dead body in the Bretail villa. Since only Harrincourt was present, the officer had no doubt for even a second that he was facing a major of the Secret Service who, for some reason, was dressed as a legionnaire private. Harrincourt, on the other hand, didn't dare contradict the officer and followed him. I decided to use the misunderstanding for the benefit of the investigation. I called General Aubert right then from the Bretail villa.

"I explained everything that had happened, and we agreed that we would not reveal the officer's misunderstanding. Let the prowling villains believe that the legionnaire at large was Major Yves. Aubert skillfully made this misrepresentation believable at the soiree of the city's military commander. From Field Marshal Cochran to Macquart, everyone believed Harrincourt to be Major Yves. This way, playing the part of the imbecile Chalky, I could sit back and watch who approached the alleged Major Yves. After the soiree, Lorsakoff and Macquart figured that "Yves" had double-crossed both of them and fled with the watch that Grison had already talked to Lorsakoff about on the phone. Magde Russel, wonderfully disguised as an Arab coffee brewer, eavesdropped on a conversation between Lorsakoff and Macquart. Based on that conversation, she also believed "Yves" to be a traitor. She also learned that the map was hidden in the wristwatch. So she followed the company to Aut-Aurirt, too. On the order from Aubert, the men of the Service smuggled Grison's body to the alley apartment that he rented under the name of Dupont. I started to suspect the importance of the watch only when I noticed that on the road to Aut-Taurirt Laporter stole it while Harrincourt was washing. I stole it from Laporter the very same day, examined it thoroughly, and even disassembled it, but I could not uncover the secret. In Laporter's knapsack, I found Harrincourt's beloved shirt, and I secretly returned it along with the watch to our friend, Pigeon.

When we arrived at the garrison, I had to disclose my identity to Magde Russel who had done a wonderful job. Mahmud, Mademoiselle Russel's manservant, also made valuable contributions in the case. Unfortunately, he is now in the hospital with a serious bout of malaria. He managed to mislead even me by instructing a couple of guerillas. These said to everyone that Abu el Kebir, the coffee-brewer, had died. And they simply denied having seen the snake charmer Mahmud. Later I included Finley in the case, through whom I got hold of the waxed canvas bag."

Troppauer swallowed a bite of food so hard that he almost choked on it:

"My poems!" he exclaimed desperately.

"They are safe," said Yves with a smile. "I needed time to read them."

"And how did you like them, if I may ask?"

"Excellent! Especially the one entitled, '*I am musing in the dream-world of the Sahara.*'"

"I got that one right by accident," Troppauer mumbled, and he swallowed a hard-boiled egg whole. Later, when he got his poems back, he insistently tried to kiss the Major's hands.

5

"Light was shed on another aspect of the case as well," Yves continued. "I mean the Russel expedition. A ring of adventurers surrounded Russel on his trip. But the explorer apparently suspected something because when he went out to explore the last stage of the road, he left all his companions behind with the exception of the trustworthy and honest Dr. Bretail. Whatever happened at the camp, I know from Illomor.

"They drank *kivi* in the evening, and the drunken, neurasthenic Ilyich danced together with the natives. And then he collapsed in exhaustion. Byrel was also soaked, and he started a brawl with the natives. He shot a couple of them, but he was eventually stabbed to death.

"After that, Laporter and his henchmen tied up the neurasthenic Ilyich. In the morning, they made him believe that he had killed Byrel and the two natives in the rage of *kivi*. Illomor, who, by the way, speaks French pretty well, sat there in silence and played the comedy of 'pledge.' The poor, weakling Ilyich was an excellent medium, and the villains continued to take advantage of him. Later, they learned the whereabouts of Russel's drawing and decided to finish off Bretail. Illomor, who served as permanent courier between the *Sokota* tribe and the spies, happened to be in Oran at the time. They mixed a large dose of sleep drug in Ilyich's cognac, which the Kid used as self-medication against suffering from the sirocco. However, fear alone might have sufficed to induce the trance and make the boy believe everything when the naked, spear-shaking pygmy stepped out of the cupboard, put down a revolver and said: 'Kill.' The boy did not kill but fell asleep. In the evening, the villains murdered Captain Corot, Dr. Bretail, and his wife. It was either Pencroft or Lorsakoff. They convinced Ilyich that he had killed all three of them in the stupor of *kivi*. With this, they made him give the same testimony as Pencroft. Thus, two witnesses told a tale of 'jealousy.' They also would have liked to make use of Ilyich in Aut-Taurirt, so they made him join the Legion together with Pencroft. However, they later noted that the boy's nerves could no longer hold up against the pressures, and they put him away."

It was morning. The sun's yellow, broiling rays opened up in front of the window and flooded the room. They all sat there in silence and, with exhausted minds, remembered the recent horrors.

"We have had a couple of busy weeks," Pigeon remarked quietly, and secretly, under the tablecloth, he squeezed Magde's hand.

CHAPTER TWENTY-NINE

1

"And now, turn the watch over, private. Tell me how much you want for it, and Ms. Magde Russel may also have a word in hammering out a deal," Major Yves said. "I have a pretty far-reaching mandate."

"Unfortunately the watch was lost," Pigeon replied.

They all looked at him alarmed.

"What did you just say?" Delahay asked leaning on his elbow. "You must think very carefully about your words."

"The watch was lost, but it will be found immediately," Pigeon continued, "if I am honorably discharged from the Legion due to general physical weakness so that I can, in part, support my old family and, in part, establish a new one. If you do not grant this, the watch will never be recovered because I have hidden it so well."

Yves wrinkled his forehead. Harrincourt's request exceeded all military notions.

"All right, consider it done," he said finally. "Any other wish?"

"Yes. I want Hümér Troppauer's poems. I insist on this one."

"I expected no less from you," the poet mumbled.

"Private Troppauer will also receive a distinguished decoration for his meritorious role in crushing the mutiny," Delahay interjected.

"Then, after you get the watch from me, you will have to buy it from Ms. Magde Russel. I deserve a reward only as an excited finder."

"Everything will work out just fine," Yves said. "We'll enter your terms into the record, and I will be able to grant you the unusual request based on my authority as a plenipotentiary in the matter."

They completed the document. The officers attested that Major Yves made commitment to grant the above wishes on behalf of Department D of the General Staff.

"And now, tell us where the watch is," Yves urged Pigeon.

"Where could a wristwatch be?" Pigeon wondered. "Except on the wrist!" He pulled up the sleeve of his jacket, and the watch was indeed on his wrist.

2

At dawn, Pencroft was executed along with Kobienski in the yard of the Court Martial in Oran. Macquart's and Lorsakoff's verdicts were commuted to life in prison, and Gardone, stripped of his rank, was released from prison two years later.

This concluded the drama.

Before Pigeon and his fiancée left Oran, they had visited the "haunted" Bretail villa and walked through the dust-covered, abandoned, sepulchral smelling rooms in anguish.

"Oh, that worked like an elevator," Magde said with a smile.

"I beg your pardon?"

"A gramophone was in the room, operated by an electrical system. A small device always returned the arm of the pick-up needle to the beginning of the recording. Whenever the lights were on in the hall, the gramophone was turned on, and if the lights were turned off, it stopped playing."

"But if I opened the door?"

"That's precisely the elevator system. On the door, just like in the case of a door of an elevator, two wires were in contact. If someone opened the door, it disrupted the circuit. If the door was closed, the wires made contact again, and the gramophone continued playing. I had this system custom-made because I predicted the murderers would return to the villa to search for the map. My poor mother sang on that record, and I thought that the murderer would certainly flee in terror from a ghost who disappears when the door is opened on her. However, I shared this with one of the murderers, Grison, when he came here."

"One more question. In the desert? When your footprints disappeared? How did you do that?"

The girl laughed.

"Oh, you big kid! I simply scooped up sand in my hat, and, while walking backward, I spread it over my footprints."

Pigeon stared down at the ground.

"I won't be a sleuth after all," he finally said quietly.

They closed down the villa, and they left Oran.

And for a long time, nobody wanted to move into that house.

3

After returning to Paris and, in addition to his terms being granted, receiving the Legion's medal of honor, Pigeon declared:

"From now on, I will take care of my health. I don't want to be sick!"

Yet, the wedding had to be postponed by two weeks because Pigeon came down with a severe case of influenza. He was sick for the first time since he had left Paris. Death warned him with a smile that it did not like jokes. However, Harrincourt's nature prevailed; he recovered and married Magde Russel. After the wedding, the small family lived in their old home. For the Russel map, Magde received enough not only to pay off the mortgage on the house but also to secure their future.

They were often visited by Latouret, the retired Master Sergeant, with his fierce, singed mustache, and by Troppauer the poet, who read his own poems to the patient family.

Harrincourt purchased a few acres of vineyard near Paris that was not visited by their boring, aristocratic, illustrious acquaintances. A peculiar company gathered in the vineyard, and did so quite often. For example: An executioner with the looks of a count, "Major" Hlavách; the old-timer Pilotte; Minkus; the giant Nadov; Master Sergeant Latouret; Sergeant Battista; and, every time he was in Paris, Major Yves. On these occasions, the host played the harmonica, his wife served good red *chablis* to everyone, and, to the playful tune of the buzzing "philharmonic," Yves started singing and the rest followed, just like when they had marched in the murderous, yellow dust of the Sahara, in the "good old days":

"*Le sac, ma foi, toujours au dos…!*"

GLOSSARY

Adjudant = adjutant

Allons! = Come on! Proceed! Let's go!

A moi! = Help! [Come] here! To me!

A mon commandement = At my command

À terre! = On the ground! ("[Put your weapons] on the ground!"; "Drop your weapons!") Also means: ashore, down to earth, earthbound

Aux armes! = To arms!

Bleu = verbatim: blue. Here, it is a derogatory term, approximately meaning "cockroach." May also mean "rookie."

Boulot = small, round bread

Cafard = severe depression or apathy – used especially of white men in the tropics.

Capitaine = captain

Cellule = prison cell

Centimes = French equivalent of pennies/cents (100 centimes = 1 Franc).

Chef = chief; here: commander, commanding officer, immediate superior.

Corvée = guard unit, service, unpaid labor, chore, drudgery, fatigue party

Debout! = Up! On your feet!

Eh bien! = Well! (Verbatim: Very Good!)

En avant! = Forward!

En avant! Marche! = Forward! March!

En joue! Feu! = Ready, aim! Fire!

En route! = Let's go!

Fini = It's over. (finished, done)

Fixe! En joue! = Halt! Aim! (Verbatim: Stop! Ready!)

Garde à vous! = Attention!

Halte! Fixe! = Halt! Don't move!

Hamada = a type of desert landscape consisting of high, largely barren, rocky plateaus, with minimal sand (Arabic).

Képi = cap with a flat circular top and a visor; typical of French military (including legionnaires') and police uniforms. The *képi blanc* (white cap) is a symbol of the French Foreign legion.

Kesra = a Moroccan bread

L'amour m'a rendu fou = Love made me crazy

Le sac, ma foi, toujours au dos! = My pack, my faith, always on my back! (Legionnaires' song.)

Marche! = March!

Mon chef = Sir ("My Chief")

Mon excellence = Your Excellency

Musette = haversack

Nom de Dieu! = Good Lord!

Nom du nom! = Exclamation of anger or surprise, similar to "Damn it!" or "Hells bells!"

Oui = yes

Oui, mon commandant = Yes, Sir! Verbatim: "Yes, my commander!"

Paquetage = cleaning [duty], polishing, "the drill." Verbatim: "[the] package"

Pas de gymnastique! = Don't dawdle!

Passat = a type of wind. Originally, "trade wind" (German)

Pelote = a form of punishment; verbatim: "[the] ball"

Peloton = squadron, company; verbatim: platoon, pack

Rompez! = Dismissed! Fall out! Disperse!

Sacrebleu! = an exclamation literally meaning "Holy blue!" *i.e.,* "Holy heavens!"

Sapeur = sapper (field fortification, demolition specialist branch in the army)

Simoom = strong, dust-laden whirlwind in North Africa.

Spahi: light cavalry of the French Foreign Legion recruited mainly from the indigenous populations of French colonial North Africa.

Si l'on savait = If one could understand/know. This was a line in a popular French song (*On ne sait pas qui l'on est*) by Jean Delettre & Michel Emer, performed by Marie Dubas in 1935. It's full quoted line is *Si l'on savait qui l'on est* (If we knew who we are). Perhaps the most popular song performed by Marie Dubas was *Mon légionnaire*, which is more widely known today as sung by Édith Piaf.

"*Tiens, voilà du boudin*" = "Here you are some blood sausage." *Le boudin* colloquially meant the rolled up in a red blanket that topped the backpacks of Legionnaires.

Travaux forcés = hard labor (punishment)

Un, deux, trois = one, two, three.

Vicomte = viscount (member of the nobility ranking below an earl and above a baron)

ABOUT THE TRANSLATOR

Balint Kacsoh was born in Budapest, Hungary in 1959. He attended Semmelweis University of Medicine and graduated with an M.D. in 1984. He earned a Ph.D. at the Hungarian Academy of Sciences in 1997 in Basic Medical Sciences - Physiology/Endocrinology. He has lived in the United States since 1986 and has worked at Mercer University School of Medicine since 1992 where he is a full professor.

End Notes

[1] In several countries throughout Europe and Latin America, name days are celebrated similar to birthdays. Children's given names (baptismal names) appear in the calendar. Traditionally, these were saints' feast days in the Roman Catholic calendar. However, in modern times, traditional, "pagan," and/or popular names unrelated to religion were also assigned to specific days in the calendar, and each country developed its unique tradition. To understand the tradition, imagine that everyone named Patrick would have a birthday-like name day celebration on the 17th of March, and that everyone named Nicholas would have a name day celebration on the 6th of December. There are websites dedicated to name day traditions, *e.g.*, http://www.happynameday.info.

[2] Wikipedia has an article about Jenő Rejtő in English (search either as "Jeno Rejto," or as "P. Howard"). In Hungarian, the following book is an important source of information about Rejtő's life: Tibor Hámori: *Piszkos Fred és a többiek... Történetek Rejtő Jenő életéből*. [*Dirty Fred and the rest of the bunch... Stories from the life of Jenő Rejtő*] Ságvári Endre Könyvszerkesztőség, Budapest, 1982. ISBN 963-422-502-0

[3] Bryan Cartledge: Mihály Károlyi and István Bethlen. Hungary: The Peace Conferences of 1919-23 and Their Aftermath (Makers of the Modern World, Haus Histories). Haus Publishing, London, 2009. ISBN-10: 1905791739; ISBN-13: 978-1905791736

[4] János Bús, Péter Szabó: *Béke Poraikra*. [*May They Rest in Peace*] *Varietas '93 Kft*, Budapest, 1999. ISBN 963-03-8934-7

[5] The name Harrincourt probably is a misspelled version of the French town of *Havrincourt*.

⁶ Swedish gymnastics: A type of physical therapy used in orthopedics in which specific movements are used to achieve joint mobilization, increase flexibility, and decrease pain.

⁷ In the original, the text was: "life insurance policy that would pay only if 'in the course of his professional duties, naval cadet Jules Manfred Harrincourt should die.'" The reference to Harrincourt's profession as a naval cadet is in conflict with the novel's plot and was, therefore, omitted.

⁸ *La Canebière* was a particularly elegant avenue in Marseille in the 1930s. It was the place where King Alexander I of Yugoslavia was assassinated on October 9, 1934, five years before P. Howard wrote *The Frontier Garrison*.

⁹ *Avocat* = attorney

¹⁰ *Mon chef* = Sir ("my chief")

¹¹ *Sapeur* = sapper (field fortification, demolition specialist branch in the army)

¹² *Rompez!* = Dismissed! Fall out! Disperse!

¹³ *Paquetage* = cleaning [duty], polishing, "the drill." Verbatim: "[the] package"

¹⁴ *Spahi*: light cavalry of the French Foreign Legion recruited mainly from the indigenous populations of French colonial North Africa.

¹⁵ *En avant! Marche!* = Forward! March!

¹⁶ *Pelote* = a form of punishment; verbatim: "[the] ball"

¹⁷ *En joue! Feu!* = Ready, aim! Fire!

[18] *Pas de gymnastique! En avant! Marche!* = Don't dawdle! Forward, march!

[19] *Si l'on savait* = If one could understand/know. This was a line in a popular French song (*On ne sait pas qui l'on est*) by Jean Delettre & Michel Emer, performed by Marie Dubas in 1935. It's full quoted line is *Si l'on savait qui l'on est* (If we knew who we are). Perhaps the most popular song performed by Marie Dubas was *Mon légionnaire*, which is more widely known today as sung by Édith Piaf.

[20] In the original: "*Louis left for the New Hebrides.*" The song's title was slightly changed to match that in Chapter 1 for consistency.

[21] *Nom du nom!* = Exclamation of anger or surprise, similar to "Damn it!" or "Hells bells!"

[22] In the original text, the author wrote "*ma reggel*" = "today in the morning." However, the story line clearly indicates "tomorrow morning."

[23] Aut-Taurirt, as occurs in the original book might be a spelling error. The geographical name Taourirt is encountered in Morocco and Algeria. The loose African geographical references in the book clearly indicate fiction.

[24] In the original, this sentence was followed by "who felt that the events justified addressing his comrade informally." Unlike modern English (and similar to Russian, German, or French), Hungarian conjugates the verbs and uses different pronouns to address others formally (*magázás*) or informally (*tegezés*). Since this aspect of the original cannot be translated, the reference to it was deleted from the English version.

²⁵ In the original, eight *soldiers* were mentioned. It made no sense that even though one of them survived, later eight *corpses* were mentioned in the story.

²⁶ *Oui, mon commandant* = Yes, Sir! Verbatim: "Yes, my commander!"

²⁷ *Halte! Qui va là?* = Halt! Who goes there?

²⁸ *Aux armes!* = To arms!

²⁹ *Halte! Fixe!* = Halt! Don't move!

³⁰ *Nom de Dieu!* = Good Lord!

³¹ The original version does not include "who call themselves soldiers."

³² The original version does not include "*Mon excellence*" ["your Excellency"]

³³ Simoom: strong, dust-laden whirlwind in North Africa.

³⁴ *Garde à vous!* = Attention!

³⁵ Hubert Lyautey (1854 – 1934) was the first French Resident-General in Morocco from 1912 to 1925 and, from 1921, a Marshal of France.

³⁶ The original is an incomplete sentence that is not marked by an ellipse, and thus might be unintentionally incomplete. "*Éppen őexcellenciája*" means "Exactly his Excellency" implying that "It is exactly his Excellency who knows it the best."

³⁷ *Peloton* = squadron, company; verbatim: platoon, pack

---

[38] *Fini* = It's over. (finished, done)

[39] *Kesra* = a Moroccan bread

[40] The correct French spelling is *Roussel.*

[41] In the original: 45-degree heat. 45 °C = 113 °F. Most metric units in the text were changed to currently used units in the United States.

[42] *Boulot* = small, round bread

[43] *À terre!* = On the ground! ("[Put your weapons] on the ground!"; "Drop your weapons!") Also means: ashore, down to earth, earthbound

[44] The Oasis town of Murzuk is located in present-day southwest Libya.

[45] *Un, deux, trois* = one, two, three. *Allons!* = Come on! Proceed! Let's go! Here: Ready, set, go!

[46] "Le boudin" is the official march of the French Foreign Legion. *"Tiens, voilà du boudin"* = "Here you are some blood sausage." *Le boudin* colloquially meant the rolled up red blanket that topped the backpacks of Legionnaires. In the original book, the lyrics of the march were misquoted as *"Tin t'auras du boudin."*

[47] *Sacrebleu!* = Damn! The exclamation literally means "Holy blue!" *i.e.,* "Holy heavens!"

[48] *Musette* = haversack

[49] *A mon commandement, en avant, marche!* = At my command, forward, march!

[50] *Centimes* = French equivalent of pennies/cents (100 centimes = 1 Franc).

[51] *Vicomte* = viscount (member of the nobility ranking below an earl and above a baron)

[52] *Gaius Suetonius Paulinus* was a consul in the 1st century A.D. He was the first Roman to lead an army across the Atlas Mountains, and was among the first European explorers of the Sahara.

[53] *Oui, mon adjudant!* = Yes, Sir! (Yes, Adjutant!)

[54] *Passat* = a type of wind. Originally, "trade wind" (German)

[55] *Fixe! En joue!* = Halt! Aim! (Verbatim: Stop! Ready!)

[56] *Hamada* = a type of desert landscape consisting of high, largely barren, rocky plateaus, with minimal sand (Arabic).

[57] *Eh bien!* = Well! (Verbatim: Very Good!)

[58] *Bleu* = verbatim: blue. Here, it is a derogatory term, approximately meaning "cockroach." May also mean "rookie."

[59] *Le sac, ma foi, toujours au dos!* = My pack, my faith, always on my back! (Legionnaires' song.)

[60] *L'amour m'a rendu fou* = Love made me crazy

[61] *Chef* = chief; here: commander, commanding officer, immediate superior.

[62] *Corvée* = guard unit, service, unpaid labor, chore, drudgery, fatigue party

[63] *Travaux forcés* = hard labor (punishment)

[64] *Debout! En route! En avant, marche!* = Up! (On your feet!) Let's go! Forward, march!

[65] *A moi!* = Help! [Come] here! To me!

[66] *Képi* = cap with a flat circular top and a visor; typical of French military (including legionnaires') and police uniforms. The *képi blanc* (white cap) is a symbol of the French Foreign legion.

[67] *Cellule* = prison cell

[68] The original text here named the sister Fanny. However, early in the book, the sister's name was mentioned as Anette.

[69] *Cafard* = severe depression or apathy – used especially of white men in the tropics.

20674612R10156

Printed in Great Britain
by Amazon